What Timmy Did

Other books by Marie Belloc Lowndes:

The Chink in the Armor
The End of Her Honeymoon
From Out the Vasty Deep
Good Old Anna
Jane Oglander
Lilla: A Part of Her Life
The Lodger
The Lonely House
Love and Hatred
Mary Pechell
The Red Cross Barge
Studies in Love and Terror
What Timmy Did
The Uttermost Farthing

What Timmy Did

Marie Belloc Lowndes

ÆGYPAN PRESS

1922

What Timmy Did
A publication of
ÆGYPAN PRESS

www.aegypan.com

"Deliver my soul from the sword, my darling from the power of the dog."

— *Psalms* xxii, 20.

Chapter I

*T*he telephone bell rang sharply in the sunlit and charming, if shabby, hall of Old Place.

To John Tosswill there was always something incongruous, and recurringly strange, in this queer link between a little country parish mentioned in Domesday Book and the big bustling modern world.

The bell tinkled on and on insistently, perhaps because it was now no one's special duty to attend to it. But at last the mistress of the house came running from the garden and, stripping off her gardening gloves, took up the receiver.

Janet Tosswill was John Tosswill's second wife, and, though over forty, a still young and alert looking woman, more Irish than Scotch in appearance, with her dark hair and blue eyes. But she came of good Highland stock and was proud of it.

"London wants you," came the tired, cross voice she knew all too well.

"I think there must be some mistake. This is Old Place, Beechfield, Surrey. I don't think anyone can be ringing us from London."

She waited a moment impatiently. Of course it was a mistake! Not a soul in London knew their telephone number. It had never been put on their notepaper. Still, she went on listening with the receiver held to her ear, and growing more and more annoyed at the futile interruption and waste of time.

She was just going to hang up the receiver when all at once the expression of her face altered. From being good-humored, if slightly impatient, it became watchful, and her eyes narrowed as was their way when Janet Tosswill was "upset" about anything. She had suddenly heard, with startling clearness, the words: — "Is that Old Place, Beechfield? If so, Mr. Godfrey Radmore would like to speak to Mrs. Tosswill."

She was so surprised, so taken aback that for a moment she said nothing. At last she answered very quietly: — "Tell Mr. Radmore that Mrs. Tosswill is here waiting on the 'phone."

There was another longish pause, and then, before anything else happened, Janet Tosswill experienced an odd sensation; it was as if she felt the masterful, to her not overattractive, presence of Godfrey Radmore approaching the other end of the line. A moment later, she knew he was there, within earshot, but silent.

"Is that you, Godfrey? We thought you were in Australia. Have you been home long?"

The answer came at once, in the deep, resonant, once familiar voice — the voice no one had heard in Old Place for nine years — nine years with the war having happened in between.

"Indeed no, Janet! I've only been back a very short time." (She noticed he did not say how long.) "And I want to know when I may come down and see you all? I hope you and Mr. Tosswill will believe me when I say it wasn't my fault that I didn't come to Beechfield last year. I hadn't a spare moment!"

The tone of the unseen speaker had become awkward, apologetic, and the listener bit her lips — she did not believe in his explanation as to why he had behaved with such a lack of gratitude and good feeling last autumn.

"We shall be very glad to see you at any time, of course. When can we expect you?"

But the welcoming words were uttered very coldly.

"It's Tuesday today; I was thinking of motoring down on Friday or Saturday. I've got a lot of business to do before then. Will that be all right?"

"Of course it will. Come Friday."

She was thawing a little, and perhaps he felt this, for there came an eager, yearning note into the full, deep voice which sounded so oddly near, and which, for the moment, obliterated the long years since she had heard it last.

"How's my godson? Flick still in the land of the living, eh?"

"Thank heaven, yes! That dog's the one thing in the world Timmy cares for, I sometimes think."

He felt that she was smiling now.

She heard the question: — "Another three minutes, sir?" and the hasty answer: — "Yes, another three minutes," and then, "Still there, Janet?"

"Of course I am. We'll expect you on Friday, Godfrey, by teatime, and I hope you'll stay as long as you can. You won't mind having your old room?"

"Rather not!" and then in a hesitating, shamefaced voice: — "I needn't tell *you* that to me Old Place *is* home."

It was in a very kindly voice that she answered: "I'm glad you still feel like that, Godfrey."

"Of course I do, and of course I am ashamed of not having written more often. I often think of you all — especially of dear old George —" There came a pause, then the words: — "I want to ask you a question, Janet."

Janet Tosswill felt quite sure she knew what that question would be. Before linking up with them all again Godfrey wanted to know certain facts about George. While waiting for him to speak she had time to tell herself that this would prove that her husband and Betty, the eldest of her three step-daughters, had been wrong in thinking that Godfrey Radmore knew that George, Betty's twin, had been killed in the autumn of 1916. At that time all correspondence between Radmore and Old Place had ceased for a long time. When it had begun again in 1917, in the form of a chaffing letter and a check for five pounds to the writer's godson, Betty had suggested that nothing should be said of George's death in Timmy's answer. Of course Betty's wish had been respected, the more so that Janet herself felt sure that Godfrey did not know. Why, he and George — dear, sunny-natured George — had been like fond brothers in the long ago, before Godfrey's unfortunate love-affair with Betty.

And so it was that when she heard his next words they took her entirely by surprise, for it was such an unimportant, as well as unexpected, question that the unseen speaker asked.

"Has Mrs. Crofton settled down at The Trellis House yet?"

"She's arriving today, I believe. When she first thought of coming here she wrote John such a nice letter, saying she was a friend of yours, and that you had told her about Beechfield. Luckily, The Trellis House was to let, so John wrote and told her about it."

Then, at last, came a more intimate question. The man's voice at the other end of the telephone became diffident — hesitating: — "Are you all right? Everything as usual?"

She answered, dryly. "Everything's quite as usual, thank you. Beechfield never changes. Since you were last here there have only been two new cottages built." She paused perceptibly, and then went on: — "I think that Timmy told you that Betty was with the Scottish Women's Hospital during the war? She's got one of the best French decorations."

Should she say anything about George? Before she could make up her mind she heard the words — "You can't go on any longer now. Time's up." And Radmore called out hastily: — "Till Friday then — so long!"

Janet Tosswill hung up the receiver; but she did not move away from the telephone at once. She stood there, wondering painfully whether she had better go along and tell Betty *now*, or whether it would be better to wait till, say, lunch, when all the young people would be gathered together? After all Betty had been nineteen when her engagement to Godfrey Radmore had been broken off, and so very much had happened since then.

And then, in a sense, her mind was made up for her by the fact that a shadow fell across the floor of the hall, and looking up, she saw her old friend and confidant, Dr. O'Farrell, blocking up the doorway with his big burly body.

"D'you remember Godfrey Radmore?" she asked as their hands met.

"Come now, you're joking surely. Remember Radmore? I've good cause to; I don't know whether I ever told you —" there came a slight, very slight note of embarrassment into his hearty Irish voice — "that I wrote to the good fellow just after the Armistice, about our Pat. That the boy's doing as well out in Brisbane as he is, is largely owing to Radmore's good offices."

Mrs. Tosswill was surprised, and not quite pleased. She wondered why Dr. O'Farrell had not told her at the time that he was writing to Godfrey. She still subconsciously felt that Godfrey Radmore belonged to Old Place and to no one else in Beechfield.

"I didn't know about Pat," she said slowly. "But you'll be able to thank him in person now, for he's coming on Friday to stay with us."

"Is he now?" The shrewd Irishman looked sharply into her troubled face. "Well, well, you'll have to let bygones be bygones — eh, Mrs. Toss? I take it he's a great man now."

"I don't think money makes for greatness," she said.

"Don't you?" he queried dryly. "I do! Come admit, woman, that you're sorry *now* you didn't let Betty take the risk?"

"I'm not at all sorry —" she cried. "It was all his fault. He was such a strange, rough, violent young fellow!"

The words trembled on the old doctor's lips — "Perhaps it will all come right now!" But he checked himself, for in his heart of hearts he did not in the least believe that it would all come right. He knew well enough that Godfrey Radmore, after that dramatic exit to Australia, had cut himself clean off from all his friends. He was coming back now as that wonderful thing to most people — a millionaire. Was it likely, so the worldly-wise old doctor asked himself, that a man whose whole circumstances had so changed, ever gave a thought to that old boyish love affair with Betty Tosswill? — violent, piteous and painful as the affair had been. But had Betty forgotten? About that the doctor had his doubts, but he kept them strictly to himself.

He changed the subject abruptly. "It isn't scarlet fever at the Mortons — only a bit of a red rash. I thought you'd like to know.

"It's good of you to have come and told me," she exclaimed. "I confess I did feel anxious, for Timmy was there the whole of the day before yesterday."

"Ah! and how's me little friend?"

Janet Tosswill looked around — but no, there was no one in the corridor of which the door, giving into the hall, was wide open.

"He's gone to do an errand for me in the village."

"The boy is much more normal, eh?" He looked at her questioningly.

"He still says that he sees things," she admitted reluctantly, "though he's rather given' up confiding in me. He tells old Nanna extraordinary tales, but then, as you know, Timmy was always given to romancing, and of course Nanna believes every word he says and in a way encourages him."

The doctor looked at Timmy's mother with a twinkle in his eye. "Nanna isn't the only one," he observed. "I was told in the village just now that Master Timmy had scared away the milk from Tencher's cow."

A look of annoyance came over Mrs. Tosswill's face. "I shall have to speak to Timmy," she exclaimed. "He's much too given to threatening the village people with ill fortune if they have done anything he thinks wrong or unkind. The child was awfully upset the other day because he discovered that the Tenchers had drowned a half-grown kitten."

"He's a queer little chap," observed the old doctor, "a broth of a boy, if ye'll allow me to say so — I'd be proud of Timmy if I were his mother, Mrs. Toss!"

"Perhaps I *am* proud of him," she said smiling, "but still I always tell John he's a changeling child — so absurdly unlike all the others."

"Ah, but that's where *you* come in, me good friend. 'Twas a witch you must have had among ye're ancestresses in the long ago."

He gripped her hand, and went out to his two-seater, his mind still full of his friend's strange little son.

Then all at once — he could not have told you why — Dr. O'Farrell's mind switched off to something very different, and he went back into the hall again.

"A word more with ye, Mrs. Tosswill. What sort of a lady has taken The Trellis House, eh? We don't even know her name."

"She's a Mrs. Crofton — oddly enough, a friend or acquaintance of Godfrey Radmore. He seems to have first met her during the war, when he was quartered in Egypt. She wrote to John and asked if there was a house to let in Beechfield, quoting Godfrey as having told her it was a delightful village."

"And how old may she be?"

"Her husband was a Colonel Crofton, so I suppose she's middle-aged. She's only been a widow three months — if as long."

Janet Tosswill waited till Dr. O'Farrell was well away, and then she began walking down the broad corridor which divided Old Place. It was such a delightful, dignified, spacious house, and very dear to them all, yet Janet was always debating within herself whether they ought to go on living in it, now that they had become so poor.

When she came to the last door on the left, close to the baize door Which shut off the commons from the living rooms, she waited a moment. Then, turning the handle, she walked into what was still called the schoolroom, though Timmy never did his lessons there.

Betty Tosswill, the eldest of John Tosswill's three daughters, was sitting at a big mid-Victorian writing-table, examining the house-books. She had just discovered two "mistakes" in the milkman's account, and she felt perhaps unreasonably sorry and annoyed. Betty had a generous, unsuspicious outlook on human nature, and a meeting with petty dishonesty was always a surprise. She looked up with a very friendly, welcoming smile as her step-mother came into the room. They were very good friends, these two, and they had a curiously close bond in Timmy, the only child of the one and the half-brother of the other. Betty was now twenty-eight and there were only two persons in the world whom she had loved in her life as well as she now loved her little brother.

As her step-mother came close up to her — "Janet? What's the matter?" she exclaimed, and as the other made no answer, a look of fear came over the girl's face. She got up from her chair. "Don't look like that, Janet, — you're frightening me!"

The older woman tried to smile. "To tell the truth, Betty, I've had rather a shock. You heard the telephone bell ring?"

"You mean some minutes ago?"

"Yes."

"Who was it?"

"Godfrey Radmore, speaking from London."

"Is that all? I was afraid that something had happened to Timmy!" But, even so, the color flamed up into Betty Tosswill's face.

Her step-mother looked away out of the window as she went on: — "It was stupid of me to have been so surprised, but somehow I thought he was still in Australia."

"He was in England last year." Betty, not really knowing what she was doing, bent over the peccant milkman's book.

"He's coming down here on Friday. I think he realizes that I haven't forgiven him for not coming to see us last year. Still we must let bygones be bygones."

Then she wondered with a sharp touch of self-reproach what had made her say such a stupid thing — a thing which might have, and indeed had, two such different meanings? What she had *meant* had been that she must forget the hurt surprise she and her husband had felt that Godfrey Radmore, on two separate occasions, had deliberately avoided coming down from London to what had been, after all, so long his home; in fact, as he himself had said just now, the only home he had ever known.

But what was this Betty was saying? — her face rather drawn and white, all the bright color drifted out of it — "Of course we must, Janet! Besides Godfrey was not to blame — not at the last."

Janet knew what Betty meant. That at the end it was she who had failed him. But when their engagement had been broken off, Godfrey had been worse than penniless — in debt, and entirely through his own fault. He had gambled away what little money he had, and it had ended in his going off to Australia — alone.

Then an astounding thing had happened. Godfrey had had a fortune left him by an eccentric old man in whose employment he had been as secretary for a while. His luck still holding, he had gone through most of the war, including Gallipoli, with only one wound, which had left no ill effects. A man so fortunate ought not to have neglected his old friends.

Janet Tosswill, the step-mother completely merging into the friend, came forward, and put her arms round the girl's shoulders. "Look here, Betty. Wouldn't you rather go away? I don't suppose he'll stay longer than Monday or Tuesday —"

"I shouldn't think of going away! I expect he's forgotten all about that old affair. It's a long time ago, Janet — nine years. We were both so young, that I've forgotten too — in a sense." And then, as she saw that the other was far more moved than she herself was outwardly, she repeated: "It really has faded away, almost out of sight. Think of all that has happened since then!"

The other muttered, "Yes, that's true," and Betty went on, a little breathlessly, "I'll tell you who'll be pleased — that's Timmy. He's got a regular hero-worship of Godfrey." She was smiling now. "I hope he asked after his godson?"

"Indeed he did. After Flick too! By the way he wanted to know if Mrs. Crofton was settled down in The Trellis House. I wonder if she's an Australian?"

"I don't think so," said Betty. "I think he met them in Egypt during the war. He mentioned them in one of his letters to Timmy, and then, when he was in England last year, he must have stayed with them, for that's where Flick came from. Colonel Crofton bred terriers. I remember reading Timmy a long letter signed 'Cecil Crofton' telling him all about how to manage Flick, and he mentioned Godfrey."

"I don't remember that — I must have been away."

They were both glad to have glided on to a safe, indifferent subject.

"I'll go back to my carnations now, but first I'd better tell your father the news."

"You — you — needn't remind father of anything that happened years ago, Janet — need you?"

Janet Tosswill shook her head, and yet when she had shut the door behind her in her husband's study, almost the first words she uttered, after having told him of Godfrey Radmore's coming visit, were: — "I shall never, never forgive him for the way he treated Betty. I hate the thought of having to be nice to him — I wish Timmy wasn't his godson!"

She spoke the words breathlessly, defiantly, standing before her old John's untidy writing table.

As she spoke, he rather nervously turned some papers over under his hand: — "I don't know that he behaved as badly as you think, my dear. Neither of them had any money, and at that time he had no prospects."

"He'd thrown away his prospects! Then I can't forgive him for his behavior last year — never coming down to see us, I mean. It was so — so ungrateful! Handsome presents don't make up for that sort of thing. I used to long to send the things back."

"I don't think you're fair," began Mr. Tosswill deprecatingly. "He did write me a very nice letter, Janet, explaining that it was impossible for him to come."

"Well, I suppose we must make the best of it — particularly as he says that he's come back to England for good."

She went out of the room, and so into the garden — back to the border she had left unwillingly but at which she now glanced down with a sensation of disgust. She felt thoroughly ruffled and upset — a very unusual condition for her to be in, for Janet Tosswill was an equable and happy-natured woman, for all her affectionate and sensitive heart.

She told herself that it was true the whole world had altered in the last nine years — everything had altered except Beechfield. The little Surrey village seemed to her mind exactly the same as it was when she had come there, as a bride, fourteen years ago, except that almost everybody in it, from being comfortably off, had become uncomfortably poor. Then all at once, she smiled. The garden of Old Place was very different from the garden she had found when she first came there. It had been a melancholy, neglected, singularly ugly garden — the kind of garden which only costly bedding-out had made tolerable in some prosperous early Victorian day. Now it was noted for its charm and beauty even among the many beautiful gardens of the neighborhood, and during the War she had made quite a lot of money selling flowers and fruit for the local Red Cross. Now she was trying to coax her husband to take one of the glebe fields on a long lease in order to start a hamper trade in fruit, vegetables and flowers. Dolly, the one of her three step-daughters whom she liked least, was fond of gardening, in a dull plodding way, and might be trained to such work.

But try though she did to forget Godfrey Radmore, her mind swung ceaselessly back to the man with whom she had just had that curious talk on the telephone. She was sorry — not glad as a more worldly woman would have been — that Godfrey Radmore was coming back into their life.

Chapter II

*W*hile Janet Tosswill was thinking so intently of Godfrey Radmore, he himself was standing at the window of a big bedroom in one of those musty, expensive, old-fashioned hotels, which, perhaps because they are within a stone's throw of Piccadilly, still have faithful patrons all the year round, and are full to bursting during the London Season. As to Radmore, he had chosen it because it was the place where the grandfather who had brought him up always stayed when he, Godfrey, was a little boy.

Tall, well-built after the loose-limbed English fashion, and with a dark, intelligent, rather grim cast of face, Radmore looked older than his age, which was thirty-two. Yet, for all that, there was an air of power and of reserved strength about him that set him apart from his fellows, and a casual observer would have believed him cold, and perhaps a thought calculating, in nature.

Yet, standing there, looking out on that quiet, narrow street, he was seething with varying emotions in which he was, in a sense, luxuriating, though whether he would have admitted any living being to a share in them was another matter.

Home! Home at last for good! — after what had been, with two short breaks, a nine years' absence from England, and from all that England stands for to such a man.

He had left his country in 1910, an angry, embittered lad of twenty-three, believing that he would never come back or, at any rate, not till he was an old man having "made good."

But everything — everything had fallen out absolutely differently from what he had expected it to do. The influence of Mars, so fatal to millions of his fellow beings, had brought him marvelous, unmerited good fortune. He had rushed home the moment War was declared, and after putting in some time in a training which he hated to remember, he had at last obtained a commission. Within a fortnight of having reached his Mecca — the Front, he was back in England in the — to him — amazing guise of wounded hero. But he had sent for none of his old friends for he was still ashamed. After the Armistice he had rushed through England on his way to Australia, putting in a few days with a Colonel and Mrs. Crofton, with whom he had been thrown in Egypt. More to do his host a kindness than for any other reason, Radmore had sent his godson, Timothy Tosswill, a pedigree puppy, from the queer little Essex manor-house where the Croftons were then making a rather futile attempt to increase their slender means by breeding terriers.

The days had slipped by there very pleasantly, for Radmore liked his taciturn host, and Mrs. Crofton was very pretty — an agreeable playfellow for a rich and lonely man. So it was that when it came to the point he had not cared to look up any of the people associated with his early youth.

But now he was going to see them — almost had he forced himself upon them. And the thought of going home to Old Place shook and stirred him to the heart.

Today he felt quite queerly at a loose end. This perhaps, partly because the lately widowed Mrs. Crofton, with whom he had spent a good deal of his time since his arrival in London three weeks ago, had left town. She had not gone far, only to the Surrey village where he himself was going on Friday.

When pretty Mrs. Crofton had told Radmore that she had taken a house at Beechfield, he had been very much surprised and taken aback.

It had seemed to him an amazing coincidence that the one place in the wide world which to him was home should have been chosen by her. But at once she had reminded him, in her pretty little positive way, that it was he himself who, soon after they had become first acquainted in Egypt, had drawn such an attractive picture of the Surrey village. That, in fact, was why, in July — it was now late September — when she, Enid Crofton, had had to think of making a new home, Beechfield had seemed to her the ideal place. If only she could hear of a house to let there! And by rare good chance there had been such a house — The Trellis House! A friend had lent her a motor, and she had gone down to look at it one August afternoon, and there and then had decided to take it. It was so exactly what she wanted — a delightful, old, cottage place, yet with all modern conveniences, lacking, alas! only electric light.

All this had happened, so she had explained, after her last letter to him, for she and Radmore had kept up a desultory correspondence.

And now, with Janet Tosswill's voice still sounding in his ears, Godfrey Radmore was not altogether sorry to feel a touch of loneliness, for at times his good fortune frightened him.

Not only had he escaped through the awful ordeal of war with only one bad wound, while many of his friends and comrades — the best and bravest, the most happily young, had fallen round him — but he had come back to find himself transformed from a penniless adventurer into a very rich man. An old Brisbane millionaire, into whose office he had drifted in the January of 1914, and with whom he had, after a fashion, made friends, had re-made his will in the memorable autumn of that year, and had left Radmore half his vast fortune. Doubtless many such wills were made under the stress of war emotion, but — and it was here that Radmore's strange luck had come in — the maker of this particular will had died within a month of making it. And, as so often happens to a man who had begun by losing what little he had owing to folly and extravagance, Godfrey Radmore, though exceptionally generous and kindly, now lived well within his means, and had, if anything, increased his already big share of this world's goods.

Now that he was home for good, he intended to buy a nice old-fashioned house with a little shooting, and perchance a little fishing. The place, though not at Land's End, must yet not be so near London that a fellow would be tempted to be always going to town. It seemed to him amazing that he now had it within his power to achieve what had always been his ideal. But when he had acquired exactly the kind of place he wanted to find, what those whom he had set seeking for him had assured him with such flattering and eager earnestness he would very soon discover — what then? Did he mean to live there alone? He thought yes, for he did not now feel drawn to marriage.

As a boy — it now seemed æons of years ago — it had been far otherwise. But Betty Tosswill had been very young, only nineteen, and when he had fallen on evil days she had thrown him over in obedience to her father's strongly expressed wish. He had suffered what at the time seemed a frightful agony, and he had left England full of revolt and bitterness.

But today, when the knowledge that he was so soon going to Beechfield brought with it a great surge of remembrance, he could not honestly tell himself that he was sorry. Had he gone out to Australia burdened with a girl-wife, the difficult struggle would have been well-nigh intolerable, and it was a million to one chance that he would ever have met the man to whom he owed his present good fortune. What he now longed to do was to enjoy himself in a simple, straightforward way. Love, with its tremors, uncertainties, its blisses and torments, was not for him, and in so far as he might want a pleasant touch of half sentimental, half sexless comradeship, there was his agreeable friendship with Mrs. Crofton.

Enid Crofton? The thought of how well he had come to know her in the last three weeks surprised him. When he had first met her in Egypt she had been the young, very pretty wife of Colonel Crofton, an elderly "dug-out," odd and saturnine, whose manner to his wife was not always overkindly. No one out there had been much surprised when she had decided to brave the submarine peril and return to England.

Radmore had not been the only man who had felt sorry for her, and who had made friends with her. But unlike the other men, who were all more or less in love with her, he had liked Colonel Crofton. During his visit to Fildy Fe Manor, the liking had hardened into serious regard. He had been surprised, rather distressed, to find how much less well-off they had appeared here, at home, than when the Colonel had been on so-called active service. It had also become plain to him — though he was not a man to look out for such things — that the husband and wife were now on very indifferent terms, the one with the other, and, on the whole, he blamed the wife — and then, just before he had started for home again, had come the surprising news of Colonel Crofton's death!

In her letter to one who was, after all, only an acquaintance, the young widow had gone into no details. But, just by chance, Radmore had seen a paragraph in a week-old London paper containing an account of the inquest. Colonel Crofton had committed suicide, a result, it was stated, of depression owing to shell-shock. "Shell-shock" gave Radmore pause. He felt quite sure that Colonel Crofton had never — to use a now familiar paraphrase — heard a shot fired in anger. The fact that his war service had been far from the Front had always been a subject of bitter complaint on the old soldier's part.

Radmore had written a sympathetic note to Mrs. Crofton, telling her the date of his return, and now — almost without his knowing how and why — they had become intimate, meeting almost daily, lunching or dining together incessantly, Radmore naturally gratified at the admiration his lovely companion — she had grown even prettier since he had last seen her — obviously excited.

And yet, though he had become such "pals" with her, and though he missed her society at his now lonely meals to an almost ridiculous extent, Radmore would have been much taken aback had an angel from heaven told him that the real reason he had sought to get in touch with Old Place was because Enid Crofton had already settled down at Beechfield.

Chapter III

*A*fter Timmy Tosswill had been to the village shop and done his mother's errand, he wandered on, his dog, Flick, at his heels, debating within himself what he should do next.

Like most children who lead an abnormal, because a lonely, childhood, he was in some ways very mature, in other ways still very babyish. He was at once secretive and — whenever anything touched his heart — emotionally expansive. To the indifferent observer Timmy appeared to be an exceptionally intelligent, naughty, rather spoilt little boy, too apt to take every advantage of a certain physical delicacy. This was also the view taken of him by his half-brothers, and by two out of his three step-sisters. But the three who really loved him, his mother, his nurse, and his eldest half-sister, Betty, were convinced that the child was either possessed of a curious, uncanny gift of — was it second sight? — as his old nurse entirely and his mother half, believed, or, as Dr. O'Farrell asserted, some abnormal development of his subconscious self. All three were ruefully aware that Timmy was often — well, his mother called it "sly," his sister called it "fanciful," his nurse by the good old nursery term, "deceitful."

It was this unlovable attribute of his which made it so difficult to know whether Timmy believed in the positive assertions occasionally made by him concerning his intimate acquaintance with the world of the unseen. That he could sometimes visualize what was coming to pass, especially if it was of an unpleasant, disturbing nature, was, so his mother considered, an undeniable fact. But sometimes the gift lay in abeyance for weeks, even for months. That had been the case, as Mrs. Tosswill had told Dr. O'Farrell, for a long time now — to be precise, since March, when, to the dismay of those about him he had predicted an accident in the hunting field which actually took place.

Timmy walked on up the steep bit of road which led to the upper part of the beautiful old village which was, like many an English village, shaped somewhat like a horseshoe — and then suddenly he stopped and gazed intently into a walled stable-yard of which the big gates were wide open.

Beechfield was Timmy Tosswill's world in little. He was passionately interested in all that concerned its inhabitants, and was a familiar and constant, though not always a welcome visitor to every cottage. Most of the older village men and women had a certain grudging affection for the odd little boy. They were all well aware of, and believed in, the gift which made him, as the nurse had once explained to a crony of hers, "see things which are not there," though not one of them would have cared to mention it to him.

Timmy had a special reason for wishing to know what was going on in this stable-yard, so, after a moment's thought, he walked deliberately through the gates as if he had some business there, and then he saw that two men, one of whom was a stranger to him, were tidying up the place in a very leisurely, thoroughgoing manner.

The back door of The Trellis House, as the quaint-looking, long, low building to the right was incongruously named, opened into the stable-yard and by the door was a bench. Timmy walked boldly across the yard and established himself on the bench and his dog, Flick, jumped up and sat sedately by him. The little boy then took a small black book out of his pocket. The book was called "The Crofton Boys" and Timmy had chosen it because the name of the new tenant of The Trellis House was Mrs. Crofton, a friend, as he was aware, of his godfather, Godfrey Radmore. He wondered if she had any boys.

The two men, busy with big new brooms, came up close to where Timmy was sitting. When the child, obviously "one of the gentry," had walked into the stable-yard, they had abruptly stopped talking; but now, seeing that he was reading intently, and apparently quite uninterested in what they were doing, they again began speaking to one another, or rather one of them, a hard-bitten, shrewd-looking man, much the older of the two, began talking in what was, though Timmy was not aware of it, a Cockney dialect.

"You won't find 'er a bad 'un to work for, m'lad. I speak of folks as I find them. I'm not one to take any notice of queer tales!"

"Queer tales. What be the queer tales, Mister Piper?"

Timmy knew this last speaker. He was the baker's rather sharp younger son, and Mrs. Crofton had just engaged him as handy man.

The older man lowered his voice a little, but Timmy, who, while his eyes seemed glued to the pages of the book he held open, was yet listening with all his ears, heard what followed quite clearly.

"It ain't for me to spread ill tales after what I've told you, eh? But the Colonel's death was a reg'lar tragedy, 'twas, and some there were who said that 'is widder wasn't exactly sorry. 'E were a melancholy cove for any young woman to 'ave to live with. But there, as my old mother used to say, 'any old barn-door can keep out the draft!'"

The younger man looked up: — "What sort o' tragedy?" he asked.

"The Colonel pizened 'isself, and the question was — did 'e do it o' purpose? Some said yes, and some said no. I was in it by a manner of speaking."

"You was in it?"

The boy left off working, and gazed at the other eagerly: — "D'you mean you saw him do it?"

"I was the first to see 'im in his agony — I calls that being in it. And I was called upon to give evidence at the inquest held on the corpse."

The man looked round him furtively as he spoke. The little boy sitting by the back door of the house caused him no concern, but he did not want what he said to be overheard by the two new maid-servants who had arrived at The Trellis House that morning.

"There's always a lot of talk when folks die sudden," he went on, in a sententious tone. "It was as plain as the nose on your face that the Colonel, poor chap, 'ad 'ad what they called shell-shock. I'd heard 'im a-talking aloud to 'isself many a time. 'E was a-weary of life 'e was. So 'tis plain 'e just thought 'e'd put an end to it, like many a better man afore 'im."

And then the youth said something that rather surprised himself, but his mind had been working while the other had been talking.

"Did anyone say different?" was his question and the other answered in a curious tone: "Now you're askin'! Yes, there was some folk as did say different. They argued that the Colonel never took the pizen knowingly. 'E was very keen over terriers — we bred 'em. The best of 'em, a grand sire, was the very spit of that little dawg sitting up on that there bench. Colonel bred 'em for profit, not pleasure. Mrs. Crofton, she 'ated 'em, and she lost no time either in getting rid of 'em after 'e was gone. They got on 'er nerves, same as 'e'd done. She give the best — prize-winner 'e was — to the Crowner as tried the corpse. 'E'd known 'em both — was a bit sweet on 'er 'isself."

The youth laughed discordantly. "Ho! Ho! She's that sort, is she?"

But the other spoke up at once with a touch of sharpness in his voice.

"She's a good sort to them as be'aves themselves, my lad. She give me a good present. Got me a good, new soft place, too, that's where I'm going tomorrer. I'm 'ere to oblige 'er, that's what I am — just to put you, young man, in the way of things. Look sharp, please 'er, mind your manners, and you may end better off than you know!"

The lad looked at the speaker with a gleam of rather hungry curiosity in his lackluster eyes.

"Mark my words! Your missus won't be a widder long. Ever 'eard of a Major Radmore?"

The speaker did not notice that the little boy sitting on the bench stiffened unconsciously.

"Major Radmore?" repeated the listener. "Folk in Beechfield did know a chap called Radmore. Lives in Australia, he does. He sent home some money for a village club 'e did, but nothing 'as been done about it yet. Some do say old Tosswill's sticking to the cash — a gent as what they calls trustee of it all. But then who'd trust anyone with a load o' money? The chap I'm thinking of used to live at Tosswill's a matter of ten years ago."

"Then 'tis the same one!" exclaimed the other eagerly, "and, if so, you'll not lack good things. Likely as not the Major's your future master. 'E's got plenty, and a generous soul too. Gave me a present last year when he was a stopping at Fildy Fe Manor. The Major, 'e bought one of our dawgs, and I sent it off for 'im to Old Place, Beechfield, damn me if I don't remember it now — name of Tosswill too." He stopped short, and then, as if he had thought better of what he was going to say, he observed musingly: "Some says Jack Piper's a blabber — but they don't know me! But one thing I'll tell you. The're two after the Missus, for all the Colonel's 'ardly cold, so to speak, but I put my money on the dark one."

He had hardly uttered these cryptic words when a pretty young woman opened the door which gave on to the stable-yard from the house: "Dinner-time!" she called out merrily.

Both men dropped the brooms they were holding, and going towards the door disappeared.

As they did so, Timmy heard the words: — "*She's* a peach — thinks herself one too — oh! the merry widder!"

The little boy waited a moment. He took a long look round the sunny, and now unnaturally tidy, stable-yard. Then he got up, shut his book, and put it sedately into his pocket. Flick seemed unwilling to move, so Timmy turned and called sharply: — "Flick! come along at once!"

The dog jumped down and ran up to his master. Timmy walked across the big, flat, white stones, kicking a pebble as he went. At last, when he got close to the open gate, he hop-scotched, propelling the pebble far into the road.

He was extremely disturbed and surprised. He went over and over again what he had heard the two men say. The absurd suspicion of his father filled him with angry hurt disgust. Why only yesterday the plan of the village clubhouse had come from the architect! And then that extraordinary disconcerting hint about his godfather? Godfrey Radmore belonged in Timmy's imagination, first to himself, secondly to his parents, and then, in a much less close way, to the rest of the Tosswill family. A sensation of strong-dislike to the still unknown new tenant of The Trellis House welled up in his secretive little heart, and instead of going on round the village, he turned back and made his way straight home.

As he walked along the short avenue which led to the front door of Old Place he saw his mother kneeling on her gardening mat. He stepped up on to the grass hoping to elude her sharp eyes and ears, but she had already seen him.

"Hullo, Timmy!" she called out cheerfully. "What have you been doing with yourself all this time?"

"I've been sitting reading in the stable-yard of The Trellis House."

"That seems rather a funny thing to do, when you might have been here helping your Mummy," but she said the words very kindly. Then suddenly the mention of The Trellis House reminded her of Godfrey Radmore. "I've got a great piece of news!" she exclaimed. "Guess who's coming here to spend the weekend with us, Timmy?"

He looked at her gravely and said: — "I think I know, Mum."

She felt taken aback, as she so often was with her strange little son.

"I don't think you do," she cried briskly.

"I think it's" — he hesitated a moment — "Major Radmore, my godfather."

She was very, very surprised. Then her quick Scotch mind fastened on the one unfamiliar word. "Why *Major* Radmore?" she asked.

Timmy looked a little confused. "I — I don't know," he muttered unwillingly. "I thought he was a soldier, Mum."

"Of course he *was* a soldier. But he isn't a soldier now."

"Isn't it teatime?" asked Timmy suddenly.

"Yes, I suppose it is."

As they walked towards the house together Janet was telling herself uneasily that unless Timmy had met Dr. O'Farrell, it was impossible for him to have learnt through any ordinary human agency that Godfrey Radmore was coming to Beechfield. Though a devoted, she was not a blind mother, and she was disagreeably aware that her little son never "gave himself away." She did not wish to start him on a long romancing explanation which would embody — if one were to put it in bald English — a lie. So she said nothing.

They were close to the door of the house when he again took her aback by suddenly saying: — "I don't think Mrs. Crofton can be a very nice sort of lady, Mum."

(Then he had seen Mrs. Crofton, and *she* had told him.)

"Why not, Timmy?"

"I have a sort of feeling that she's horrid."

"Nonsense! If only for your godfather's sake, we must all try and like her. Besides, my boy, she's in great trouble. Her husband only died two or three months ago."

"Some people aren't sorry when their husbands die," remarked Timmy.

She pretended not to hear. But as they walked through into the hall she heard him say as if to himself: "Some people are glad. Mrs. George Pott" — the woman who kept the local beer-shop — "danced when *her* husband died."

"I wish, Timmy," said his mother sharply, "that you would not listen to, or repeat low village gossip."

"Not even if it's true, Mum?"

"No, not even if it's true."

When Janet had first come to Old Place as a bride, eager to shoulder what some of her friends had told her would be an almost intolerable burden, her husband's six children had been a sad, subdued, nursery-brought-up group, infinitely pathetic to her warm Scotch heart. At once she had instituted, rather to the indignation of the old nurse who was yet to become in due time her devoted henchwoman, a daily dining room tea, and the custom still persisted.

And now, to Timmy's surprise, his mother opened the drawing room door instead of going on to the dining room. "Tell Betty," she said abruptly, "to pour out tea. I'll come on presently."

She shut the door, and going over to the roomy old sofa, sat down, and leaning back, closed her eyes. It was a very unusual thing for her to do, but she felt tired, and painfully excited at the thought of Godfrey Radmore's coming visit. And as she lay there, there rose up before her, wearily and despondently, the changes which nine years had brought to Old Place.

Janet Tosswill, like all intelligent step-mothers, sometimes speculated as to what her predecessor had really been like. Her husband's elder children were so amazingly unlike one another, as well as utterly unlike her own son Timmy.

Betty, the eldest of her step-children, was her favorite, and she had also been deeply attached to Betty's twin-brother, George. The two had been alike in many ways, though Betty was very feminine and George essentially masculine, and each of them had possessed those special human attributes which only War seems to bring to full fruition.

George had been out in France seven months when he had been killed at Beaumont Hamel, and he had already won a bar to his Military Cross by an action which in any other campaign would have given him the Victoria Cross. As for Betty, she had shown herself extraordinarily brave, cool, and resourceful when after doing some heavy home war work, she had gone out with one of the units of the Scottish Women's Hospital.

But Janet Tosswill admired and loved the girl more than ever since Betty had come back, from what had perforce been a full and exciting life, to take up the dull, everyday routine existence at Old Place where, what with a bad investment, high prices, and the sudden leap in the income-tax, from living pleasantly at ease they had become most unpleasantly poor.

Jack, who came next to Betty, though a long way after, and who had just missed being in the war, was a very different type of young Englishman from what George had been. He was clever, self-assertive, and already known as a brilliant debater and as a sound speaker at the Oxford Union. There need be no trouble as to Jack Tosswill's future — he was going to the Bar, and there was little doubt that he would succeed there. One of his idiosyncrasies was his almost contemptuous indifference to women. He was fond of his sisters in a patronizing way, but the average pleasant girl, of whom the neighborhood of Beechfield had more than its full share, left him quite cold.

The next in age — Dolly — was the most commonplace member of the family. Her character seemed to be set on absolutely conventional lines, and the whole family, with the exception of her father, who did not concern himself with such mundane things, secretly hoped that she would marry a young parson who had lately "made friends with her." As is often the case with that type of young woman, Dolly was feckless about money, and would always have appeared badly and unsuitably dressed but for the efforts of her elder sister and step-mother.

Rosamund, the youngest and by far the prettiest of the three sisters, was something of a problem. Though two years younger than Dolly, she had already had three or four love affairs, and when only sixteen, had been the heroine of a painful scrape — the sort of scrape which the people closely concerned try determinedly to forget, but which everyone about them remembers to his or her dying day.

The hero of that sorry escapade had been a man of forty, separated from his wife. On the principle that "truth will out even in an affidavit," poor Rosamund's little world was well aware that the girl, or rather the child, had been simply vain and imprudent. But still, she had disappeared for two terrible long days and nights, and even now, when anything recalled the episode to her step-mother or to Betty, they would shudder with an awful inward tremor, recollecting what they had both gone through. That she had come back as silly and innocent a girl as she had left, and feeling as much shame as she was capable of feeling, had been owing to the tardily awakened sense of prudence and honor in the man to whom she had run away in a fit of temper after a violent quarrel with — of all people in the world — her brother Jack.

Rosamund now ardently desired to become an actress, and after much secret discussion with his wife, her father had at last told her that if she were of the same opinion when she reached the age of twenty-one he would put no obstacle in her way.

As to Tom, the youngest of Janet Tosswill's step-children, he was "quite all right." Though only fifteen months younger than Rosamund, whereas she was as much of a woman as she ever would be, he was still a cheery, commonplace schoolboy. He had been such a baby when Janet had married that sometimes she almost felt as if he were her own child and that though Tom's relation to her own son was peculiar. Theoretically the two boys ought to have been pals, or at any rate good friends. But in practice they were like oil and water — and found it impossible to mix. When Tom was at home, as now, on his holidays, he spent most of his time with a schoolfellow of his own age who lived about two miles from Beechfield. In some ways Timmy was older now than Tom would ever be.

Chapter IV

*T*immy went on into the dining room to find his brothers and sisters all gathered there excepting Dolly. But as he sat down, and as Betty began to pour out tea, Dolly came in from the garden with the words: — "Guess who I've met and had a talk with?"

She looked round her eagerly, but no one ventured an opinion. There were so many, many people whom Dolly might have met and had a talk with, for she was the most gregarious member of the Tosswill family.

At last Timmy spoke up: — "I expect you've seen Mrs. Crofton," he observed, his mouth already full of bread and butter.

Dolly was taken aback. "How did you know?" she cried. "But it's quite true — I *have* seen Mrs. Crofton!"

"What is she like?" asked Jack indifferently.

"How old is she?" This from Betty, who somehow always seemed to ask the essential question.

"D'you think she'll prove a 'stayer'?" questioned Tom.

He had hoped that someone with a family of boys and girls would have come to The Trellis House. It was a beautiful little building — the oldest dwelling-house in the village, in spite of its early Victorian name. But no one ever stayed there very long. Some of the older village folk said it was haunted.

"Did you speak to her, or did she speak to you?" asked Rosamund.

And then again Timmy intervened.

"I know more about her than anyone of you do. But I don't mean to tell you what I know," he announced.

No one took any notice of him. By common consent efforts were always made in the family circle to keep Timmy down — but such efforts were rarely successful.

"Well, tell us what's she like?" exclaimed Rosamund. "I did so hope we should escape another widow."

She had hoped for a nice, well-to-do couple, with at least one grown-up son preferably connected, in some way, with the stage.

Dolly Tosswill, still standing, looked down at her audience.

"She's quite unlike what I thought she would be," she began. "For one thing, she's quite young, and she's awfully pretty and unusual-looking. You'd notice her anywhere."

"Did you meet her in the post office?" asked Betty.

"No, at church. She only arrived this morning, and she said she felt so lonely and miserable that when she heard the bell ring she thought she'd go along and see what our church was like."

"Oh, then she's 'pi'?" in a tone of disgust from Rosamund.

"I'd noticed her in church, though she was sitting rather back, close to the door," went on Dolly, "and I'd wondered who she was, as she looked so very unlike any of the Beechfield people."

"How do you mean — unlike?" asked Tom.

"I can't explain exactly. I thought she was a summer visitor. And then something so funny happened —"

Dolly was sitting down now, and Betty handed her a cup of tea, grieving the while to see how untidy she looked with her hat tilted back at an unbecoming angle.

"What happened?"

"Well, as we came out of the church together, all at once that old, half-blind, post office dog made straight for her! He gave a most awful howl, and she was so frightened that she ran back into the church again. But of course I didn't know she was Mrs. Crofton *then*. I got the dog into the post office garden and then I went back into the church to tell her the coast was clear. But she waited a bit, for she was awfully afraid that he might get out again."

"What a goose she must be" — this from Jack.

"She asked if she were likely to meet any other dog in the road; so I asked her where she lived, and then she told me she was Mrs. Crofton, and that she had only arrived this morning. I offered to walk home with her, and then we had quite a talk. She has the same kind of feeling about dogs that some people have about cats."

"That's rather queer!" said Tom suddenly, "for her husband bred wire-haired terriers. Colonel Crofton sold Flick to Godfrey Radmore last year — don't you remember?"

He appealed to Betty, who always remembered everything.

"Yes," she said quietly, "I was just thinking of that. Colonel Crofton wrote Timmy such a nice letter telling him how to manage Flick. It does seem strange that she should have that feeling about dogs."

Again Timmy's shrill voice rose in challenge. "I should hate *my* wife not to like dogs," he cried pugnaciously.

"It'll take you all your time to make her like *you*, old man," observed Tom.

"I've asked her in to supper tonight," went on Dolly, in her slow, deliberate way, "so we shall have to have Flick locked up."

"Whatever made you ask her to supper, Doll?" asked Jack sharply.

Jack Tosswill had a hard, rather limited nature, but he was very fond of his home, and unlike most young men, he had a curious dislike to the presence of strangers there. This was unfortunate, for his step-mother was very hospitable, and even now, though life had become a real struggle as to ways and means, she often asked people in to meals.

"Her cook didn't turn up," exclaimed Dolly. "And when she asked me if I knew of any woman in the village who could come in and cook dinner for her this evening, I said I was sure Janet would like her to come in and have supper."

"And I hope," chimed in Rosamund decidedly, "that we shall all dress for dinner. Why should she think us a hugger-mugger family?"

"I don't mean to change. I shall only wash my hands!" This from Timmy, who was always allowed to sit up to dinner. His brothers and sisters were too fond of their step-mother to say how absurdly uncalled-for they thought this privilege.

As everyone pretended not to have heard his remark, Timmy repeated obstinately: "I shall only wash my hands."

"Mrs. Crofton won't care how *you* look," observed Jack irritably. "If we didn't now live in such a huggery-muggery way, I should always dress. I do everywhere else."

Betty looked at him, and her face deadened. Though she would hardly have admitted it, even to herself, she regretted the way in which everything at Old Place was now allowed to go "slack." She knew it to be bad for her sisters. It wasn't as if they did any real housework or gave useful help in the kitchen. Dolly tried to do so in a desultory way, but in the end it was she, Betty, who kept everything going in this big, rambling old house, with the help of the old nurse and a day girl from the village.

Timmy gave a little cackle, and Jack felt annoyed. He looked across at his half-brother with a feeling akin to dislike. But Jack Tosswill was truly attached to his step-mother. He was old enough to remember what a change she had made in the then dull, sad, austere Old Place. Janet had at once thrown herself into the task of being sister, rather than step-mother, to her husband's children, and bountifully had she succeeded!

Still, with the exception of Betty, they all criticized her severely, in their hearts, for her weakness where her own child was concerned. And yet poor Janet never made the slightest difference between Timmy and the others. It was more the little boy's own clever insistence which got him his own way, and secured him certain privileges which they, at his age, had never enjoyed. Timmy also always knew how to manage his delicate, nervous father. John Tosswill realized that Timmy might some day grow up to do him credit. Timmy really loved learning, and it was a pleasure to the scholar to teach his clever, impish, youngest son.

*M*eanwhile Janet, who had remained on in the drawing room, got up from the sofa and, going into the corridor, opened the dining room door. For some moments she stood there, unseen, watching the eager party gathered round the table, and as she did so, she looked with a curious, yearning feeling at each of the young folk in turn.

How changed, how utterly changed, they all were since Godfrey Radmore had last been in that familiar room! The least changed, of course, was Betty. To her step-mother's partial eyes, Betty Tosswill, at twenty-eight, was still an extraordinarily charming and young-looking creature. Had her nose been rather less retroussé, her generous, full-lipped mouth just a little smaller, her brown hair either much darker, or really fair, as was Rosamund's, she would have been exceptionally pretty. What to the discriminating made her so much more attractive than either of her younger sisters was her look of intelligence and quiet humor. But of course she looked not only older, but different, from what she had looked nine years ago. Betty had lived a full and, in a sense, a tragic life during four of the years which had elapsed since she and Radmore had parted in this very room.

Janet's eyes traveled past Betty to Jack. Just at that moment he was looking with no very pleasant expression across at his little brother, and yet there was something softer than usual in his cold, clear-cut face. Janet Tosswill would have been touched and surprised indeed had she known that it was the thought of herself that had brought that look on Jack's face. Jack was twenty-one, but looked like a man of thirty — he was so set, he knew so exactly what he wanted of life. As she looked at him, she wondered doubtfully whether he would ever make that great career his schoolmaster had so confidently predicted for him. He was so — so — she could only find the word "conventional" to describe him.

Janet Tosswill passed over Dolly quickly. Today Dolly looked a little different from the others, for she was wearing a hat, and it was clear that she had just come in from the village. Her step-mother noticed with dissatisfaction that the over large brooch fastening Dolly's blouse was set in awry, and that there were wisps of loose hair lying on her neck.

As for Rosamund, she looked ill-humored, frankly bored today — but oh, how pretty and dainty, next to the commonplace Dolly! Rosamund's gleaming fair hair curled naturally all over her head; she had lovely, startled-looking eyes which went oddly with a very determined, if beautifully molded, mouth and chin.

Betty was convinced that, given a chance, Rosamund would make a success on the stage, but Betty was prejudiced. There had always been a curious link of sympathy between the two sisters, utterly different as they were, and many as were the years that separated them.

Tom was the only one of the flock who presented no problem. He was far more human than Jack, but, like Jack, absolutely steady and dependable.

Janet Tosswill's mind swung back to Godfrey Radmore. She wondered how he would like the changes in Old Place, whether they would affect him pleasantly or otherwise. She was woman enough to regret sharply their altered way of life. When Godfrey had lived in Old Place, there had been a good cook, a capable parlor maid, and a well-trained housemaid, as well as a bright-faced "tweenie" there, and life had rolled along as if on wheels. It was very different now.

She wondered if Betty or Timmy had told the others of Radmore's coming visit. It was so strange, in a way, so painful to know that to most of them, with the possible exception of Jack, he was only a name.

Suddenly Betty, turning around, saw her step-mother. "Dolly has met Mrs. Crofton, and she's utterly unlike what any of us thought she would be!" she cried out. "She's young, and very pretty — quite lovely in fact! Dolly asked her into supper tonight, as her cook has not yet arrived."

She had a sort of prevision that Janet was now going to tell the others about Godfrey Radmore, and she wanted to get away out of the room first. But this was not to be. Janet Tosswill had a very positive mind — she was full of what she had come in to say, and the new tenant at The Trellis House interested her not at all, so as soon as she had sat down, she exclaimed, "Perhaps Timmy has told you my news?"

Then all turned to her, except Betty and Timmy himself.

"What news?" came in eager chorus.

"Godfrey Radmore is in England. He telephoned from London just now, and he's coming down on Friday to spend a long weekend!"

Rosamund was the only one who stole a look at Betty.

"Godfrey Radmore here?" repeated Jack slowly. "It's queer he would want to come — after the odd way he's behaved to us."

"Yes, it is rather strange," Janet tried to speak lightly. "But there it is! The whole world has turned topsy-turvy since any of us saw him last."

"I wonder if he's still very rich," went on Jack.

Janet Tosswill felt startled. "Why shouldn't he be?" she asked.

"Oh, I don't know — it only occurred to me that he might have lost some of this money in the same way that he lost that first fortune of his."

"It wasn't a fortune" — Betty's quiet voice broke in very decidedly — "and most of it was lost by a friend of his, not by Godfrey himself at all. He was too proud to say anything about it to father, but he wrote and told George."

A curious stillness fell over the company of young people. They were all in their different ways very much surprised, for Betty never mentioned her twin-brother. All at once they each remembered about Betty and Godfrey — all except Timmy, who had never been told.

"And now what's this about Mrs. Crofton?" asked Janet at last, breaking a silence that had become oppressive. "Do I understand that she's coming to supper tonight?"

It was Betty who answered: "I hope you don't mind? Dolly thought it the only thing to do, as the poor woman's cook hadn't arrived."

"We mustn't forget to ask her in for lunch or dinner on one of the days that Godfrey is here," observed Janet. "I gather they're friends. He asked if she'd already come."

*T*immy was supposed to prepare his lessons between tea and dinner, but unlike the ordinary boy, he much preferred to wake early and work before breakfast. This was considered not good for his health, and there was a constant struggle between himself and his determined mother to force him to do the normal thing. So after she had finished her tea, she beckoned to her son, and he unwillingly got up and followed her into the drawing room. But before he could settle down at his own special table Betty came in.

"Janet, I want to ask you something before I go into the village. There are one or two things we must get in, if Mrs. Crofton is coming this evening —"

The little boy did not wait to hear his mother's answer. He crept very quietly out of the open window, which was close to his table, and then made his way round to the first of the long French windows of the dining room. He was just in time to hear his brother Tom ask in a very solemn tone: "I say, you fellows! Wasn't Betty once engaged to this Radmore chap?"

Timmy, skillfully ensconced behind the full old green damask curtains, listened, with all his ears, for the answer.

"Yes," said Jack at last, with a touch of reluctance. "They were engaged, but not for very long. Still, they'd been fond of one another for an age and George was his greatest friend —"

Rosamund broke in: "Do tell us what he's like, Jack! I suppose you can remember him quite well?"

Jack hesitated, rather uncomfortably.

"Of course I remember Radmore very well indeed. He had quite a tidy bit of money, as both his parents were dead. His snuffy old guardian had been at Balliol with father. So father was asked to coach him. And then, well, I suppose as time went on, and Betty began growing up, he fell in love with her."

"And she with him?" interposed Rosamund.

"A girl is apt to like any man who likes her," said Jack loftily. "But I believe 'twas he made all the fuss when the engagement was broken off."

"But why was it broken off?" asked Rosamund.

"Because he'd lost all his money racing."

"What a stupid thing to do!" exclaimed Tom.

"The row came during the Easter holidays," went on Jack meditatively, "and there was a fearful dust-up. Like an idiot, Radmore had gone and put the whole of the little bit of money he had saved out of the fire on an outsider he had some reason to think would be bound to romp in first — and the horse was not even placed!"

"Poor fellow!" exclaimed Rosamund.

"He rushed down here," went on Jack, "to say that he had made up his mind to go to Australia. And he was simply amazed when father and Janet wouldn't hear of Betty going with him."

"Would she have liked to go?" asked Tom.

"Well, yes — I believe she would. But of course it was out of the question. Father could have given her nothing, even then, so how could they have lived? There was a fearful rumpus, and in the end Godfrey went off in a tearing rage."

"Shaking the dust of Old Place off his indignant feet, eh?" suggested Tom.

"Yes, all that sort of thing. George was having scarlet fever — in a London hospital — so of course he was quite out of it."

"Then, at last Godfrey reopened communication via Timmy?" suggested the younger boy.

"Timmy's got the letter still," chimed in Rosamund. "I saw it in his play-box the other day. It was rather a funny letter — I read it."

"The devil you did!" from Tom, indignantly.

She went on unruffled: — "He said he'd been left a fortune, and wanted to share it with his godson. How much did he send? D'you remember?" She looked round.

"Five pounds!" said Dolly.

"I wish *I* was his godson," said Tom.

"And then," went on Dolly, in her precise way, "the War came, and nothing more happened till suddenly he wrote again to Timmy from Egypt, and then began the presents. I wonder if we ought to have thanked him for them? After all, we don't *know* that they came from him. The only present we *know* came from him was Flick."

"And a damned silly present, too!" observed Jack, dryly.

"Do you think he's still in love with Betty?" asked Rosamund.

"Of course he's not. If he was, he would have written to her, not to Timmy. Nine years is a long time in a man's life," observed Jack sententiously.

"My hat! yes!" exclaimed Tom. "Poor Betty!"

Jack got up, and made a movement as if he were thinking of going out through the window into the garden. So Timmy, with a swift, sinuous movement, withdrew from the curtain, and edging up against the outside wall of the house, walked unobtrusively back into the drawing room.

When his mother — who had gone out to find something for Betty to take into the village — came back, she was pleased and surprised to find her little son working away as if for dear life.

Chapter V

Close on eight that same evening, Timmy Tosswill stood by the open center window of the long drawing room, hands duly washed, and his generally short, rough, untidy hair well brushed, whistling softly to himself.

He was longing intensely for his godfather's arrival, and it seemed such a long time off to Friday. A photograph of Radmore, in uniform, sent him at his own request two years ago, was the boy's most precious personal possession. Timmy was a careful, almost uncannily thrifty child, with quite a lot of money in the Savings Bank, but he had taken out 10/- in order to buy a frame for the photograph, and it rested, alone in its glory, on the top of the chest of drawers that stood opposite his bed.

There had been a time when Timmy had hoped that he would grow up to look like his godfather, but now he was aware that this hope would never be fulfilled, for Radmore, in this photograph, at any rate, had a strongly-featured, handsome face, very unlike what his mother had once called "Timmy's wizened little phiz."

It seemed strange to care for a person you had never seen since you were a tiny child — but there it was! To Timmy everything that touched his godfather was of far greater moment than he would have admitted to anyone. Radmore was his secret hero; and now, tonight, he asked himself painfully, why had his hero left off loving Betty? The story he had overheard this afternoon had deeply impressed him. For the first time he began to dimly apprehend the strange and piteous tangle we call life.

Suddenly there broke on the still autumn air the distant sound of sharp barks and piteous whines. Much against his will, the little boy had had to bow to the edict that Flick should be shut up in the stable. Dolly, who so seldom bothered about anything, had seen to this herself, because Mrs. Crofton, who was coming to supper, hated dogs. Timmy inhospitably hoped that the new tenant of The Trellis House would very seldom honor Old Place with a visit. It would be impossible for them always to hide Flick away like this!

He moved further into the pretty, old-fashioned room. Like most old-fashioned country drawing rooms of the kind, it was rather overfull of furniture and ornaments. The piano jutted out at right angles to a big, roomy sofa, which could, at a pinch, hold seven or eight people, the pinch usually being when, for the benefit of Timmy, the sofa was supposed to be a stagecoach of long ago on its way to London. The Tosswills had been great people for private theatricals, charades, and so on — Timmy's own mother being a really good actress and an excellent mimic, but she did not often now indulge in an exhibition of her powers.

At last Timmy looked round at the clock. It was ten minutes to eight, and his mother would not be down for another five minutes. So he went back to the window. All at once he saw in the gathering twilight, two people walking up the avenue which led to the house. The little boy felt surprised. "Who can they be?" was his immediate thought.

As far as he could make out the one was an elderly-looking gentleman — Timmy could just see the rough grey Norfolk jacket and knickerbockers — by whose side there walked, sedately, a wire-haired terrier. What an extraordinary thing! Surely that dog, walking by the stranger, was *Flick* — Flick, having escaped from the stable, and behaving for all the world as if the stranger were his master. But again there fell on his ears Flick's distant squeals of anger and annoyance and he felt a queer sensation of relief.

Timmy turned his attention to the other figure, that of the young lady who, dressed all in black, tripped gracefully along by the side of her companion. Evidently some tiresome old gentleman, and his equally tiresome daughter. He told himself crossly that his absent-minded, kind-hearted father, or his incurably hospitable mother, forgetting all about Mrs. Crofton, had asked these two people in to supper. If that was so, Timmy, who was as much at home in the kitchen as in the drawing room, knew that there would not be quite enough to go round comfortably. This was all the more irritating, as he himself was looking forward tonight to tasting, for the first time, an especially delicious dish. This was lobster pie, for which Old Place had been famed before the War, but which, owing to the present price of lobsters, was among the many delightful things which the War had caused to vanish from poor little Timmy's world. One of the few sensible people in the world who know what other people really like in the way of a present had sent by parcels-post a lot of lobsters to Timmy's mother — hence the coming lobster pie tonight.

Realizing that the strangers must be very near the front door by now, he edged towards the door of the drawing room, meaning to make a bolt for it into what was still called the schoolroom. He did not wish to be caught by himself in the drawing room. But he was caught, for the door suddenly opened, and his mother came in.

Janet Tosswill "paid for dressing" as the old saying is. She looked charming tonight, in a rather bright blue evening dress, and Timmy, slipping his hand into hers, said softly: "You do look nice, Mum."

She smiled, touched and pleased, for her child was not given to compliments. Also, she had told herself, when glancing at her slim, active figure in the early Victorian cheval glass which had belonged to her husband's mother, that this blue dress was really *very* old-fashioned, and would probably appear so to Mrs. Crofton.

In view of Timmy's pleasant compliment, she did not like to ask him if he had washed his hands and brushed his hair. She could only hope for the best: "I hope we shall like Mrs. Crofton," she said meditatively. "You know she's a friend of your godfather, my dear."

"Yes, I know that," he announced, in rather an odd voice, and she felt just a little surprised. How did Timmy know that? Then she remembered her husband had read aloud Mrs. Crofton's pretty, well-turned letter — the letter which explained that the writer was looking out for a country house, and would like to find one at Beechfield if possible, as her friend, Godfrey Radmore, had described it as being the most beautiful village in England.

Timmy let go his mother's hand — then he looked searchingly into her face: "Do you suppose," he asked, "that my godfather is in love with Mrs. Crofton?"

She was taken aback, and yes, shocked, by the question: "Of course not. Whatever put such an extraordinary idea into your head, Timmy?"

The words had hardly left her lips when the door opened, and the village girl, who was staying on for two hours beyond her usual time because of this visitor, announced in a breathless voice: — "Mrs. Crofton, ma'am."

Timmy saw at once that the visitor was the young lady he had seen walking up the avenue. Then the old gentleman and his dog — the dog which was so extraordinarily like Flick — had only brought her as far as the door. And then, while his mother was shaking hands with Mrs. Crofton, and shepherding her towards the sofa, Timmy managed to have a good, long look at the new tenant of The Trellis House.

Grudgingly he admitted to himself that she was what most people — such people, for instance, as Rosamund and Betty — would call "very pretty."

Mrs. Crofton had a small three-cornered face, a ridiculously little, babyish mouth, and a great deal of dark, curly hair which matched in a queer kind of way the color of her big, pathetic-looking eyes. Timmy told himself at once that he did not like her — that she looked "a muff." It distressed him to think that his hero should be a friend of this weak-looking, sly little thing — for so he uncompromisingly described Enid Crofton to himself.

Hostess and guest sat down on the big, roomy sofa, while Timmy moved away and opened a book. He was afraid lest his mother should invite him to leave the room, for he wanted to hear what they were saying. Timmy always enjoyed hearing grown-up people's conversation, especially when they had forgotten that he was present. All at once his sharp ears heard Mrs. Crofton's low, melodious voice asking the question he had been half-expecting her to ask: "Do you expect Mr. Radmore soon?"

"Yes, he's coming down on Friday." There was a pause, then Timmy heard his mother say: "Have you known Godfrey Radmore long?"

Janet really wanted to know. Somehow, she found it difficult to imagine a friendship between Godfrey and this little fribble of a woman. But as to that, Janet Tosswill showed less than her usual intelligence. She still thought of Godfrey Radmore as of the rather raw, awkward, though clear-headed and determined lad of twenty-three — the Radmore, that is, of nine years ago.

"My husband and I first met him in Egypt," said Mrs. Crofton hesitatingly. The delicate color in her cheeks deepened. "One day he began to talk about himself, and he told me about Beechfield, what a beautiful village it was, how devoted he was to you all!"

Janet Tosswill glanced at the clock. "It's already five minutes past eight!" she exclaimed. "I must go and hurry my young people — their father likes them to be absolutely punctual. The gong will go in a minute."

After his mother had left the room, Timmy crept up close to the sofa, and so suddenly appeared, standing with his hands behind his back, before the visitor. She felt just a little startled; she had not known the strange-looking boy was still there. Then she told herself quickly that this surely must be Godfrey Radmore's godson — the child to whom he had sent one of her late husband's puppies.

There came over pretty Mrs. Crofton a slight feeling of apprehension and discomfiture — she could not have told why.

"When did you last see my godfather?" he asked abruptly, in an unchildish voice, and with a quaintly grown-up manner.

"Your godfather?" she repeated hesitatingly, and yet she knew quite well who he meant.

"I mean Major Radmore," he explained.

She wondered why the disagreeable little fellow had asked such an indiscreet question.

Then, reluctantly, she made up her mind she had better answer it truly: "I saw him the day before yesterday." She forced herself to go on lightly. "I suppose you're the young gentleman to whom he sent a puppy last year?"

He nodded, and then asked another disconcerting question: "Did you leave your dog outside? Dolly thought you didn't like dogs, so my terrier, Flick, has been shut up in the stable. I suppose you only like your own dog — I'm rather like that, too."

"I haven't got a dog," she answered nervously. "It's quite true that I don't like dogs — or, rather, I should like them if they liked me, but they don't."

"Then the dog that was with you belonged to the old gentleman?"

"Old gentleman?" repeated Mrs. Crofton vaguely. This time she didn't in the least know what the child was talking about, and she was relieved when the door opened, and the Tosswill family came streaming through it, accompanied by their step-mother.

Laughing introductions took place. Mrs. Crofton singled out instinctively her gentle, cultivated-looking host. She told herself with a queer sense of relief, that he was the sort of man who generally shows a distantly chivalrous regard for women. Next to her host, his eldest son, Jack Tosswill, came in for secret, close scrutiny, but Enid Crofton always found it easy and more than easy, to "make friends" with a young man.

She realized that she was up against a more difficult problem in the ladies of the family. She felt a little frightened of Mrs. Tosswill, of whom Godfrey Radmore had spoken with such affection and gratitude. Janet looked what Mrs. Crofton called "clever," and somehow she never got on with clever women. Betty and Dolly she dismissed as of no account. Rosamund was the one the attractive stranger liked best. There is no greater mistake than to think that a pretty woman does not like to meet another pretty woman. On the contrary, "like flies to like" in this, as in almost everything else.

But how did they regard her? She would have been surprised indeed had she been able to see into their hearts.

Mr. Tosswill, who was much more wide-awake than he looked, thought her a poor exchange for the amusing, lively, middle-aged woman who had last lived at The Trellis House, and who had often entertained there a pleasant, cultivated guest or two from London. Jack, though sufficiently human to be attracted by the stranger's grace and charm, was inclined to reserve his judgment. The three girls found her very engaging, and their step-mother, if more critical, was quite ready to like her. As is often the case with people who only care for those near and dear to them, the world of men and women outside Janet Tosswill's own circle interested her scarcely at all. She would make up her mind as to what any given individual was like, and then dismiss him or her once for all from her busy, overburdened mind.

One thing, however, both Janet and the three girls did notice — that was the way their new acquaintance was dressed. Her black frock was not only becoming, but had that indefinable look which implies thought, care, and cost — especially cost. All four ladies decided immediately that Mrs. Crofton must be much better off than she had implied in the letter she had written to Mr. Tosswill some weeks ago.

Timmy, alone of them all, on that first evening, felt strongly about their visitor. Already he was jealous of the pretty, pathetic-looking young widow. It irritated him to think that she was a friend of his godfather.

After they had all gone into the dining room, and had sorted themselves out, the guest being seated on her host's right, with Jack on the other side of her, Janet announced: "This is supper, not dinner, Mrs. Crofton. I hope you don't mind lobster? When I first came to Old Place, almost the first thing I learnt was that it was celebrated for its lobster pie! Since the War we have not been able to afford lobsters, but a kind friend sent us six from Littlehampton yesterday, so I at once thought of our dear old lobster pie!"

Mrs. Crofton declared that, far from minding, she adored lobsters! And then after she had been served, Timmy's fears were set at rest, for his mother, very improperly the rest of the family thought, served him next, and to a generous helping.

As the meal went on, the mistress of Old Place realized that she had made one mistake about Mrs. Crofton; their visitor was far more intelligent, though in a mean, rather narrow way, than she had at first supposed. Also, Mrs. Crofton was certainly very attractive. As the talk turned to London doings, his step-mother was amused to notice that Jack was becoming interested in their guest, and eagerly discussed with her a play they had both seen.

And the visitor herself? During supper she began to feel most pleasantly at home, and when she walked into the long, high-ceilinged sitting room, which had such a cozy, homelike look she told herself that it was no wonder Godfrey Radmore liked the delightful old house, and these kindly, old-fashioned, and — and unsuspicious people.

Two tall Argand lamps cast a soft radiance over the shabby furniture and faded carpet. It was a lovely evening, a true St. Martin's summer night, and the middle one of the three long French windows was widely open on to the fragrant, scented garden.

Mrs. Crofton, a graceful, appealing figure in her soft, black chiffon gown, hesitated a moment — she wondered where they wanted her to sit? And then Mrs. Tosswill came forward and, taking her hand, led her to the big sofa, while one of the girls fetched an extra cushion so that she might sit back comfortably. The talk drifted to the War, and Enid Crofton was soon engaged in giving an animated account of some of her own experiences — how she had managed to spend a very exciting fortnight not far from the Front, in a hospital run by a great lady with whom she had a slight acquaintance. Soon, sooner than usual, Mr. Tosswill and his three sons came into the drawing room, and they were all talking and laughing together happily when a most unlucky, and untoward, accident happened! Timmy's dog, Flick, having somehow escaped from the stable, suddenly ran in from the dark garden, straight through the window opposite the sofa round which the whole of the party was now gathered together. When about a yard from Mrs. Crofton, he stopped dead, and emitted a series of short, wild howls, while his hair bristled and stood on end, and his eyes flamed blood red.

They were all so surprised — so extremely taken aback by Flick's behavior — that no one moved. Then Mrs. Crofton gave a kind of gasp, and covering her face with her hands, cowered back in the corner of the sofa.

Timmy jumped up from the stool where he had been sitting, and as he did so, his mother called out affrightedly: "Don't go near Flick, Timmy — he looks mad!"

But Timmy was no coward, and Flick was one of the few living things he loved in the world. He threw himself on the floor beside his dog. "Flick," he said warningly, "what's the matter, old chap? Has anything hurt you?" As he spoke he put out his skinny little arms, and Flick, though still shivering and growling, began to calm down.

The little boy waited a moment, Flick panting convulsively in his arms, then he gathered the dog to him, and, getting up from the floor, walked quickly through the open window into the garden.

For a moment no one stirred — and then Mr. Tosswill, who had been sitting rather apart from the rest of the party, got up and shut the window.

"What a curious thing," he said musingly. "I have always regarded Flick as one of the best tempered of dogs. This is the first time he has ever behaved like this."

Mrs. Crofton dragged herself up from her comfortable seat. Her face looked white and pinched. In spite of her real effort to control herself, there were tears in her eyes and her lips were trembling. "If you are on the telephone," she said appealingly, "I should be so grateful if you should send for a fly. I don't feel well enough to walk home." She tried to smile. "My nerves have been upset for some time past."

Janet felt vexed and concerned. "Jack will drive you home in our old pony cart," she said soothingly. "Will you go and bring it round, Tom?"

Tom slipped off, and there arose a Babel of voices, everyone saying how sorry they were, Dolly especially, explaining eagerly how she herself had personally superintended the shutting up of the dog. As for Betty, she went off into the hall and quietly fetched Mrs. Crofton's charming evening cloak and becoming little hood. As she did so she told herself again that Mrs. Crofton must be much better off than they had thought her to be from her letter. Every woman, even the least sophisticated, knows what really beautiful and becoming clothes cost nowadays, and Mrs. Crofton's clothes were eminently beautiful and becoming.

As Betty went back into the drawing room, she heard the visitor say: — "I was born with a kind of horror of dogs, and I'm afraid that in some uncanny way they always know it! It's such bad luck, for most nice people and all the people I myself have cared for in my life, have been dog lovers."

And at that Dolly, who had a most unfortunate habit of blurting out just those things which, even if people are thinking of, they mostly leave unsaid, exclaimed: — "Your husband bred terriers, didn't he? Flick came from him."

Mrs. Crofton made no answer to this, and Janet, who was looking at her, saw her face alter. A curious expression of — was it pain? — it looked more like fear, — came over it. It was clear that Dolly's thoughtless words had hurt her.

Suddenly there came the sound of a tap on the pane of one of the windows, and Mrs. Crofton, whose nerves were evidently very much out of order, gave a suppressed cry.

"It's only Timmy," said Timmy's mother reassuringly, and then she went and opened the window. "I hope you've shut Flick up," she said in a low voice.

"Of course I have, Mum. He's quite quiet now."

As the boy came forward, into the room, he looked straight up into Mrs. Crofton's face, and as she met the enquiring, alien look, she told herself, for the second time that evening, what a pity it was that these nice people should have such an unpleasant child.

Tom came in to say that the pony cart was at the door, and that Jack was waiting there for Mrs. Crofton.

They all went out in the hall to see her off. It was a bright, beautiful, moonlight night, and Rosamund thought the scene quite romantic.

Mr. Tosswill handed his guest into the pony cart with his usual, rather aloof, courtesy; and after all the good-byes had been said, and as Jack drove down the long, solitary avenue, Enid Crofton told herself that in spite of that horrible incident with the dog — it was so strange that Flick should come, as it were, to haunt her out of her old life, the life she was so anxious to forget — she had had a very promising and successful evening. The only jarring note had been that horrid little boy Timmy — Timmy and his hateful dog.

And then suddenly Enid Crofton asked herself whether Godfrey Radmore was likely to go on being as fond of Timmy Tosswill as he seemed to be now. She had been surprised at the reminiscent affection with which he had spoken of his little godson. But there is a great difference between an attractive baby-child of three and a forward, spoilt, undersized boy of twelve. About a week ago, while they were enjoying a delicious little dinner in the Berkeley Hotel grill-room, he had said: — "Although of course none of them know it, for the present at any rate, Master Timmy is my heir; if I were to die tonight Timmy Tosswill would become a very well-to-do young gentleman!"

Even at the time they had been uttered, the careless words had annoyed Enid Crofton; and now the recollection of them made her feel quite angry. All her life long money had played a great part in this very pretty woman's inmost thoughts.

Chapter VI

*B*etty Tosswill sat up in bed and told herself that it was Friday morning. Then she remembered what it was that was going to happen today.

It was something that she had thought, deep in her heart, would never happen. Godfrey Radmore was coming back — coming back into her life, and into all their lives. Though everything seemed just the same as when he had left Old Place, everything was different, both in a spiritual and material sense. The War had made a deep wound, nay, far more than one wound, in the spiritual body politic of Old Place. And it was of a very material thing that Betty Tosswill thought first, and most painfully, this morning. This was the fact that from having been in easy circumstances they were now very poor.

When Godfrey Radmore had gone out of their lives there had been a great, perhaps even then a false, air of prosperity over them all. John Tosswill was a man who had always made bad investments; but in that far-off time, "before the War," living was so cheap, wages were so low, the children were all still so young, that he and Janet had managed very well.

Only Betty knew the scrimping and the saving Jack, at Oxford, and Tom, at Winchester, now entailed on the part of those who lived at Old Place. Why, she herself counted every penny with anxious care, and the stupid, kindly folk who asked, just a trifle censoriously, why she wasn't "doing something," now that "every career is open to a girl, especially to one who did so well in the War," would perhaps have felt a little ashamed had they discovered that she was housemaid, parlor maid, often cook, to a large and not always easily pleased family. They never had a visitor to stay now — they simply couldn't afford it — and she hated the thought of Godfrey, himself now so unnaturally prosperous, coming back to such an altered state of things.

Besides, that was not all. Betty covered her face with her hands, and slow, bitter, reluctant tears began to ooze through her fingers. She had tried not to think of Godfrey and of his coming, these last two or three days. She had put the knowledge of what was going to happen from her, with a kind of hard, defiant determination. But now she was sorry — sorry, that she had not taken her step-mother's advice, and gone away for a long weekend. Betty Tosswill felt like a man who, having suffered intolerably from a wound which has at last healed, learns with sick apprehension that his wound is to be torn open.

Although not even Janet, her one real close friend and confidant, was aware of it, Godfrey had not been the only man in Betty's life. There had been two men, out in France, who had loved her, and lost no time in telling her so. One had been killed; the other still wrote to her at intervals, begging her earnestly, pathetically, to marry him, and sometimes she half thought she would.

But always Godfrey Radmore stood before the door of her heart, imperiously, almost contemptuously, "shooing off" any would-be intruder. And yet today she told herself, believing what she said, that she no longer loved him. She remembered now, as if they had been uttered yesterday, the cruel words he had flung at her during their last hour together when he had taunted her with not giving up everything and going off with him — and that though she had known that there was, even then, a part of his acute, clever brain telling him insistently that she would be a drag on him in his new life. . . . She had also been cut to the heart that Godfrey had not written to her father when his one-time closest friend, her twin-brother, George, had been killed.

Today for the first time, Betty Tosswill told herself that perhaps she had been mistaken in doing right instead of wrong, in coming here to help Janet with her far from easy task with the younger children, instead of getting a good job, as she knew she could have done, after the War.

There is a modern type of young woman, quite a good young woman, too, who, in Betty's position, would have thought that it was far better that she should go out and earn, say, three or four pounds a week, sending half the money, or a third of the money, home. But poor Betty was no self-deceiver — she was well aware that what was wanted at Old Place in the difficult months, aye, and even years, which would follow the end of the Great War, was personal service.

And so she had come home, making no favor of it, settling into her often tiring and tiresome duties, trying now and again to make Rosamund and Dolly do their share. In a way they did try, but they were both very selfish in their different ways, and only Janet knew all that everyone of them owed to Betty's hard, continuous work, and sense of order. Not that the girl was perfect by any means; now and again she would say a very sharp, sarcastic word, but on the whole she was wonderfully indulgent, kindly and understanding — more like a mother than a sister to the others.

Everyday life is a mosaic of infinitely little things, whatever those who write and talk may say. Betty had come back and settled down to life at home, mainly because her step-mother could no longer "carry on." Janet could not get servants, and if she could have got them, she could not now have paid them. Then there had been the silly, vulgar but highly dangerous affair between Rosamund and their too attractive married "billet." Had Betty been at home that business would almost certainly have been checked in the bud. As for Dolly, she was worse than no good in the home. But — a certain secret hope was cherished both by Janet and by Betty concerning Dolly. The bachelor vicar of the next parish seemed to find a strange pleasure in her society. He was away now in Switzerland and he had written to Dolly a minute account of his long, tiresome journey.

She wondered, with a feeling of pain at her heart, what Godfrey would think of them all. There had been such an air of charm and gaiety about the place nine years ago. Now, beautiful in a sense as was the stately Georgian house, lovely as was the garden, thanks to Janet's cleverness and hard work, there was an air of shabbiness over everything though Betty only fully realized it on the very rare occasions when she got away for a few days for a change and rest with old friends.

This summer her brother Jack had said a word to her, not exactly complainingly, but with a sort of regret. "Don't you think we could afford new furniture covers for the drawing room?" and Betty had shaken her head. They could afford *nothing* for the house — she alone knew how very difficult it was to keep up Jack's own modest allowance.

There had been a discussion between herself and Janet as to whether Mr. Tosswill should start taking pupils again in his old age, but they had decided against it, largely because they felt that the class of pupils whom he had been accustomed to take before the war, and who could alone be of any use from the financial point of view, could not now be made really comfortable at Old Place. Betty was ashamed of feeling how much it hurt her pride to know how concerned Godfrey would be to find how poor they had become. She would not have minded this if he had been poor himself. But she hated the thought of a rich Godfrey, who flung money about over foolish, extravagant presents, discovering, suddenly, how altered were their circumstances since the day when he had rushed out of the house throwing the big check kind John Tosswill had shamefacedly handed to him, on to the floor.

*A*fter Betty had had her own cold bath, and had prepared a tepid one for her father, she dressed quickly, and going over to the dressing-table in the large, low-ceilinged room — a room which, in spite of the fact that everything in it was old and worn, had yet an air of dainty charm and dignity, for everything in it was what old-fashioned people call "good" — she looked dispassionately at herself in the glass.

Her step-mother had said, "You haven't changed one bit!" But that was not true. Of course she had changed — changed very much, out-wardly and inwardly, since she was nineteen. For one thing, the awful physical strain of her work in France had altered her, turned her from a girl into a woman. She had seen many terrible things, and she had met with certain grim adventures she could never forget, which re-mained all the more vivid because she had never spoken of them to a living being.

And then, as she suddenly told herself, with a rather bitter feeling of revolt, the life she was leading now was not calculated to make her retain a look of youth. Last week, in a fit of temper, Rosamund had said to her: — "I only wish you could see yourself! You look a regular 'govvy'!" She had laughed — the rather spiteful words passing her by — for she had never cared either for learning or teaching. But now, as she gazed critically in her mirror, she told herself that, yes, she really did look rather like a nice governess — the sort of young woman a certain type of smart lady would describe as her "treasure." Forty or fifty years ago that was the sort of human being into which she would have turned almost automatically when poverty had first knocked at the door of Old Place. Now, thank God, people who could afford to pay well for a governess wanted a trained teacher, not an untrained gentlewoman for their children.

But Betty did not waste much time staring at herself. Throwing her head back with what had become a characteristic gesture, she went off and called her sisters and brothers before running lightly down the back stairs.

Nanna was already pottering about the kitchen. She had laid and lit the fire, and put the kettle on to boil for Mrs. Tosswill's early cup of tea. The old woman looked up as Betty came into the kitchen, and a rather touching expression came over her old face. She had a strong, almost a maternal affection for her eldest nurseling, and she wondered how Miss Betty was feeling this morning. Nanna had been told of the coming visitor by Timmy, but with that peculiar touch of delicacy so often found in her class, she had said nothing about it to Betty.

"Well, Nanna? I expect Mrs. Tosswill has told you that Mr. Radmore is coming today, and that he's to have George's room."

Nanna nodded. "It's quite ready, Miss Betty. I went in there yesterday afternoon while you was all out. He'll find everything there just as he left it. Eh, dear, I do mind how those dear boys loved their stamps and butterflies."

Betty sighed, a sharp, quick sigh. After calling Jack she had thought of going into the room which had been her brother's and Godfrey's joint room in the long, long ago. And then she had decided that she couldn't bear to do so. The room had never been slept in since George had spent his last happy leave for now there was never any occasion to put a visitor in what was still called by Nanna "Master George's room."

"I expect he'll arrive for tea," said Betty, "and I was wondering whether we couldn't make one of those big seed cakes he and George used to be so fond of."

"That's provided for, too," said Nanna quietly.

And then, all at once, almost as though she were compelled to do so by something outside herself, Betty went across the kitchen and threw her arms round her old nurse's neck and kissed her.

"There, there," said Nanna soothingly, "do you mind much, my dearie!"

"No, I don't think I do." Betty winked away the tears. "It's George I'm really thinking of, Nanna."

"But the dear lad is in the Kingdom of the Blessed, my dear. You wouldn't have him back — surely?"

"Not if he's really happier where he is," said the girl, "but oh, Nanna, it's so hard to believe that." She went across to the big old-fashioned kitchen range, and poured the boiling water into a little silver teapot. Then she took the tray to her step-mother's room.

Next she went down into the drawing room — she always "did" that room while Nanna laid the breakfast with the help of the village girl who, although she was supposed to come in at seven, very seldom turned up till eight. And then, while Betty was carefully dusting the quaint, old-fashioned Staffordshire figures on the mantelpiece, the door opened, and Nanna came in and shut it behind her. "There isn't any wine," she began mysteriously. "Gentlemen do like a little drop of wine after their dinner."

"I think what father and Jack can do without, Mr. Radmore can do without, too," said Betty. For the first time her color heightened. "In any case, I don't see how we can get anything fit to drink by this evening."

"I was thinking, Miss Betty, that you might borrow a bottle of port wine at Rose Cottage."

"I don't think I can do that," said Betty decidedly, "you see, Miss Pendarth's port is very good port, and we could never give her back a bottle of the same quality."

And then, as Nanna sidled towards the door, the old woman suddenly remarked, a little irrelevantly: — "I suppose you've told Miss Pendarth that Mr. Godfrey is coming, Miss Betty?"

Betty looked round quickly. "No," she said, "I haven't had a chance yet. Thank you for reminding me."

The old woman slipped away, and Betty suddenly wondered whether Nanna had really come in to ask that question as to Miss Pendarth. Somehow Betty suspected that she had.

Chapter VII

*I*t was about eleven, when most of her household chores were done, that Betty started off to pay an informal call on Miss Pendarth, in some ways the most outstanding personality in the village of Beechfield.

"Busybody" — "mischief-maker" — "a very kind lady" — "a disagreeable woman" — "a fearful snob" — "a true Christian" — were some of the epithets which had been, and were still, used, to describe the woman to whose house, Rose Cottage, Betty Tosswill, with a slight feeling of discomfort bordering on pain, began wending her way.

Olivia Pendarth and her colorless younger sister, Anne, the latter now long dead, had settled down at Beechfield in the nineties of the last century. When both over thirty years of age, they had selected Beechfield as a dwelling-place because of its quiet charm and nearness to London. Also because Rose Cottage, which, in spite of its unassuming name, was, if a small yet a substantial, red-brick house with a good garden, paddock and stables, exactly suited them, as to price, and as to the accommodation they then wanted. The surviving sister was now rather over sixty, and her income was very much smaller than it had been, but it never even occurred to her to try and sell what had become to her a place of mingled painful and happy memories.

In every civilized country a village is the world in little, though it is always surprising to the student of human nature to find how many distinct types are gathered within its narrow bounds. And if this is true of village communities all over Europe, it is peculiarly true of an English village.

Miss Pendarth was a clever woman. Too clever to be really happy in the life to which she had condemned herself. She had been born many years too early to follow up any of the various paths now open to the intelligent, educated woman. Yet she belonged, by birth and upbringing, to that age-long tradition of command which perhaps counts for most of all to the one class which has remained in England much the same for generations.

The Pendarths had once been very great people in Cornwall, and long records of the family are to be found in all county histories. Olivia Pendarth was wordlessly very proud of their lineage, and it is no exaggeration to say that she would have died rather than in any way disgrace it.

A woman of great activity, she had perforce no way of expending her energies excepting in connection with the people about her, and always in intention at least she spent herself to some beneficent purpose. Yet there was a considerable circle who much disliked her and whom she herself regarded with almost limitless scorn. These were the folk, idle people most of them, and very well-to-do, who, having made fortunes in London, now lived within a radius of five to ten miles round Beechfield.

Miss Pendarth was on excellent terms with what one must call, for want of a better name, the cottage class. To them she was a good, firm, faithful friend, seeing them through their many small and great troubles, and taking real pains to help their sons and daughters to make good starts in life. Many a village mother had asked Miss Pendarth to "speak" to her naughty girl or headstrong son, and as she was quite fearless, her words often had a surprising effect. She neither patronized nor scolded, and it was impossible to take her in.

But when dealing with the affairs of those of her neighbors, who were well-to-do, and who regarded themselves as belonging to her own class, it was quite another matter. With regard to them and their affairs she was what they often angrily accused her of being — a busy-body and even a mischief-maker. Her lively mind caused her to take a great interest — too great an interest — in the private affairs of people some of whom she disliked, and even despised. She was also not as scrupulous as she might have been in repeating unsavory gossip. Yet, even so, so substantially good a woman was she, that what some people called Miss Pendarth's interfering ways had more than once brought about a reconciliation between husband and wife, or between an old-fashioned mother and a rebellious daughter. It was hopeless to try to keep from her the news of any local quarrel, love-affair, or money trouble — somehow or other she always found out everything she was likely to want to know — and she almost always wanted to know everything.

There was another fact about Miss Pendarth, and one which much contributed to her importance even with the people who disliked and feared her: she was the only inhabitant of the remote Surrey village who was in touch with the world of fashion and society — who knew people whose "pictures are in the papers." Now and again, though more and more rarely as time went on, she would leave Rose Cottage to take part in some big family gathering of the important and prosperous clan to which, in spite of her own lack of means, she yet belonged, and with whom she kept in touch. But she herself never entertained a visitor at Rose Cottage, for a reason of which she herself was painfully aware and which the more careless of those about her did not in the least realize. This reason was that she was very, very poor. Before the War, her little settled income had enabled her to live in comfort in a house which was her own. But now, had not her one servant been friend as well as maid, she could not have gone on living in Rose Cottage; and during the last year, as Betty Tosswill perhaps alone had noticed, certain beautiful things, fine bits of good old silver, delicate inlaid pieces of furniture, and a pair of finely carved gilt mirrors, had disappeared from Rose Cottage.

The house was situated in the village street, with, however, a paved forecourt, in which stood two huge Italian oil jars gay from April to November with narcissi, tulips, or pink geraniums. Miss Pendarth was proud of the fine old Sussex ironwork gate and railing which separated her domain from the village street. The gate was exactly opposite the entrance to the churchyard, while at right angles stood the village post office. From the windows of her drawing room upstairs, the mistress of Rose Cottage was able to see a great deal that went on in the village of Beechfield.

Miss Pendarth's appearance, as is so often the case with an elderly, unmarried Englishwoman of her class, gave no clue to her clever, decisive, and original character. She had a thin, rather long mouth, what old-fashioned people call a good nose, and grey eyes, and she had kept the slight, rather stiff, figure of her girlhood. She still wore her hair, which was only now beginning to turn really grey, braided in the way which had been becoming to her thirty years before. The effect, if neat, was rather wiglike, and the one peculiar-looking thing about her appearance. She always wore, summer and winter, a mannish-looking tailor-made coat and skirt, and a plainly cut flannel or linen shirt. At night — and she dressed each evening — she alternated between two black dresses, the one a velvet dress gown, the other a sequin-covered satin tea-gown.

Such was the woman to whom Betty Tosswill had thought it just as well to go herself with the news of Godfrey Radmore's coming visit to Old Place, and as she walked slowly up the village street, the girl tried to remind herself that Miss Pendarth had a very kind side to her nature. Of all the letters Betty had received at the time of her brother's death, she had had none of more sincerely expressed sympathy than that from this old friend whom she was now going to see. And yet? Yet what pain and distress Miss Pendarth had caused them all at the time of the Rosamund trouble! Instead of behaving like a true friend, and, as far as possible, stopping the flow of gossip, she had added to its volume, causing the story to be known to a far larger circle than would otherwise have been the case. But Betty, honesty itself, was well aware that her step-mother had made a serious mistake in not telling Miss Pendarth what there was to tell. A confidence she never betrayed.

Betty also reminded herself ruefully that in the faraway days when Godfrey Radmore had been so often an inmate of Old Place, there had been something like open war between himself and Miss Pendarth, and when she had heard of his extraordinary good fortune, she had not hidden her regret that it had fallen on one so unworthy.

As Betty went up to the iron gate and unlatched it, she half hoped that the owner of Rose Cottage would be out. Miss Pendarth, unlike most of her neighbors, always kept her front door locked — you could not turn the handle and walk right into the house.

Today she answered Betty's ring herself, and with a smile of welcome lighting up her rather grim face she drew the girl into the hall and kissed her affectionately.

"I was just starting to pay my first call on Mrs. Crofton. But I'm so glad. Perhaps you'll be able to tell me something about her. I hear she had supper with you the day she arrived!"

As she spoke, she led the way into a little room off the hall. "I've been trying to make out to what branch of the Croftons she belongs," she went on reflectively. "There was a man called Cecil Crofton in my second brother's regiment a matter of forty years ago."

"She looks quite young," said Betty doubtfully.

"Old enough to know better than to get herself talked about the first hour she arrived," observed Miss Pendarth grimly.

"I don't think she can have done that —"

"Not only did she bring a man with her, a Captain Tremaine, — but just before he left they had some kind of quarrel which was overheard by two of the tradespeople who were calling to leave their cards."

"How — how horrid," murmured Betty. But what really shocked her was that Miss Pendarth should listen to that sort of gossip.

"It was horrid and absurd too, for the man had turned the key in the lock of the sitting room, and it stuck for a minute or two when one of them tried to unlock the door in answer to the maid's knock!"

"What an extraordinary thing!"

"I could hardly believe the story, but now that I've seen Mrs. Crofton, I'm not so very much surprised!"

"Then you have seen her?" Betty smiled.

"I've just had a glimpse of her," admitted Miss Pendarth grudgingly, "as she came out of church, a day or two ago, with your sister Dolly."

"She's extraordinarily pretty, isn't she?"

"Too theatrical for my taste. But still, yes, I suppose one must admit that she will prove a very formidable rival to most of our young ladies. I'm told she's a war widow — and she certainly behaves as if she were."

"I don't think it's fair to say that!" Betty crimsoned. She felt a close kinship to all those women who had lost someone they loved in the War.

"You mean not fair to the war widows?"

"Yes, that is what I do mean. Only a few of them behave horridly —"

There was a pause. Betty was trying to bring herself to introduce the subject which filled her mind. But Miss Pendarth was still full of the new tenant of The Trellis House.

"I hear that Timmy's dog gave her a fearful fright."

Betty felt astonished, well used as she was to the other's almost uncanny knowledge of all that went on in the village. Who could have told her this particular bit of gossip?

"I wonder," went on the elder lady reflectively, "what made Mrs. Crofton come to Beechfield, of all places in the world. Somehow she doesn't look the sort of woman who would care for a country life."

"Godfrey Radmore first told her of Beechfield," said Betty, and in spite of herself, she felt the color rise again hotly to her cheeks.

"Godfrey Radmore?" It was Miss Pendarth's turn to be genuinely surprised. *"Godfrey Radmore!* Then she's Australian? I thought there was something odd about her."

Betty smiled, but she felt irritated. In some ways Miss Pendarth was surely very narrow-minded!

"No, she's not Australian — at least I'm pretty sure she's not. They met during the War, in Egypt. Her husband was quartered there at the same time as Godfrey." She paused uncomfortably — somehow she found it very difficult to go on and say what, after all, she had come here to say this morning.

"I suppose," said Miss Pendarth at last, "that Godfrey Radmore is back in Brisbane by now. One of the strange things about this war has been the way in which those who could have been best spared, escaped."

In spite of herself, Betty smiled again. "Godfrey has come back to England for good," she said quietly, "he's coming today for a long weekend."

"D'you mean," asked Miss Pendarth, "that he's coming to stay with this Mrs. Crofton at The Trellis House?"

"Oh, no!" exclaimed Betty. (What odd ideas Miss Pendarth sometimes had.) "He's coming to Old Place of course: he telephoned to Janet from London, and proposed himself."

"I think it's very good of you all to put up with him," said Miss Pendarth dryly, "I've never said so before, my dear, but I thought it exceedingly ungrateful of him not to have come down here when he was in England a year ago, I mean when he sent that puppy to your brother Timmy."

Betty remained silent, and for once her old friend felt — what she too seldom did feel — that she might just as well have kept her thoughts to herself.

Miss Pendarth was really attached to Betty Tosswill, but she was one of those people — there are many such — who find it all too easy to hurt those they love.

They both got up.

"I'm afraid you think me very uncharitable," said the older woman suddenly.

Betty looked at her rather straight. "I sometimes think it strange," she said slowly, "that anyone as kind and clever as I know you are, does not make more allowances for people. For my part, I wonder that Godfrey is coming here at all. As I look back and remember all that happened — I don't think that anyone at Old Place behaved either kindly or fairly to him — I mean about our engagement."

Miss Pendarth was moved as well as surprised by Betty's quiet words. The girl was extraordinarily reserved — she very rarely spoke out her secret thoughts. But Miss Pendarth was destined to be even more surprised, for Betty suddenly put out her hand, and laid it on the other's arm.

"I want to tell you," she said earnestly, "that as far as I am concerned, everything that happened then is quite, quite over. I don't think that Godfrey would have been happy with me, and so I feel that we both had a great escape. I want to tell you this because so many people knew of our engagement, and I'm afraid his coming back like this may cause a lot of silly, vulgar talk."

Miss Pendarth was more touched than she would have cared to admit even to herself. "You can count on me, my dear," she said gravely, "and may I say, Betty, that I feel sure you're right in feeling that you would have been most unhappy with him?"

As Betty walked on to the post office she was glad that *that* little ordeal was over.

*J*ohn Tosswill was one of those men who instinctively avoid and put off as long as may be, a difficult or awkward moment. That was perhaps one reason why he had not made a better thing of his life. So his wife was not surprised when, after luncheon, he observed rather nervously that he was going out, and that she must tell Godfrey Radmore how sorry he was not to be there to welcome him.

As she remained silent, he added, rather shamefacedly: — "I'll be back in time to have a few words with him before dinner."

Poor Janet! She still loved her husband as much as she had done in the days when he, the absent-minded, gentle, refined scholar, made his way into her heart. Nay, in a sense, she loved him more, for he had become entirely dependent on her. But though she loved and admired him, she no longer relied on him, as she had once done; he had a queer way of failing her at the big moments of life, and now, today, she felt it too bad of him to shirk the moment of Godfrey Radmore's return. His presence would have made everything easier, for he had never admitted either to himself or her, that Godfrey had behaved in a strange or untoward manner.

As she turned over the leaves of a nursery-man's catalogue and gazed at the list of plants and bulbs she could not afford to buy, long-forgotten scenes crowded on her memory.

Radmore had been the violent, unreasonable element in the painful episode, for Betty had behaved well, almost too well. The girl would have thrown in her lot with her lover, but both her father and step-mother had been agonized at the thought of trusting her to a man — and so very young a man — who had made such a failure of his life. That he was going out to Australia practically penniless — nay, worse than penniless, saddled with debts of so-called honor — had been, or so they had judged at the time, entirely his own fault.

John Tosswill, who had a very clear and acute mind when any abstract question was under discussion, had told Betty plainly that she would only be a dangerous hindrance to a man situated as Radmore would be situated in a new country, and she had submitted to her father's judgment.

But how ironical are the twists and turns of life! If only they had known what the future was to bring forth, how differently Betty's father and step-mother would have acted! Yet now today, Janet tried to tell herself that Betty had had a happy escape. Godfrey had been like a bull in the net during those painful days nine years ago. He had shown himself utterly unreasonable, and especially angry, nay enraged, with her, Janet, because he had been foolish enough to hope that she would take his part against Betty's father.

*A*cting on a sudden impulse, she went upstairs, and, feeling a little ashamed of what she was doing, went into the room which was to be Godfrey Radmore's. Then she walked across to where stood Timmy's play-box, in order to find the letter which Betty's one-time lover had written to his godson.

The play-box had been George's play-box in the days of his preparatory school, and it still had his name printed across it.

She turned up the wooden lid. Everything in the box was very tidy, for Timmy was curiously grown-up in some of his ways, and so she very soon found the letter she was seeking for.

It was a quaint, humorous epistle — the letter of a man who feels quite sure of himself, and yet as she read it through rapidly, there rose before her the writer as he had last appeared in a railing whirlwind of rage and fury, just before leaving Old Place — he had vowed at the time — forever. She remembered how he had shouted at her, hurling bitter reproaches, telling her she would be sorry one day for having persuaded Betty to give him up. But though she, Janet Tosswill, had not forgotten, he had evidently made up his mind, the moment he had met with his unexpected and astonishing piece of good luck, to let bygones be bygones. For, after that first letter to his godson, gifts had come in quick succession to Old Place, curious unexpected, anonymous gifts, but even Dolly had guessed at once from whom they came.

No wonder the younger children were all excited and delighted at the thought of his coming visit! Radmore was now looked upon as a fairy godfather might have been. They were too young, too self-absorbed, to realize that these wonderful gifts out of the blue never seemed to wing their way to Betty or Janet. Yet stop, there had been an exception. Last Christmas each had received an anonymous fairing — Betty, a beautiful little watch, set in diamonds, and Janet, a wonderful old lace flounce. Both registered parcels had come from London, Godfrey Radmore being known at the time to be in Australia. But neither recipient of the delightful gift had ever cared to wear or use it.

Chapter VIII

*A*nd meanwhile the man of whom every single human being in Old Place, with the exception of the little village day girl, was thinking this afternoon, was coming ever nearer and nearer to Beechfield in an ecstasy of sentient joy at being "at home" again.

As Radmore motored along the Portsmouth Road through the warmly-beautiful autumn countryside, a feeling of exultation, of intense personal love for, and pride in, the old country, filled his heart. Why had he stayed in London so long when all this tranquil, appealing loveliness of wood, stream, hill and hollow lay close at hand? There are folk who deny the charm of Surrey — by whom this delicious county, with its noble stretches of wild, fragrant uplands, and wide, deep valleys, is dismissed as suburban. But though they would deny it vehemently, the eyes of such folk are holden.

As he was borne along through the soft, lambent air, everything he passed appealed to his heart and imagination. Each of the small, yet dignified, eighteenth-century houses, which add such distinction and grace to each Surrey township — Epsom, Leatherhead, Guildford — gave him a comfortable feeling of his country's well-being, of the essential stability of England. Now and again, in some woodland glade where summer still lingered, he would pass by happy groups engaged in black-berrying; while on the road there waited the char-à-bancs, the motorcycles, the pony-traps, which had brought them.

Once, when they came to such a spot, he, Radmore, called out to his chauffeur to stop. They were close to the crest of Boxhill, and below them lay spread out what is perhaps the finest, because the richest in human and historic associations, view in Southern England. As he stood up and gazed down and down and down, to his right he saw what looked from up here such a tiny toylike town, and it recalled suddenly a book he had once read, as one reads a Jules Verne romance, "The Battle of Dorking," a soldier's fairy-tale that had come perilously near being a prophecy.

Before Radmore's eyes — blotting out the noble, peaceful landscape, rich in storied beauty — there rose an extraordinarily vivid phantasmagoria of vast masses of armed men in field grey moving across that wide, thickly peopled valley of lovely villages and cozy little towns. He saw as in a vision the rich stretches of arable land, the now red, brown, and yellow spinneys and clumps of high trees, the meadows dotted with sleek cattle, laid waste — while sinister columns of flames and massed clouds of smoke rose from each homestead.

"Drive on!" he called out, and the chauffeur was startled by the harsh note in his employer's generally kindly voice.

On they sped down the great flank of the huge hill, past the hostelry where Nelson bid a last farewell to his Emma, on and on along narrow lanes, and between high hedges starred with autumn flowers. And then, when in a spot so wild and lonely that it might have been a hundred miles from a town — though it was only some ten miles from Beechfield — something went wrong with the engine of the car.

Janet had proposed that tea should be at five o'clock, so as to give the visitor plenty of time to arrive. But from four onwards, all the younger folk were in a state of excitement and expectation — Timmy running constantly in and out of the house, rushing to the gate, from whence a long stretch of road could be seen, till his constant gyrations got on his mother's nerves, and she sharply ordered him to come in and be quiet.

At a quarter to five the telephone bell rang and Jack languidly went to answer it. Then he came back into the drawing room. "Radmore's had a breakdown," he said briefly, "he's afraid he can't get here till seven."

Here was a disappointing anti-climax!

"Then we'd better all go and have our tea," said Timmy sententiously, and everyone felt, in a dispirited way, that, as usual, Timmy had hit the nail on the head.

They all trooped into the dining room, but Timmy was the only one who did full justice to the cakes and scones which had been made specially in Godfrey Radmore's honor: all the others felt cross and disappointed, especially Tom and Rosamund, who had given up going to a tennis-party.

Tea was soon over, for everyone talked much less than usual, and then they all scattered with the exception of Timmy and Betty. Janet had someone to see in the village; Tom persuaded Rosamund that they would still be welcome at the tennis-party; Betty stayed to clear the table. She, alone of them all, was glad of even this short respite, for, as the day had gone on, she had begun to dread the meeting inexpressibly. She knew that even Tom — who had only been seven years old when Godfrey went away — would be wondering how she felt, and watching to see how she would behave. It was a comfort to be alone with only Timmy who was still at table eating steadily. Till recently tea had been Timmy's last meal, though, as a matter of fact, he had nearly always joined in their very simple evening meal. And lately it had been ordained that he was to eat meat. But much as he ate, he never grew fat.

"Hurry up!" said Betty absently. "I want to take off the tablecloth. We can wash up presently."

Timmy got up and shook himself; then he went across to the window, Flick following him, while Betty after having made two tray journeys into the kitchen, folded up the tablecloth. Timmy might have done this last little job, but he pretended not to see that his sister wanted help. He thought it such a shame that he wasn't now allowed the perilous and exciting task of carrying a laden tray. But there had been a certain dreadful day when. . .

Betty turned round, surprised at the child's stillness and silence. Timmy was standing half in and half out of the long French windows staring at something his sister could not see.

Then, all at once, Betty's heart seemed to stop still. She heard a voice, familiar in a sense, and yet so unlike the voice of which she had once known every inflection.

"Hullo! I do believe I see Timothy Godfrey Radmore Tosswill!" and the window for a moment was darkened by a tall, stalwart figure, which looked as if it were two sizes larger than that which Betty remembered.

The stranger took up Timmy's slight, thin figure as easily as a little girl takes up a doll, and now he was holding his godson up in the air, looking up at him with a half humorous, half whimsical expression, while he exclaimed: — "I can't think where you came from? You've none of the family's good looks, and you haven't a trace of your mother!"

Then he set Timmy down rather carefully and delicately on the edge of the shabby Turkey carpet, and stepped forward, into the dining room.

"I wonder if I may have a cup of tea? Is Preston still here?"

"Preston's married. She has five children. Mother says it's four too many, as her husband's a cripple." Timmy waited a moment. "We haven't got a parlor maid now. Mother says we lead the simple life."

"The devil you do!" cried Radmore, diverted, and then, not till then, did he suddenly become aware that he and his godson were not alone.

"Why, Betty!" he exclaimed in a voice he tried to make quite ordinary, "I didn't see you. Have you been there the whole time?" — the whole time being but half a minute at the longest.

And then he strode across the room, and, taking her two hands in his strong grasp, brought her forward, rather masterfully, to the window through which he had just come.

"You're just the same," he said, but there was a doubtful note in his voice, and then as she remained silent, though she smiled a little tremulously, he went on: —

"Nine years have made an awful difference to me — nine years *and* the war! But Beechfield, from what I've been able to see of it, seems exactly the same — not a twig, not a leaf, not a stone out of place!"

"We didn't expect you for another hour at least," said Betty, in her quiet, well-modulated voice.

She was wondering whether he remembered, as she now remembered with a kind of sickening vividness, the last time they had been together in this room — for it was here, in the dining room of Old Place, that they had spent their last miserable, heart-broken moment together, a moment when all the angry bitterness had been merged in wild, piteous tenderness, and heart-break. . .

"I had a bit of luck," he answered cheerfully, "as I went out of the house where I had managed to get on to a telephone, there came a car down the road, and I asked the man who was driving it if he would give me a lift. My luck held, for he was actually breaking his journey for half an hour here, at Beechfield!"

He was talking rather quickly now, as if at last aware of something painful, awkward, in the atmosphere.

"Others all out?" he asked. "Perhaps you'll show me my room, godson?"

"Wouldn't you like to see Nanna?" asked Timmy officiously. "She's so looking forward to seeing you. She wants to thank you for the big Shetland shawl she supposes you sent her last Christmas, and she has an idea that the little real silver teapot she got on her birthday came from you too. It has on it 'A Present for a Good Girl.'"

*A*s Radmore followed Timmy up the once familiar staircase, he felt extraordinarily moved.

How strange the thought that while not only his own life, but the lives of all the people with whom he had been so intimately associated, had changed — this old house had remained absolutely unaltered! Nothing had been added — as far as he could see — and nothing taken away, and yet the human atmosphere was quite other than what it had been ten years ago.

Just now, in the moment of meeting, he had avoided asking Betty about George. Betty's twin had been away at the time of Radmore's break with Old Place — away in a sense which in our civilized days can only be brought about by one thing, an infectious illness. At the time the agonizing debate was going on at Beechfield, he had been in a fever hospital close on a month, and they were none of them to see him for three more weeks. It had been at once a pain and a relief that he should not be there — yet what good could a boy of nineteen have done?

As to what had happened to George afterwards, Radmore knew nothing. He believed that his friend had joined the Indian Civil Service. From childhood George had always intended to make his career in India, his maternal forebears having all been in the service of John Company.

During the last few days Radmore had thought a great deal of George, wondering what had happened to him during the war — whether, for instance, he had at last managed, as did so many Anglo-Indian officials, to get leave to join the Army? At one moment, before it had entered into his mind to write to his little godson, he had thought of opening up communications through George. But he had rejected the notion. The break had been so complete, and George, after all, was so closely connected with Betty! Considering that he had not mentioned Betty's brother, either when speaking to Janet on the telephone two or three days ago, or again just when he had made his unconventional re-entry into Old Place, it was odd how the thought of Betty's twin haunted him as he followed his little guide upstairs. Odd? No, in a sense very natural, for he and George often raced each other up these very stairs. They had been such pals in spite of the four years' difference between them.

Radmore and Timmy were now in the kind of annex or wing which had been added some fifty years after the original mansion had been built. The lower floor of this annex consisted of one big room which, even in the days of Radmore's first acquaintance with the Tosswills, was only used in warm weather. Above it were two good bedrooms — the one still called "George's room," overlooked the garden, and had a charming view of bracken-covered hill beyond.

Timmy opened the door with a flourish, and Radmore saw at once that only one of the two beds was made up; otherwise the room was exactly the same, with this one great outstanding difference — that it had a curiously unlived-in look. The dark green linoleum on the floor appeared a thought more worn, the old rug before the fireplace a thought more shabby — still, how well things lasted, in the old country!

He walked across to one of the windows, and the sight of the garden below now in its full autumn beauty, seemed to bring Janet Tosswill vividly before him.

"Your mother as great a gardener as ever?" he asked, without turning round, and Timmy said eagerly: — "I should think she is! And we're going to sell our flowers and vegetables. *We* shall get the money now; the Red Cross got it during the war."

As his godfather remained silent, the boy went on insistently: — "Fifteen shillings a week clear profit is £40 a year, and Mum thinks it will come to more than that."

Radmore turned round.

"I wonder if any of you have yet met a lady who's just come to live here — Mrs. Crofton?"

"Oh, yes, we've met her; in fact she's been to supper." Timmy spoke without enthusiasm, but Radmore did not notice that.

"I was wondering if you and I could go round and see her between now and dinner?"

"I *think* I could." There was a doubtful touch in Timmy's voice. He knew quite well he ought to stay and help his sister to wash up the tea-things and do certain other little jobs, but he also knew that if he asked Betty to let him off, she would.

"I shan't be a minute," he exclaimed, and a moment later Radmore heard the little feet pattering down the carpetless back stairs, and then scampering up again.

Timmy ran in breathlessly. "It's all right!" he exclaimed, "I can go with you — Mrs. Crofton has got The Trellis House — I'll show you the way there."

"Show me the way there?" repeated Radmore. "Why, I knew The Trellis House from garret to cellar before you were born, young man."

In the hall Timmy gave a queer, side-long look at his companion. "Do you think we'd better take Flick?" he asked doubtfully, "Mrs. Crofton doesn't like dogs."

"Oh, yes, she does," Radmore spoke carelessly. "Flick was bred by Colonel Crofton. I think she'll be very pleased to see him."

Timmy would have hotly resented being called cruel, and to animals he was most humane, yet somehow he had enjoyed Mrs. Crofton's terror the other night, and he was not unwilling to see a repetition of it. And so the three set out — Timmy, Radmore, and Flick. Somehow it was a comfort to the grown-up man to have the child with him. Had he been alone he would have felt like a ghost walking up the quiet, empty village street. The presence of the child and the dog made him feel so *real.*

The two trudged on in silence for a bit, and then Radmore asked in a low voice: — "Is that busy-body, Miss Pendarth, still alive?"

They were passing by Rose Cottage as he spoke, and Timmy at once replied in a shrill voice: — "Yes, of course she is." And then, as if as an afterthought, he remarked slyly: — "Rosamund often says she wishes she were dead. Do you hate her, too?"

"Hate's a big word," said Radmore thoughtfully, "but there was very little love lost between me and that good lady in the old days."

They passed the lichgate of the churchyard, and then, following a sudden impulse, Radmore turned into the post office.

Yes, his instinct had been right, for here, at any rate, was an old friend, but a friend who, from a young man, had become old and grey. Grasping the postmaster, Jim Cobbett, warmly by the hand Radmore exclaimed: — "I'm glad to find you well and hearty, Cobbett." There came the surprised: "Why, it's Mr. Radmore to be sure! How's the world been treating you, sir?"

"Better than I deserve, Cobbett."

"Can you stay a minute, sir — Missus would like to see you, too?" The speaker opened a door out of the tiny shop, and Radmore, followed by Timmy and Flick, walked into a cozy living room, where an old dog got up and growled at them.

"That dog," said Timmy in a hoarse whisper, "frightened poor Mrs. Crofton very much the other day as she was coming out of church."

For a moment Radmore thought the room was empty. Then, in the dim lamp-light, a woman, who had been sitting by the fireplace, got up.

"Here's Mr. Radmore come all the way from Australia, mother."

"Mr. Radmore?" repeated the woman dully, and Radmore had another, and a very painful, shock.

He remembered Mrs. Cobbett definitely, as a buxom, merry-looking young woman. She now looked older than her husband, and she did not smile at him, as the man had done, as she held out her worn, thin hand.

"A deal has happened," she said slowly, "since you went away."

"Yes," said Radmore, "a deal has happened, Mrs. Cobbett; but Beechfield seems unchanged, I cannot see any difference at all."

"Hearts are changed," she said in a strange voice.

For the first time since he had been in Beechfield, Radmore felt a tremor of real discomfort run through him.

He looked up at the mantelpiece. It was bare save for the photographs, in cheap frames, of two stolid-looking lads, whom he vaguely remembered.

"Those your boys?" he asked kindly, and then, making an effort of memory of which he felt harmlessly proud, he said: — "Let me see, one was Peter and the other was Paul, eh? I hope they're all right, Mrs. Cobbett?"

"In a sense, sir," she said apathetically. "I do believe they are. They was both killed within a month of one another — first Paul, then Pete, as we called him — so Mr. Cobbett and I be very lonely now."

As Radmore and Timmy walked away from the post office, Radmore said a trifle ruefully: — "I wish, Timmy, you had told me about those poor people's sons. I'm afraid — I suppose — that a good many boys never came back to Beechfield."

He now felt that everything was indeed changed in the lovely, peaceful little Surrey village.

"I expect," said Timmy thoughtfully, "that the most sensible thing you could do" — (he avoided calling Radmore by name, not knowing whether he was expected to address him as "godfather," "Godfrey," or "Major Radmore") — "before we see anybody else, would be to take a look at the Shrine. You have plenty of matches with you, haven't you?"

"The Shrine?" repeated Radmore hesitatingly.

"Yes, *you* know?"

But somehow Radmore didn't know.

They walked on in the now fast gathering darkness through a part of the village where the houses were rather spread out. And suddenly, just opposite the now closed, silent schoolhouse and its big playground, Timmy stopped and pointed up to his right. "There's our Shrine," he exclaimed. "If you'll give me the box of matches, I'll strike some while you look at the names."

Radmore stared up to where Timmy pointed, but, for a moment or two, he could see nothing. Then, gradually, there emerged against the high hedge a curious-looking wooden panel protected by a slanting, neatly thatched eave, while below ran a little shelf on which there were three vases filled with fresh flowers.

Timmy Tosswill struck a match and held it up, far above his little head. And Radmore saw flash out the gilded words: —

ROLL OF HONOR, 1914–1918.
PASS, FRIEND. ALL'S WELL.

The first name was "Thomas Ingleton," then came "Mons, 22nd August, 1914." Immediately below, bracketed together, came "Peter and Paul Cobbett," followed, in the one case, by the date October 15, 1915, and in the other, November 19, 1915. And then, in the wavering light, there seemed to start out another name and date.

Radmore uttered an exclamation of sharp pain, almost of anger. He did not want the child to see his shocked, convulsed face, but he said quickly: — "Not George? Surely, Timmy, not *George?*"

Timmy answered, "Then you didn't know? Dad and Betty thought you did, but Mum thought that perhaps you didn't."

"Why wasn't I told?" asked Radmore roughly. "I should have thought, Timmy, that you might have told me when you answered my first letter."

He took the box of matches out of Timmy's hand, and himself lighting a match, went up quite close to the list of names. Yes, it was there right enough.

"When did he, George, volunteer?" he asked.

"On the seventh of August, two days after the War began," said Timmy simply. "He was awfully afraid they wouldn't take him. There was such a rush, you know. But they did take him, and the doctor who saw him undressed, naked, you know, told Daddy" — the child hesitated a moment, then repeated slowly, proudly — "that George was one of the finest specimens of young manhood he had ever seen."

"And when did he go out?"

"He went out very soon; and we used to have such jolly times when he came back, because, you know, he did come back three times altogether, and the second time — Betty hadn't gone to France then — they all went up to London together and had a splendid time. I didn't go; Mum didn't think it worth the expense that I should go, though George wanted me to."

Hardly conscious that he was doing so, Radmore turned round, and began walking quietly on along the dark road, with Timmy trotting by his side. "What I believed," he muttered, half to himself, "was that George was safe in India, and probably not even allowed to volunteer."

"George never went to India," said Timmy soberly. "Betty wasn't well, I think, and as they were twins, he didn't like to go so far away from her. So he got a job in London. It was quite nice, and he used to come down once a month or so." He waited a moment, then went on. "Betty always said he was a born soldier, and that he ought to have been a soldier from the very beginning. As you care so much," he added a little diffidently, "I expect Betty would show you the letters his men wrote about him. Dad has got the letters of his Colonel and of the officers, but Betty has the others."

And then all at once Radmore felt a small skinny hand slipped into his.

"I want to tell you something," muttered Timmy. "I want to tell you two things. I want to tell you that I'm sure George is in Heaven. I don't know if you know, but I sometimes see people who are dead. I saw Pete Cobbett once. He was standing by the back door of the post office, and that old dog of theirs saw him too; it was just before we got the news that he was killed, so I thought he was back on leave. But I've never seen George — sometimes I've felt as if he were there, but I've never *seen* him."

For a moment Radmore wondered if he had heard the words aright. What could the child mean? Did Timmy claim the power to see spirits?

"Now I'll tell you the second thing," went on Timmy, his voice dropping to a whisper. "The last time George was home he came into the night nursery one night. Nanna was still busy in the kitchen, so I was by myself. I have a room all to myself now, but I hadn't then. George came in to say a special good-bye to me — he was going off the next morning very early, and Betty wanted to be the only one up to see him go; I mean really early, half past five in the morning. And then — and then — he said to me: 'You'll look after Betty, Timmy? If anything happens to me you'll take my place, won't you, old chap? You'll look after Betty all the days of her life?' I promised I would, and so I will too. But I haven't told her what George said, and you mustn't tell anybody. I've only told you because you're my godfather."

Chapter IX

Mrs. Crofton was walking restlessly about her new home — the house that was so new to her, and yet, if local tradition could be trusted, one of the oldest inhabited dwellings in that part of England.

She had felt so sure that Godfrey Radmore would manage to get away from Old Place, and call on her this afternoon, for Jack Tosswill had told her that he was arriving before tea — she felt depressed and disappointed though she had not yet given up hope.

She wondered if he would come alone the first time, or if one of the girls would accompany him. She felt just a little afraid of Rosamund — Rosamund was so very pretty with all the added, evanescent charm of extreme youth. She told herself that it was lucky that she, Enid, and Godfrey Radmore were already friends, and good friends too.

Twice she went up into her bedroom and gave a long, searching, anxious look at herself in the narrow panel mirror which she had fixed on to one of the cupboard doors. That there is no truer critic of herself, and of her appearance, than a very pretty woman, is generally true even of the vainest and most self-confident of her sex.

Enid Crofton had put on a white serge skirt, and a white woolen jumper, the only concession to her new widowhood being that the white jumper was bordered in pale grey of a shade that matched her shoes and stockings. Though her anxious surveys of herself had been reassuring, she felt nervous, and a trifle despondent. She did not like the country — the stillness even of village life got on her nerves. Still, Beechfield was very different from the horribly lonely house in Essex to which she never returned willingly in her thoughts — though sometimes certain memories of all that had happened there would thrust themselves upon her, refusing to be denied.

Fortunately for the new occupant of The Trellis House, a certain type of prettiness gives its lucky possessor an extraordinary sense of assurance and tranquility when dealing with the average man. Enid Crofton wasn't quite sure, however, if Godfrey Radmore was an average man. He had never made love to her in those pleasant, now faraway days in Egypt, when every other unattached man did so. That surely proved him to be somewhat peculiar.

During the whole of her not very long life she had been petted and spoilt, admired and sheltered, by almost everyone with whom fate had brought her in contact.

Enid Crofton's father had been a paymaster in the Royal Navy named Joseph Catlin. After his death she and her mother had lived on in Southsea till the girl was sixteen, when her mother had pronounced her quite old enough to be "out." Mrs. Catlin was still too attractive herself to feel her daughter a rival, and the two years which had followed had been delightful years to them both. Then something which they regarded as most romantic occurred. On the day Enid was eighteen, and her mother thirty-seven, there had been a double wedding, Mrs. Catlin becoming the wife of a prosperous medical man, while Enid married a young soldier who had just come in for £4,000, which he and his girl-wife at once proceeded to spend.

Today, in spite of herself, her mind went back insistently to her first marriage — that marriage of which she never spoke, but of which she was afraid she would have to tell Godfrey Radmore some day. She was shrewd enough to know that many a man in love with a widow would be surprised and taken aback were he suddenly told that she had been married before, not once, but twice.

Unknowingly to them both, the young, generous, devoted, lover-husband, to whom even now she sometimes threw a retrospective, kindly thought, had done her an irreparable injury. He had opened to her the gates of a material paradise — the kind of paradise in which a young woman enjoys a constant flow of ready money. Though she was quite unaware of it, it was those fifteen weeks spent on the Riviera, for the most part at Monte Carlo, which had gradually caused Enid to argue herself into the belief that she was justified in doing anything — *anything* which might contribute to the renewal of that delicious kind of existence — the only life, from her point of view, worth living.

Her first husband's death in a motor accident had left her practically penniless, as well as frightened and bewildered, and so she had committed the mistake of marrying, almost at once, clever, saturnine Colonel Crofton, a man over thirty years older than herself. His mad passion had died down like a straw-fed flame, and when there had come, like a bolt from their already grey sky, the outbreak of War, it had been a godsend to them both.

Colonel Crofton had at once stepped into what had seemed to them both a good income, with all sorts of delightful extras, and allowances, attached to it. And while he was in France, at the back of the Front, absorbed in his job, though resentful of the fact that he was not in the trenches, Enid had shared a small flat in London with another young and lonely wife. The two had enjoyed every moment of war-time London, dancing, flirting, taking part, by way of doing their bit, in every form of the lighter kind of war charities, their ideal existence only broken by the occasional boredom of having to entertain their respective husbands when the latter were home on leave.

Then had come the short interval in Egypt during which the Croftons had met Godfrey Radmore, and, after that for Enid, another delightful stretch of London life.

She had felt it intolerable to go back to the old, dull life, on an income which seemed smaller than ever with rising prices, and everything sacrificed, or so it had seemed to her, to Colonel Crofton's new, dog-breeding hobby. She resented too, perhaps, more bitterly than she knew herself, her husband's altered attitude to herself. From having been passionately, foolishly in love, he had become critical, and, what to her was especially intolerable, jealous. For a time she had kept up with some of her war-time acquaintances, but there was a strain of curious timidity in her nature, and she grew afraid of Colonel Crofton. Even now, when Enid Crofton, free at last, remembered those dreary months in the shabby little manor-house which Colonel Crofton had taken after the Armistice, she told herself, with a quickened pulse, that flesh and blood cannot stand more than a certain amount of dullness and discomfort. But she seldom went back in thought to that hateful time. She had wanted to obliterate, as far as was possible, all recollection of the place where she had spent such unhappy months, and where had occurred the tragedy of her husband's death. And it would have been difficult to find two dwelling-houses more different than the lonely, austere-looking, Fildy Fe Manor, which stood surrounded by water-clogged fields, some two miles from an unattractive, suburban Essex town, and the delightful, picturesque, cheerful-looking Trellis House which formed an integral part of a prosperous-looking and picturesque Surrey village.

*A*t last Mrs. Crofton settled herself down into her low-ceilinged, square little sitting room, and, looking round at her new possessions, she told herself that outwardly her new home was perfect.

The Trellis House had been for a short time in the possession of a clever, modern architect who had done his best to restore the building to what it must have been before it had been transformed, early in the 19th century, from a farm into a so-called gentleman's house. He had uncovered the old oak beams, stripped five layers of paper off the walls of the living rooms, and laid bare what paneling there was — in fact he had restored the interior of the old building, while leaving the rose and clematis covered trellis which was on the portion of the house standing at right angles to the village street, and which gave it its name.

In a sense it was too much like a stage picture to please a really fine taste. But to Enid Crofton it formed an ideal background for her attractive self. She had sold for very high prices the sound, solid, fine, 18th century furniture, which her husband had inherited, and with the proceeds she had bought the less comfortable but to the taste of the moment, more attractive oak furnishings of The Trellis House.

Enid Crofton was the kind of woman who acquires helpful admirers in every profession. The junior partner of the big firm of house-agents who had disposed of the lease of Fildy Fe Manor had helped her in every way possible, though he had been rather surprised and puzzled, considering that she knew no one there, at her determination to find a house in, or near, the village of Beechfield.

It was also an admirer, the only one who had survived from her war sojourn in Egypt — a cheery, happy, good-looking soldier, called Tremaine, now at home on leave from India — who had helped her in the actual task of settling in. Not that there had been much settling in to do — for the house had been left in perfect order by its last tenant. But

Captain Tremaine had fetched her from the hotel where she had stayed in London; he had bought her first-class ticket (Enid always liked someone to pay for her); they had shared a delightful picnic lunch which he provided in the train; and then, finally, reluctantly, he had left The Trellis House — after a rather silly, tiresome, little scene, during which he had vowed that she should marry him, even if it came to his kidnapping her by force!

While hoping and waiting, in nervous suspense, for Godfrey Radmore, she cast a tender thought to Bob Tremaine. Nothing, so she told herself with a certain vehemence, would induce her to marry him, for he had only £200 a year beside his pay, and that, even in India, she believed would mean poverty. Also she had been told that no woman remained really pretty in India for very long. But she was fond of Tremaine — he was "her sort," and far, far more her ideal of what a man should be than was the rich man she had deliberately made up her mind to marry; but bitter experience had convinced Enid Crofton that money — plenty of money — was as necessary to her as the air she breathed.

*S*uddenly there broke on her ear the peal of an old-fashioned bell, followed by a short, sharp knock on the toy knocker of her front door. Enid started up, her face full of eagerness and pleasure; something seemed to tell her that it was — it must be — Radmore!

While the maid was going to the door, her mind worked quickly. Surely it was very late for a call? He must have been wishing to see her as soon as he possibly could, or he would never have managed to get away from Old Place, and its many tiresome inmates. There came a mischievous smile over her face. Of one of those inmates, the rather priggish Jack Tosswill, she had made a real conquest. Under some flimsy excuse he had come every day, always staying for a considerable time. This very morning he had not gone till she had told him frankly that she only had lunch enough for one!

The door opened slowly, and her smile died away, giving place to a touching, pathetic expression. And then, instead of the tall, dark man she expected to see walk in, there advanced towards her a small, freckled-faced, fair-haired little boy — Timmy Tosswill, the child whom she was already beginning to regard with something akin to real distaste.

But Enid Crofton was never unpleasant in manner to anybody, and she even forced herself to smile, as she exclaimed: — "I was not expecting a visitor so late, but I'm very pleased to see you all the same, Master Timmy! How wonderful that you should have been able to reach my knocker. It's placed so very high up on the door – I think I must get it altered."

"I didn't knock," said Timmy shortly, "it was my godfather who knocked, Mrs. Crofton."

And when Radmore followed his godson into the room he was surprised, even a little touched, at the warmth of Mrs. Crofton's greeting.

She put out both her hands, "I *am* glad to see you" – and then she added, characteristically, for truth was not in her, "I was afraid you wouldn't have time to look me up forever so long!"

But though Radmore was pleased by her evident joy in seeing him, he looked at her with a curiously critical eye. He was surprised to find her in a white frock – inclined, even, to be just a little bit shocked.

And there was something else. Enid Crofton had enjoyed the War – she had admitted this just a little shamefacedly a week ago, when they two were having dinner together at the Savoy Grill, where she had been easily the prettiest woman in the room. At the time he had felt indulgently that it was a good thing that someone should have gone through that awful time untouched by the pains and scars of war. But now everything seemed different, somehow. Beechfield was a place of mourning, and in a place of mourning this smiling, beautifully dressed, almost too pretty young creature looked out of place. Still that wasn't her fault, after all.

As the three sat down, Timmy upset the narrow oak stool on which he had placed himself with a great clatter, and Radmore suddenly realized that he had made a mistake in bringing the boy. For the first time since his return to England he saw something like a frown gather on Mrs. Crofton's face. Perhaps, unlike most nice women, she didn't like children?

"I'm awfully grateful to you for having told me about Beechfield," she exclaimed. "Although I've hardly been here a week, I do feel what a delightful place it is! Everybody is so kind and friendly. Why the very first day I was here I was asked to supper at Old Place – and several people have left cards on me already. What sort of a woman is Miss –" she hesitated, "Pendarth?"

Timmy and Radmore looked at one another, but neither spoke for a moment. Then Radmore answered, rather dryly: – "In my time, Miss Pendarth was the greatest gossip and busy-body within a radius of thirty miles. She must be an old woman now."

"Oh, I don't think she would like you to call her that!" exclaimed Timmy, and both his grown-up auditors laughed. But Enid Crofton felt a little disappointed, for on Miss Pendarth's card had been written the words: – "I look forward to making your acquaintance. I think I must

have known Colonel Crofton many years ago. There was a Cecil Crofton
who was a great friend of my brother's — they joined the Ninetieth on
the same day." She had rather hoped to find a kindly friend and ally in
the still unknown caller.

And then, as if answering her secret thought, Radmore observed
carelessly: — "It's wrong to prejudice you against Miss Pendarth; I've
known her do most awfully kind things. But she had what the Scotch
call a 'scunner' against me when I was a boy. She's the sort of woman
who's a good friend and a bad enemy."

"I must hope," said his hostess softly, "that she'll be a good friend
to me. At any rate, it was nice of her to come and call almost at once,
wasn't it?"

"You've delightful quarters here," observed Radmore. "The Trellis
House was a very different place to this in my time; I can remember a
hideous, cold and white wallpaper in this room — it looks twice as large
as it did then."

"I found the things I sold made it possible for me to buy almost
everything in The Trellis House. Tappin & Edge say that I got a great
bargain."

"Yes," said Radmore hesitatingly, "I expect you did."

But all the same he felt that his pretty friend had made a mistake,
for he remembered some of Colonel Crofton's furniture as having been
very good. In the bedroom in which he had slept at Fildy Fe Manor
there had been a walnut-wood tallboy of the best Jacobean period. That
one piece must certainly have been worth more than all the furniture
in this particular room put together.

Poor Enid Crofton! The call to which she had been looking forward
so greatly was not turning out a success. Godfrey Radmore seemed a
very different man here, in Beechfield, from what he had seemed in
London. They talked in a desultory way, with none of the pleasant, cozy,
intimacy to which she had insensibly accustomed him; and though
Timmy remained absolutely quiet and silent after that unfortunate
accident with the stool, his presence in some way affected the atmosphere.

All at once Radmore asked: — "And where's Boo-boo? It's odd I never
thought of asking you in London, but somehow one expects to see a
dog in the country, even as highly civilized and smart a little dog as
Boo-boo!"

"I sold her," answered Mrs. Crofton, in a low, pained tone. "I got £40
for her, and a most awfully good home. Still," she sighed, "of course I
miss my darling little Boo —" and then a sharp tremor ran through her,
for there suddenly fell on her ears the sound of a dog, howling.

Now Enid Crofton did not believe that what she heard so clearly were real howls, proceeding from a flesh-and-blood dog. She thought that her nerves were betraying her, as they had a way of doing since her husband's death. Often when she fell asleep, there would come to her a strange and horrible nightmare. It was such a queer, uncanny kind of dream for a grown-up woman to have! She used to dream that she was a rat — and that Colonel Crofton's own terrier, a fierce brute called Dandy, was after her.

"That's Flick! Perhaps I'd better go and let him out?" Timmy jumped up as he spoke. "I thought you didn't like dogs, Mrs. Crofton, and so I shut Flick up in your stable-yard. I expect he's got bored, being in there all by himself, in the dark!"

The boy's words brought delicious relief, and then, all at once, she felt unreasonably angry. How stupid of this odious little fellow to have brought his horrid, savage dog with him — after what had happened the other night!

Timmy shot out of the room and so through the front door, and Radmore got up too. "I'm afraid we ought to be going," he said.

His white-clad hostess came up close to him: — "It's so good of you to have come to see me so soon," she murmured. "Though I do like Beechfield, and the people here are awfully kind, I feel very forlorn, Mr. Radmore. Seeing you has cheered me up very much. I hope you'll come again soon."

There fell on the still air the voice of Timmy talking to his dog outside. Mrs. Crofton went quickly past Radmore into the tiny hall; she shut the front door, which had been left ajar; and then she came back.

"It's quite true that I don't like dogs!" she exclaimed. "Poor Cecil's terriers got thoroughly on my nerves last winter. I sometimes dream of them even now."

He looked at her, surprised, and rather concerned. Poor little woman! There were actually tears in her eyes.

"Yes," she went on, as if she could not help the words coming out, "that's the real reason I sold Boo-boo. I even felt as if my poor little Boo-boo had turned against me." There was a touch of excitement, almost of defiance, in her low voice, and Radmore felt exceedingly taken aback and puzzled. This was an Enid Crofton he had never met. "Come, come — you mustn't feel like that" — he took her hand in his and held it closely.

She looked up at him and her eyes filled with tears, and then, suddenly, her heart began beating deliciously. She saw flash into his dark face a look she had seen flash into many men's faces, but never in his, till now — the excited, tender look that she had longed to see there.

She swayed a little towards him; dropping her hand, he put out his arms — in another moment, what she felt sure such a man as Radmore would have regarded as irreparable would have happened, had not the door just behind them burst open.

They fell apart quickly, and Radmore, with a sudden revulsion of feeling — a sensation that he had been saved from doing a very foolish thing — turned to see his godson, Timmy Tosswill.

Enid Crofton looked at Timmy, too, and if evil thoughts could kill, the child would have fallen dead. But evil thoughts do not kill, and so all that happened was that Timmy had a sudden, instinctive feeling that he must account for his presence.

Looking up into his godfather's face, he said breathlessly: — "The front door was shut, so I came in, through the kitchen. It's ever so late, Godfrey — after half past seven. Dad *will* be upset if you're not back to speak to him before dinner!"

*A*s the two, the tall man and the short boy, walked away into the darkness, Radmore was possessed by an extraordinary mixture of feelings. "You've had an escape! You've got well out of what would have been not only a dangerous but an absurd situation," so whispered a secret, inner voice. And yet there was a side of him which felt not only balked and disappointed, but exasperated. . .

"Do you ever think of people's faces when they're not there?" asked Timmy suddenly, and then, without waiting for an answer, he went on: — "When I shut my eyes, before I go quite off to sleep, you know, I see a row of faces. Sometimes they're people I've never seen at all; but last night I kept seeing Mrs. Crofton's face, looking just as it looked when Flick ran in and growled at her the other night. It was such an awful look — I don't think I shall ever forget it."

As Radmore said nothing, the little boy asked another question: "Do you think Mrs. Crofton pretty?" This time Timmy waited for an answer.

"Yes, I think she's very pretty. But gentlemen don't discuss ladies and their looks, old boy."

"Don't they? How stupid of them!" said Timmy. He added a little shyly, "I suppose a gentleman may talk of his sister?"

Radmore turned hot in the darkness. Was Timmy going to say something of Betty, and of that old, painful, now he hoped forgotten, episode? But Timmy only observed musingly: — "You haven't seen Rosamund yet. Of course we never say so to her, because it might make her vain, but I do think, Godfrey, that she's very, *very* pretty."

And then, rather to his companion's discomfiture, his queer little mind swung back to the woman to whose house they had just been. "Mrs. Crofton," he observed, with an air of finality, "may be pretty, but she's got what I call a blotting-paper face."

Chapter X

*R*admore felt secretly relieved that he and Timmy got home too late for him to see Mr. Tosswill alone before dinner. And when at last he came down, just a minute or two late, for he had to do things for himself to which he had become unaccustomed — unpacking his bag, putting out his evening clothes, placing of studs in his evening shirt, and so on — he found what looked to him like a large party of strangers all gathered together in the dear old drawing room.

As he walked in among them he looked first with quick interest at the three girls. Yes, Timmy was right — Rosamund was lovely. Dolly struck him as commonplace, though as a matter of fact she looked more attractive than usual. Betty looked very hot — or was it that the exquisite complexion that once had been her chief physical beauty had gone?

After a moment or two Betty slipped out of the room, leaving Radmore and Mr. Tosswill shaking hands quite cordially, if a little awkwardly.

"Well, sir, here I am again, turned up just like a bad penny!" And his host answered absently: — "Yes, yes, Godfrey — very glad to see you, I'm sure."

Then, after he had shaken hands with Janet and Tom, they all stood together on the hearthrug waiting, so Radmore supposed, for the parlor maid to come in and announce dinner.

But instead of that happening, the door opened and Timmy appeared. "Will you come into the dining room? Everything's ready now."

They all followed him, three of the younger ones — Tom, Dolly and Rosamund — laughing and whispering together. Somehow Timmy never associated himself with those of his brothers and sisters nearest to him in age.

Radmore came last of all with Janet. He felt as if he were in a strange, unreal dream. It was all at once so like and so unlike what he had expected to find it. All these quiet, demure-looking young strangers, instead of the jolly, familiar children he had left nine years ago — and, as he realized with a sharp pang — no George. He had not known till tonight how much he had counted on seeing George, or at least on hearing all about him. Instead, here was Jack, so very self-possessed — or was it superior? — in his smart evening jacket. He could hardly believe that Jack was George's brother.

For a moment he forgot Betty. Then he saw her come hurrying in. Her color had gone down, and she looked very charming, and yet — yes, a stranger too.

The table was laid very much as it had been in the old days on a Sunday, when they always had supper instead of dinner at Old Place. But today was not Sunday — where could all the servants be?

Janet, looking very nice in the bright blue gown her little son had admired, placed the guest on her right hand. To her left, Timmy, with snorts and wriggles, settled himself. The others all sorted themselves out; Betty sat the nearest to the door, on the right of her father, — lovely Rosamund on his left.

Timmy stood up and mumbled out a Latin grace. How it brought back Radmore's boyhood and early manhood days! But in those days it was Tom, a simple cherubic-looking little boy of seven, who said grace — the usual "For what we are going to receive, may the Lord make us truly thankful!" The stranger — how queer to think he was a stranger here, in this familiar room — did not care for the innovation.

They all sat down, and Radmore began to eat his soup, served in a covered cup. It was very good soup, and as he was rather tired and hungry, he enjoyed it. Then Timmy got up and removed the cup and its cover; and suddenly the guest became aware that only four people at the table had taken soup — himself, Mr. Tosswill, Jack, and Timmy. What an odd thing!

They were all rather silent, and Radmore began to have a strange, uncanny feeling that none of them could see him, that he was a wraith, projected out of the past into the present. It was a novel and most disconcerting sensation. But no one glancing at his keen face, now illumined with a half humorous expression of interest, would have guessed the mixed and painful feelings which possessed him.

He stole a look to his left. Janet, in his eyes, was almost unchanged. Of course she looked a thought older, a thought thicker — not so much in her upright figure, as in her clever, irregular-featured face. In the days of his early manhood she had never seemed to him to be very much older than himself — but now she looked a lifetime older than he felt.

Only Mr. Tosswill looked absolutely unchanged. His mild benevolent face, his deep blue eyes, his grey hair, seemed exactly the same as when Radmore had last sat down, in the Old Place dining room, to a full table. That had been in the Christmas holidays of 1910. Very well he remembered all that had happened then, for he and Betty had just become engaged.

At nineteen Betty Tosswill had belonged to the ideal type of old-fashioned English girlhood — high-spirited, cheerful, artless yet intelligent, with a strong sense of humor. She had worn a pink evening frock during those long-ago Christmas holidays, and had looked, at any rate in her young lover's eyes, beautiful.

They had been ardently, passionately in love, he a masterful, exacting lover, and though seeming older than his age, without any of the magnanimity which even the passage of only a very few years brings to most intelligent men. Poor little Betty of long ago — what a child she had been at nineteen! — but a child capable of deep and varied emotions.

At the time of their parting he had been absorbed in his own selfish sensations of anger, revolt, and the sharp sense of loss, savagely glad that she was unhappy too. But after he had gone, after he had plunged into the new, to him exciting and curious, life of the great vessel taking him to Australia, he had forced himself to put Betty out of his mind, and, after a few days, he had started a violent flirtation with the most attractive woman on board the liner. The flirtation had developed, by the time they reached Sydney, into a serious affair, and had been the determining cause why he had not written even to George. Godfrey Radmore had not thought of that woman for years. But tonight her now hateful, meretricious image rose, with horrid vividness, before him. It had been an ugly, debasing episode, and had dragged on and on, as such episodes have a way of doing.

Wrenching his mind free of that odious memory, he looked across at Betty. Yes, it was at once a relief and something of a disappointment to feel her, too, transformed into a stranger. For one thing she had had, when he had last seen her, a great deal of long fair hair. But she had cut it off when starting her arduous war work, and the lack of it altered her amazingly, all the more that she did not wear her short hair "bobbed," in what had become the prevailing fashion, but brushed back from her low forehead, and staidly held in place by a broad, black, snoodlike ribbon.

He looked to his right, down the old-fashioned, almost square dining table. Jack was the least changed, after his father, of the young people sitting at this table. Jack, nine years ago, had been a rather complacent boy, doing very well at school, the type of boy who is as if marked out by fate to do well in life. Yes, Jack had hardly changed at all, but Radmore, looking at Jack, felt a sudden intolerable jealousy for George. . . .

He came back with a start to what was going on around him, and idly he wondered what had happened to all the servants this evening. Truth to tell he had been just a little surprised and taken aback at not finding his bag unpacked and his evening clothes laid out before dinner.

Timmy had slipped out of his chair and brought him a plateful of roast mutton, and now Rosamund was playing waitress, smiling at his elbow, a lovely Hebe indeed, with dishes of potatoes and greens. He helped himself a little awkwardly, while Timmy was taking round platefuls of meat to his father, to Jack, and finally one to his own little self.

Then Betty went out of the room, and came back with a large dish of macaroni cheese, which she put on a side table. Jack got up and whispered something to her rather angrily. He was evidently remonstrating with her for not having allowed him to go and get the dish, for he motioned her rather imperiously back to her seat by her father, while he himself, calling to Dolly to help him, dealt out generous portions of macaroni cheese to those who had not taken meat.

All at once Timmy exclaimed in his shrill voice: — "I like macaroni cheese. Why shouldn't I have a little today, too? Here, Tom, you take my meat, and I'll have your macaroni cheese." He did not wait for Tom's assent to this peculiar proposal, and was proceeding to effect the exchange when Tom muttered crossly, while yet, or so Radmore fancied, casting rather longing eyes at Timmy's plate.

"You know perfectly well you've got to have meat to drive the ghosties out of your silly head."

Timmy submitted with a grunt of disappointment, and the meal proceeded. Again Radmore felt surprised and puzzled. Was it conceivable that the whole family — with the exception of Mr. Tosswill, Jack and Timmy, had become so High Church that Friday was with them a meatless day?

Chapter XI

*A*fter her visitors had gone, Mrs. Crofton had come back slowly, languidly, to her easy chair.

It was too warm for a fire, yet somehow the fire comforted her, for she felt cold as well as tired, and, yes, she could admit it to herself, horribly disappointed. How stupid men were — even clever men!

It was so stupid of Godfrey Radmore not to have come to see her, this the first time, alone. He might have found it difficult to have come without one of the Tosswill girls, but there was no reason and no excuse for his being accompanied by that odious little Timmy. It was also really unkind of the boy to have brought his horrid dog with him. Even now she seemed to hear Flick's long-drawn-out howls — those horrible howls that at the time she had not believed to be real. What a nervous, hysterical fool she was becoming! How long would she go on being haunted by the now fast-disappearing past?

There came back to Enid Crofton the very last words uttered by Piper, the clever, capable man who, after having been Colonel Crofton's batman in the War, had become their general factotum in Essex: — "Don't you go and be startled, ma'am, if you see the very spit of Dandy in this 'ere village! As me and your new lad was cleaning out the stable-yard this morning, a young gentleman came in with a dog as was 'is exact image. After a bit o'course, I remembered as what we'd sent one of Juno's and Dandy's pups to a place called Beechfield this time last year — 'tis that pup grown into a dog without a doubt!"

It was certainly a bit of rank bad luck that there should be here, in Beechfield, a dog which, whenever she saw it, brought the image of her dead husband so vividly before her.

She had just settled herself down, and was turning over the leaves of one of the many picture papers which Tremaine had bought for her on their jolly little journey on the day of her arrival at The Trellis House, when there came a ring at the door.

Who could it be coming so late — close to seven o'clock? Enid Crofton got up, feeling vaguely disturbed.

The new maid brought in a reply-paid telegram, and Mrs. Crofton tore open the orange envelope with just a faint premonition that something disagreeable was going to happen: — "May I come and stay with you for the weekend? Have just arrived in England. Alice Crofton."

Thank Heaven she had been wrong as to her premonition! This portended nothing disagreeable — only something unexpected. The sender of this telegram was the kind, opulent sister-in-law whom she always thought of as "Miss Crofton."

Going over to her toy writing-table, she quickly wrote on the reply-paid form: — "Miss Crofton, Buck's Hotel, Dover Street. Yes, delighted. Do come tomorrow morning. Excellent eleven o'clock train from Waterloo. — Enid."

As she settled herself by the fire she told herself that a visit from Miss Crofton might be quite a good thing — so far as Beechfield was concerned. Her associations with her husband's sister were wholly pleasant. For one thing, Alice Crofton was well off, and Enid instinctively respected, and felt interested in, any possessor of money. What a pity it was that Colonel Crofton had not had a fairy godmother! His only sister had been left £3,000 a year by a godmother, and she lived the agreeable life so many Englishwomen of her type and class live on the Continent. While her real home was in Florence, she often traveled, and during the War she had settled down in Paris, giving many hours of each day to one of the British hospitals there.

The young widow's mind flew back to her one meeting with Alice Crofton. It was during her brief engagement to Colonel Crofton, and the latter's sister, without being over cordial, had been quite pleasant to the startlingly pretty little woman, who had made such a fool of her brother.

But at the time of Colonel Crofton's death, his sister had been truly kind. She had telegraphed £200 to her sister-in-law from Italy, and this sum of ready money had been very useful during that tragic week — and even afterwards, for the insurance people had made a certain amount of fuss after Colonel Crofton's sad suicide, "while of unsound mind," and this had caused a disagreeable delay.

The new tenant of The Trellis House had her lonely dinner brought in to her on a tray, and then, perhaps rather too soon — for she was not much of a reader, and there was nothing to while away the time — she went upstairs to her pleasant, cozy bedroom, and so to bed.

But, try as she might, she found it impossible to fall asleep; for what seemed to her hours she lay wide awake, tossing this way and that. At last she got up, and, drawing aside the chintz curtain across one of the windows, she looked out. The window was open, and in the eerily bright moonlight the upper part of the hill on which Beechfield village lay seemed spread before her. There were twinkling lights in many of the windows – doubtless groups of happy, cheerful people behind them. She felt horribly lonely and depressed as well as wide awake tonight.

In her short, healthy life, Enid Crofton had only had one attack of insomnia. During the ten days that had followed her husband's sudden death – for the inquest had had to be put off for a day or two – she had hardly slept at all, and the doctor who had been so kind a friend during that awful time, had had to give her a strong narcotic. To his astonishment it had had no effect. She had felt as if she were going mad – the effect, so he had told her afterwards, of the awful shock she had had.

Tonight she wondered with a kind of terror whether that terrible sleeplessness which had ended by making her feel almost lightheaded was coming back.

She turned away from the window, and, getting into bed again, tried to compose her limbs into absolute repose, as the doctor had advised her to do. And then, just as she was mercifully going to sleep, there floated in, through the open window, a variant on a doggerel song she had last heard in Egypt: –

"The angels sing-a-ling-a-ling-a-ling,
 They've got the goods for me.
 The bells of hell ring ting-a-ling-a-ling
 For you, as you shall see."

Enid Crofton sat up in bed. She felt suddenly afraid – horribly, desperately afraid. As is often the case with those who have drifted away from any form of religion, she was very superstitious, and terrified of evil omens. During the War she had been fond of going first to one and then to another of the fashionable soothsayers.

They had all agreed as to one thing – this was that her husband would die, and of course she had thought he would be killed at the Front. But he had come through safe and sound, and more – more *hateful* than ever.

One fortune-teller, a woman, small, faded, commonplace-looking, yet with something sinister about her that impressed her patrons uncomfortably, had told Enid Crofton, with a curious smile, that she would have yet another husband, making the third. This had startled her very much, for the woman, who did not even know her name, could only have guessed that she had been married twice. Enid Crofton was not given to making unnecessary confidences. With the exception of her sister-in-law, none of the people who now knew her were aware that Colonel Crofton had been her second husband.

She lay down again, and in the now dying firelight, fixed her eyes on the chintz square of the window curtain nearest to her. She shut her eyes, but, as always happens, there remained a square luminous patch on their retinas. And then, all at once, it was as if she saw, depicted on the white, faintly illuminated space, a scene which might have figured in one of those cinema-plays to which she and her house-mate, during those happy days when she had lived in London, used so often to go with one or other of their temporary admirers.

On the white, luminous background two pretty little hands were moving about, a little uncertainly, over a window-ledge on which stood a row of medicine bottles. Then, suddenly the two pretty hands became engaged in doing something which is done by woman's hands every day – the pouring of a liquid from one bottle into another.

Enid Crofton did not visualize the owner of the hands. She had no wish to do so, but she did see the hands.

Then there started out before her, with astonishing vividness, another little scene – this time with a man as central figure. He was whistling; that she knew, though she could not hear the whistling. It was owing to that surprised, long-drawn-out whistling sound that the owner of the pretty hands had become suddenly, affrightedly, aware that someone was there, outside the window, staring down, and so of course seeing the task on which the two pretty little hands were engaged.

Now, the owner of that pair of now shaking little hands had felt quite sure that no one could possibly see what they were engaged in doing – for the window on the ledge of which the medicine bottles were standing looked out on what was practically a blank wall. But the man whose long, surprised whistle had so suddenly scared her, happened at that moment to be sitting astride the top of the blank wall, engaged in the legitimate occupation of sticking bits of broken bottles into putty. The man was Piper, and doubtless the trifling incident had long since slipped his mind, for that same afternoon his master, Colonel Crofton, had committed suicide in a fit of depression owing to shell shock.

Enid Crofton opened her eyes wide, and the sort of vision, or nightmare – call it what you will – faded at once.

It was a nightmare she had constantly experienced during the first few nights which had succeeded her husband's death. But since the inquest she had no longer been haunted by that scene – the double scene of the hands, the pretty little hands, engaged in that simple, almost mechanical, action of pouring the contents of one bottle into another, and the vision of the man on the wall looking down, slantwise, through the window, and uttering that queer, long-drawn-out whistle of utter surprise.

When at last Mrs. Crofton had had to explain regretfully to clever, capable Piper that she could no longer afford to keep him on, they had parted the best of friends. She had made him the handsome present of twenty-five pounds, for he had been a most excellent servant to her late husband. And she had done more than that. She had gone to a good deal of trouble to procure him an exceptionally good situation. Piper had just gone there, and she hoped, rather anxiously, that he would do well in it.

The man had one serious fault — now and again he would go off and have a good "drunk." Sometimes he wouldn't do this foolish, stupid thing for months, and then, perchance, he would do it two weeks running! Colonel Crofton, so hard in many ways, had been indulgent to this one fault, or vice, in an otherwise almost perfect servant. When giving Piper a very high character Mrs. Crofton had just hinted that there had been a time when he had taken a drop too much, but she had spoken of it as being absolutely in the past. Being the kind of woman she was, she wouldn't have said even that, had it not been that Piper had got disgracefully drunk within a week of his master's death. She had been very much frightened then, though not too frightened to stay, herself, within hail of the man till he had come round, and to make him a cup of strong coffee. When, at last, he was fit to do so, he had uttered broken words of gratitude, really touched at her kindness, and frightfully ashamed of himself.

Lying there, wide awake, in the darkness and utter stillness of Beechfield village, Enid Crofton reminded herself that she had treated Piper very well. In memory of the master whom he had served she had also given him, before selling off her husband's kennel, two prize-winners. But it is sometimes a mistake to be too kind, for on receiving this last generous gift the man had hinted that with a little capital he could set up dog-breeding for himself! She had had to tell him, sadly but firmly, that she could not help him to any ready money, and Piper had been what she now vaguely described to herself as "very nice" about it, though obviously disappointed.

At the end of their little chat, however, he had said something which had made her feel rather uncomfortable: — "I was wondering, ma'am, whether Major Radmore might perhaps be inclined for a little speculation? I wouldn't mind paying, say, up to ten percent, if 'e'd oblige me with a loan of five hundred pounds."

She had been astonished at the suggestion — astonished and unpleasantly taken aback. He had surprised her further by going on: — "I believe as what the Major is coming 'ome soon, ma'am. Perhaps then I might venture to ask you to say a word for me? Major Radmore was known in the regiment as a very kind gentleman."

"I'll do what I can, Piper." She had said the words with apparent earnestness, but, deep in her heart, she had thought the request totally unreasonable.

And now it was this conversation which came back to her as she moved restlessly about in her bed. She wondered uneasily whether she had made a mistake. Her capital was very small, and she was now living on her capital, but after all, perhaps it would have been wiser to have given Piper that £500. She was quite determined not to mix up Piper with Godfrey Radmore, but she had a queer, uncomfortable feeling that she had not done with this man yet.

At last she fell into a heavy, troubled, worried sleep — the kind of sleep from which a woman always wakes unrefreshed.

But daylight brought comfort to Enid Crofton, and after she had had her early cup of tea and had enjoyed her nice hot bath, she felt quite cheery again, and her strange, bad night faded into nothingness. She was young, she was strong, above all she was enchantingly pretty! She told herself confidently that nothing terrible, nothing *really* dreadful ever happens to a woman who is as attractive as she knew herself to be to the sex which still holds all the material power there is to hold in this strange world.

During the last three weeks, she had sometimes wondered uneasily whether Godfrey Radmore realized how very pretty she was. There was something so curiously impersonal about him — and yet last night he had very nearly kissed her!

She laughed aloud, gaily, triumphantly, as she went down to her late breakfast.

Chapter XII

*A*t the moment that Enid Crofton was telling herself that everything was going fairly well with her, and that nothing could alter the fact that she was now, and likely to remain for a long time, a woman likely to attract every man with whom she came in contact — Godfrey Radmore, following Janet Tosswill after breakfast into the drawing room of Old Place, exclaimed deprecatingly: — "I feel like Rip Van Winkle!'

"Do you?" She turned to him and smiled a little sadly. "It's *you* that have changed, Godfrey. Everything here is much the same. As for me, I never see any change from one year to another."

"But they've all grown up!" he exclaimed plaintively. "You can't think how odd it seems to find a lot of grown-up young ladies and gentlemen instead of the jolly little kids who were in the nursery with Nanna nine years ago. By the way, Nanna hasn't changed, and" — he hesitated, then brought out with an effort, "Mr. Tosswill is exactly the same."

She felt vexed that he hadn't included Betty. To her step-mother's fond eyes Betty was more attractive now than in her early girlhood. "I think the children have improved very much," she said quickly. "Jack was a horrid little prig nine years ago!"

She hadn't forgiven Radmore. And yet, in a sense, she was readjusting her views and theories about him, for the simple reason that he, Godfrey Radmore, had changed so utterly. From having been a hot-tempered, untamable, high-spirited boy, he was now, or so it seemed to her, a cool, restrained man of the world, old for his years. In fact it was he who was now a stranger — but a stranger who had most attractive manners, and who had somehow slipped very easily into their everyday life. Janet liked his deferential manner to the master of the house, she enjoyed his kindly and good-humored, if slightly satirical dealings with Jack and with pretty Rosamund, and she was very grateful to him for the way he treated queer, little Timmy, her own beloved changeling child.

And now something happened that touched her, and made her suddenly feel as if she was with the old Godfrey Radmore again.

"Look here," he said, in a low, hesitating voice, "I want to tell you, Janet, that I didn't know till yesterday about George. You'll think me a fool — but somehow I always thought of him as being safe in India." And then with sudden passion he asked: — "How can you say that everything is the same in Old Place with George not here? Why, to me, George was as much part of Old Place as — as Betty is!"

"We all thought you knew — at least I wasn't sure."

"Thank God *he* didn't think so poorly of me as that," he muttered, and then he looked away, his eyes smarting with unshed tears. "Nothing will ever be the same to me again without George in the world."

As she said nothing, he went on with sudden passion: — "Every other country in Europe has changed utterly since the War, but England seemed to me, till last night, exactly the same — only rather bigger and more bustling than nine years ago." He drew a long breath. "Timmy and I went into the post office last evening, and Cobbett asked me to go in, and see his wife. I thought I remembered her so well — and when I saw her, Janet, I didn't know her! Then I asked after her boys — and she told me."

"It's strange that a man who went through it all himself should feel like that," she said slowly.

The door opened suddenly and Rosamund's pretty head appeared: "There's a message come through saying that your car's all right, and that it will be along in about an hour," she exclaimed joyfully. To Rosamund, Godfrey Radmore was in very truth a stranger, and a very attractive stranger at that.

As a rule, after breakfast, all the young people went their various ways, but this morning they were all hanging about waiting vaguely for Godfrey to come and do something with one or all of them. Rosamund was longing to ask him whether he knew any of the London theatrical managers; Tom was wondering whether Godfrey would allow him to drive his car; Dolly and Timmy, as different in everything else as two human beings could well be, each desired to take him into the village and show him off to their friends. The only one of the young people who was not really interested in Radmore was Jack Tosswill. He was engaged just now in looking feverishly for an old gardening book which he had promised to lend Mrs. Crofton, and he was cursing under his breath because the book had been mislaid.

As Rosamund looked in, her step-mother and Radmore both stopped speaking abruptly, and so after a doubtful moment, she withdrew her head, and shut the door behind her.

"Tell me about George," he said, without looking at her.

"I think Betty would like to tell you," she answered slowly: "Ask her about him some time when you're alone together."

"Where is she now?" he asked abruptly.

"In the kitchen I think — but she won't be long."

Jack, looking ruffled and uneasy, very unlike his quiet, cool self, burst into the room. "I can't think where that old shabby green gardening book has gone, Janet. Do you know where it is?"

"You mean 'Gardening for Ladies'?"

"Yes."

"What on earth d'you want it for?"

"For Mrs. Crofton. Her garden's been awfully neglected."

"I'll find it presently. I think it's in my bedroom."

Again the door shut, and Janet turned to Radmore: "Your friend has made a conquest of Jack!" She spoke with a touch of rather studied unconcern, for she had been a little taken aback last evening when Timmy had told her casually of his own and his godfather's call at The Trellis House.

"My friend?" Radmore repeated uncertainly.

"I mean Mrs. Crofton. The coming of a new person to live in Beechfield is still quite an event, Godfrey."

"I don't think she'll make much difference to Beechfield," again he spoke with a touch of hesitation. "To tell you the truth, Janet, I rather wonder that she decided to live in the country at all. I should have thought that she would far prefer London, and all that London stands for. But I'm afraid that she's got very little money, and, of course, the country *is* cheaper than town, isn't it?"

"I suppose it is. But Mrs. Crofton can't be poor. I know she paid a premium for the lease of The Trellis House."

"That's odd." Radmore spoke in an off-hand manner, but Janet, watching him, thought he felt a little awkward. He went on: — "I know that Colonel Crofton was hard up. He told me so, quite frankly, the last time I saw him. But of course she may have had money of her own."

Janet looked at him rather hard. A disagreeable suspicion had entered her mind. She wondered whether there was anything like an "understanding" between the man she was talking to and the tenant of The Trellis House. If so, she wished with all her heart that Godfrey Radmore had kept away. Why stir up embers they had all thought were dead, if he was going to marry this very pretty but, to her mind, second-rate little woman, as soon as a decent time had elapsed?

"What are your plans for the future?" she asked. "Are you going to settle down, or are you going to travel a bit?" ("After all, he won't be able to marry Mrs. Crofton for at least another six months," she said to herself.)

"Oh, I mean to settle down." His answer was quick, decisive, final.

He went on: "My idea is to find a place, not too far from here, that I can buy; and my plan is to go about and look for it now. That's why I've hired a motor for a month. Perhaps you'd lend me Timmy, and, if it wouldn't be improper, one of the girls, now and again? We might go round and look about a bit."

And then he walked across to where she was standing, and put his hand on her arm, "How about you?" he asked, "why shouldn't I take you and Timmy a little jaunt just for a week or so — that would be rather fun, eh?"

She smiled and shook her head.

He took a step back. "Look here, Janet — do try and forgive me — I'm a more sensible chap than I was, honest Injun!"

"I'm beginning to think you are," she cried, and then they both burst out laughing.

He lingered a moment. He was longing, longing intensely, to ask her certain questions. He wanted to know about Betty — what sort of a life Betty had made for herself. He still, in an odd way, felt responsible for Betty — which was clearly absurd.

And then Janet Tosswill said something that surprised him very much. "I think you'd better go round and see some of the people in the village today. I was rather sorry you went off straight to The Trellis House last evening. You know how folks talked, even in the old days, in Beechfield?"

He looked uneasy — taken aback, and she felt, if a little ashamed, glad that she had made that "fishing" remark.

There was a pause, and then he said with a touch of formality: "Look here, Janet? I'd like you to know that though I've become quite fond of Mrs. Crofton, I'm only fond — nothing more, you understand? Perhaps I'll make my meaning clearer when I tell you that I was the only man in Egypt who knew her who wasn't in love with her."

He saw her face change and, rather piqued, he asked: "Did you think I was?"

"I thought that you and she were great friends —"

"Well, so we are in a way. I saw a great deal of her in London."

"And you went straight off to see her the moment you arrived here."

"Well, perhaps I was foolish to do that."

What an odd admission to make. He certainly had changed amazingly in the last nine years!

Then it was Janet who surprised him: "Don't make any mistake," she said quickly. "There's no reason in the world why you shouldn't marry Mrs. Crofton — after a decent interval has elapsed. All I meant to say — and I'd rather say it right out now — is that as most people know that her husband hasn't been dead more than a few weeks, you ought to be rather careful, all the more careful if — if your friendship should come to anything, Godfrey."

"But it won't!" he exclaimed, with a touch of the old heat, "indeed it won't, Janet. To tell you the truth, I don't think I shall ever marry."

"*I* certainly shouldn't if I were a rich bachelor," she said laughing; and yet somehow what he had just said hurt her.

As for Radmore, he felt just a little jarred by her words. Had she quite forgotten all that had happened in that long ago which, in a sense, seemed to belong to another life? He hadn't, and since his arrival yesterday certain things had come back in a rushing flood of memory.

"I've something to do in the garden now." Janet was smiling — she really did feel perhaps rather absurdly relieved. Like Timmy, she didn't care for Mrs. Crofton, and the mere suspicion that Godfrey Radmore had come back here to Old Place in order to carry on a love affair had disturbed her.

"By the way, how's McPherson?" he asked abruptly. "He *is* a splendid gardener and no mistake! I've never seen a garden looking more beautiful than yours does just now, Janet. I woke early this morning and looked out of my window. I suppose McPherson's about — I'll go out and speak to him."

Her face shadowed. "McPherson," she said slowly, "was one of the first men to leave Beechfield. He was perfectly fit, and he made up his mind to go at once. You know, Godfrey — or perhaps you don't know — that the Scotch glens emptied first of men?"

"D'you mean. . .?"

She nodded. "He was killed at the second battle of Ypres. He was sent to the Front rather sooner than most, for he was a very intelligent man, and really keen. I've got a boy now, a lad of seventeen — not half a bad sort, but it does seem strange to give him every Saturday just double the money I used to give McPherson!"

She went out, through into the garden, on these last words, and again there came over Radmore a feeling of poignant sadness. How strange that he should have spent those weeks in London, knowing so little, nay, not knowing at all, what the War had really meant to the home country.

He opened the door into the corridor, and listened, wondering where they had all gone. He had some business letters to write, and he told

himself that he would go and get them done in what he still thought
of in his mind as George's room. He had noticed that the big plain deal
writing table was still there.

He went upstairs, and when he opened the bedroom door, he was
astonished to find Rosamund kneeling in front of George's old play-
box, routing among what looked like a lot of papers and books.

"I'm hunting for a prescription for father," she said, looking up.
"Timmy thinks he put it in here one day after coming back from the
chemist's at Guildford." She looked flushed, and decidedly cross, as she
went on: "No one's taught Timmy to put things in their proper place,
as we were taught to do, when we were children!"

Radmore felt amused. She certainly was very, very pretty, and did not
look much more than a child herself.

"Look here," he said good-naturedly, "let me help. I don't think you're
going the right way to work." He felt just a little bit sorry for Timmy;
Rosamund was raking about as if the play-box was a bran-pie.

Bending down he took up out of the box a bundle of envelopes,
copybooks, and Christmas cards. Then he sat himself down on a chair
in the window, and began going through what he held, carefully and
methodically.

Suddenly through the open door there came a cry of "Miss Rosamund, I want you!"

Rosamund got up reluctantly. "Nanna's a regular tyrant!"

"Leave all this to me," he said. "I'll find the prescription if it's here."

She went off, and almost at once he came to a folded bit of paper.
Perhaps this was the prescription? He opened it, and this is what he
read: —

March 12, 1919. This is the happiest day of my life. One of my
godmothers has died and left me £50. I am going to buy two
nanny-goats, a boy and a girl. They will have kids, and I shall make
munny. We shall then have a propper cook, and I shall never help
Betty wash up anymore. I wish my other godmother would die.
She is very genrus and kind — she would go strait to Heaven. But
she is very hellfy.

Poor little Timmy! Dear little unscrupulous child of nature! Would
Timmy wish him, Godfrey Radmore, dead, if some accident were to
reveal to him what a great difference it would make to them all? He
hoped not. But he couldn't feel sure, for, from being well-to-do the
Tosswills must have become poor, painfully and, to his mind, unnaturally poor.

Further search proved the prescription was not in the play-box, and he went downstairs. Still that same unnatural silence through the house. Where could Timmy be? Somehow he felt that he wanted to see Timmy and find out about the nanny-goats. He feared his godson's expectations of wealth had not been fulfilled, but he supposed that there was a "propper cook," probably the lack of her had been quite temporary.

He wandered into the drawing room. In the old days all five sitting rooms had been in use. Now four of them were closed, and the drawing room was everybody's meeting place. Dolly was there working a carpet-sweeper languidly.

"Where's everybody?" he asked.

"I think Betty and Timmy are still in the scullery. I don't know where Rosamund is."

"I suppose *I* can go into the scullery?"

She looked at him dubiously. "Yes, if you'd like to — certainly. Betty loves cooking and all that sort of thing. I hate it — so in our division of labor, I do the other kind of housework." She looked ruffled and he told himself, a little maliciously, that she was not unlike a lazy, rather incompetent, housemaid. "If it's Timmy you want," she continued, "I'll go and see if he can come."

"Please don't trouble. I'll find him all right."

Radmore went out into the passage. As the baize door, which shut off the kitchen quarters, opened, he saw his godson and Rosamund before they saw him, and he heard Rosamund say, in a cross tone: "It only means that someone else will have to help her; I think it's very selfish of you, Timmy."

From being full of joy Timmy's face became downcast and sullen.

"Hullo!" Radmore called out, "I want you to show me the garden, Timmy. Where's Betty?"

"She's in the scullery, of course. I tell you I *have* done, Rosamund. You *are* a cruel pig —"

"Come, Timmy, don't speak to your sister like that."

It ended in the three of them going off — Rosamund to look for the prescription, and the other two into the garden.

*N*anna waddled into the scullery: "I'll wipe up them things, Miss Betty," she said good-naturedly; "you go out to Mr. Godfrey and Master Timmy — they was asking for you just now."

Betty hesitated — and then suddenly she made up her mind that, yes, she would do as Nanna suggested.

In early Victorian days women of Betty Tosswill's class and kind worked many of their most anxious thoughts and fears, hopes and fancies, into the various forms of needlework which were then considered the only suitable kind of occupation for a young gentlewoman; and often Betty, when engaged on the long and arduous task of washing up for her big family party, pondered over the problems and secret anxieties which assailed her. Though something of a pain, it had also been to her a great relief to realize that the living flesh and blood Godfrey Radmore of today had ousted the passionately devoted, if unreasonable and violent, lover of her early girlhood. In the old days, intermingled with her deep love of Radmore, there had been a protective, almost maternal, feeling, and although Radmore had been four years older than herself, she had always felt the older of the two. But now, in spite of the responsible, anxious work she had done in France during the War, she felt that the rôles were reversed, and that her one-time lover had become infinitely older than she was herself in knowledge of the world.

Old Nanna hoped that Miss Betty would go upstairs and change her plain cotton dress for something just a little prettier and that she would put on, maybe, a hat trimmed with daisies which Nanna admired. But Betty did nothing of the sort. She washed her hands at the sink, and then she went out into the hall, and taking up her big plain old garden hat went straight out into the keen autumnal air.

And then, as she caught sight of the tall man and of the little boy, she stayed her steps, overwhelmed by a flood of both sweet and bitter memories.

During the year which had followed the breaking of her engagement there had been corners and byways of the big, rambling old garden filled with poignant, almost unbearable, associations of the days when she and Godfrey had been lovers. There had been certain nooks and hidden oases where it had been agony to go. She had considered all kinds of things as being possible. Perhaps her most certain conviction had been that he would come back some day with a wife whom she, Betty, would try to teach herself to love; but never had she visioned what had now actually occurred, that is Radmore's quiet, commonplace falling-back into the day-to-day life of Old Place.

All at once she heard Timmy's clear treble voice: — "Hullo! There's Betty."

Radmore turned and said something Betty did not hear, and the child went off like an arrow from the bow. Then Radmore, turning, came towards her quickly. She had no clue to the strange look of pain and indecision on his face, and her heart began to beat, strangely.

When close to her: — "Betty," he said in a low voice, "I want to tell you that I didn't know about George till last night. How could you think I did?"

"I suppose one does think unjust things when one's in great trouble," she answered.

He felt hurt and angry and showed it. "I should have thought you would all have known me well enough to know that I should have written at once — at once. Why, the whole world's altered now that I know that George is no longer in it! Perhaps that sounds foolish and exaggerated, as I never wrote to him. But I think *you'll* know what I mean, Betty? It was all right, as long as I knew he was somewhere, happy."

She said almost inaudibly: — "I think that he is happy somewhere. You know — but no, you don't know — that George was a born soldier. Those months after he joined up, and until he was killed, were, I do believe, by far the happiest of his life. He always said they were."

As he made no answer she went on: — "I'll show you some of his letters if you like, and father will show you the letters that were sent to us — afterwards."

By now they had left the garden proper, and were walking down an avenue which was known as the Long Walk. It was here that they two, with George always as a welcome third, used to play "tip and run" and "hide and seek" with the then little children.

"Tell me something about the others," he said abruptly. "I'm moving in a world unrealized."

She smiled up into his face. Somehow that confession touched her, and brought them nearer to one another.

"Jack frightens me a bit, you know — he's so unlike George. And then the girls? Is it true what Timmy says — that Rosamund wants to be an actress?"

There was a slight tone of censorious surprise in his voice, and Betty reddened.

"I don't see why she shouldn't be an actress if she wants to be! Father's making her wait till she's twenty-one."

"Let me see," he said hesitatingly, "Dolly's older than Jack, isn't she?"

"Oh, no. Dolly will only be twenty next Thursday."

There came over her an overwhelming impulse to tell him something — the sort of thing she could only have told George.

"You know that pretty old church at Oakford?"

He nodded.

"Well, Mr. Runsby is dead. They've got a bachelor clergyman now, and Janet and I think that he's becoming very fond of Dolly! He's away just now, or you would have already seen him. He's very often over here."

"I should have thought —" He hesitated in his turn, but already he was falling again into the way of saying exactly what he thought right out to Betty — "that with you and Rosamund in the house, no one would look at Dolly!"

Betty blushed, and for a fleeting moment Godfrey saw the blushing, dimpling Betty of long ago.

"Rosamund has the utmost contempt for him. As for me, he never sees me — I'm always in the kitchen when he comes here." She added with a touch of the quiet humor he remembered, "I don't think Dolly's in any danger from me!"

"*Why* are you always in the kitchen, Betty?" he asked. "Is it really necessary?"

"Yes, it really is necessary," she answered frankly. "Father's got much poorer, and everything's about a hundred times as dear as it was before the War. But you mustn't think that I mind. I like it in a way — and it won't last forever. Some of father's investments are beginning to recover a little even now, and prices are coming down —"

They had now come back to the garden end of the Long Walk. "I must go now," she said. "Would you like me to send out one of the girls to entertain you?"

He shook his head. "No, I think I'll stroll about the village for a bit."

They both felt as if the first milestone of their new relationship had been set deep in the earth, and both were glad and relieved that it was so.

Radmore walked about a bit, admiring Janet's autumnal herbaceous borders, and then he remembered a door that he had known of old which led from the big kitchen garden into the road. If it was open he could step out without walking across the front of the house.

He turned into the walled garden, and walked quickly down a well-kept path past the sun-dial to the door. It was open. He walked through it, and then, with a rather guilty feeling — a feeling he did not care to analyze — he made his way round the lower half of the village till he reached the outside wall of The Trellis House.

There he hesitated for a few moments, but even while he was hesitating he knew that he would go in. Before he could turn the handle the door in the garden wall was opened by Enid Crofton herself. Radmore was surprised to see that she was dressed in a black dress, with the orthodox plain linen collar and cuffs of widowhood. It altered her strangely.

He was at once disappointed and a little relieved also, to find Jack Tosswill in the garden with her. But soon the three went indoors, and then, as had often been Mrs. Crofton's experience with admirers in the past, each man tried to sit the other out.

At last the hostess had to say playfully: — "I'm afraid I must turn you out now, for I'm expecting my sister-in-law, Miss Crofton."

And then they both, together, took their departure; Radmore feeling that he had wasted an hour which might have been so very much more profitably spent in going to see some of his old friends among the cottagers. As to Jack Tosswill, he felt perplexed, and yes, considerably put out and annoyed. He had been a good deal taken aback to see how close was the acquaintance between Mrs. Crofton and Godfrey Radmore.

Chapter XIII

*T*here is nothing like a meal, especially a good meal, for inducing between two people an agreeable sense of intimacy. When Enid Crofton and her elderly sister-in-law passed from the dining room of The Trellis House into the gay-looking little sitting room, with its old-fashioned, brightly colored chintz furnishings, and quaint reproductions of eighteenth-century prints, the two ladies were far more at ease the one with the other than before luncheon.

Enid, in the plain black woolen gown, with its white linen collar and cuffs, which she had discarded almost at once after her husband's funeral, felt that she was producing a pleasant impression. As they sat down, one on each side of the cheerful little wood fire, and began sipping the excellent coffee which the mistress of the house had already taught her very plain cook to make as it should be made, she suddenly exclaimed: —

"I do want to thank you again for the money you sent me when poor Cecil died! It was most awfully good of you, and very useful, too, for the insurance people did not pay me for nearly a month."

These words gave her visitor an opening for which she had waited during the last hour: "I'm glad my present was so opportune," said Miss Crofton in her precise, old-fashioned way. "As we have mentioned money, I should like to know, my dear, how you are situated? I was afraid from something Cecil told me last time he and I met that you would be very poorly left."

She stopped speaking, and there followed a long pause. Enid Crofton was instinctively glad that she was seated with her back to the window. She was afraid lest her face should betray her surprise and discomfiture at the question. And yet, what more natural than that her well-to-do, kind-hearted sister-in-law should wish to know how she, Enid, was now situated?

Cecil Crofton's widow was not what ordinary people would have called a clever woman, but during the whole of her short life she had studied how to please, cajole, and yes — deceive, the men and women about her. Unfortunately for her, Alice Crofton was a type of woman with whom she had never before been brought in contact; and something deep within her told her that she had better stick as close to the truth as was reasonably possible with this shrewd spinster who was, in some ways, so disconcertingly like what Enid Crofton's late husband had been, in the days when he had been a forlorn girl-widow's protecting friend and ardent admirer.

Yet, even so, she began with a lie: "When my mother died last year she left me a little money. I thought it wise to spend it in getting this house, and in settling down here." She said the words in a very low voice, and as Miss Crofton said nothing for a moment, she added timidly: — "I do hope that you think I did right? I know people think it wrong to use capital, but the War has changed everything, including money, and one simply can't get along at all without paying out sums which before the War would have seemed dreadful."

"That's very true," said Miss Crofton finally.

Enid, feeling on sure ground now, went on: "Why, I had to pay a premium of £200 for the lease of this little house. But I'm told I could get that again — even after living for a year or two in it."

Miss Crofton began looking about her with a doubtful air: "I suppose you mean to spend the winter here," she said musingly, "and then let the house each summer?"

"Yes," said Enid, "that is my idea."

As a matter of fact, she had never thought of doing such a thing, though she saw the point of it, now that it was put by her sister-in-law. She hoped, however, that long before next summer her future would be settled on most agreeable lines.

"Then I suppose the balance of what your mother left you forms a little addition to your pension, and to what poor Cecil was able to leave you?"

As the other hesitated, Miss Crofton went on, in a very friendly tone: — "I hope you won't think it interfering that I should speak as I am doing? I expected to find you much less comfortably circumstanced, and I was going to propose that I should increase what I had feared would be a very small income, by two hundred a year."

Enid was as much touched by this unexpected generosity as it was in her to be, and it was with an accent of real sincerity that she exclaimed: — "Oh, Alice, you *are* kind! Of course two hundred a year would be a *great* help. Nothing remains of what my mother left me. But you must not think that I'm extravagant. I sold a lot of things, and that made it possible for me to take over The Trellis House exactly as you see it. But even during the very few days I have been here I have begun to find how expensive life can be, even in a village like this."

"All right," said Miss Crofton. She got up from her easy chair with a quick movement, for she was still a vigorous woman. "Then that's settled! I'll give you a check for £100 today — and one every six months as long that is, as you're a widow." Then she smiled a little satirically, for Enid had made a quick movement of recoil which Alice Crofton thought rather absurd.

"It's early to think of such a thing, no doubt," she said coolly. "But still, I shall be very much surprised, Enid, if you do not re-make your life. I myself have a dear young friend, very little older than you are, who has been married three times. The War has altered the views and prejudices even of old-fashioned people."

"I want to ask you something," said Enid, "d'you think I ought to tell people that I have already been married twice?"

Miss Crofton told herself quickly that such questions are always put with a definite reason, and that she probably would not be called upon to pay her sister-in-law's allowance for very long.

"I don't think you are in the least bound to tell anyone such a fact about yourself, unless" — she hesitated, — "you were seriously thinking of marrying again. In such a case as that I think you would be well advised, Enid, to tell the man in question the fact before you become obliged to reveal it to him."

There was a pause, and then Miss Crofton abruptly changed the subject by saying something which considerably disturbed her young sister-in-law.

"I should be much obliged, my dear, if you would tell me a few details as to my poor brother's death. Your letter contained no particulars at all," and as the other made no immediate answer, Miss Crofton went on: — "I know there was an inquest, for one of my friends in Florence saw a report of it in an English paper. Perhaps you would kindly let me see any newspaper account or cuttings you may have preserved?"

"I have kept *nothing*, Alice!" Enid Crofton uttered the words with a touch of almost angry excitement. Then, perhaps seeing that the other was very much surprised, she said more quietly: — "The inquest was a purely formal affair — the Coroner himself told me that there must always be an inquest when a person died suddenly."

"Oh, but surely the question was raised, and that very seriously, as to whether Cecil took what he did take on purpose, or by accident? I understood from my friend that the account of the inquest she saw in some popular Sunday paper was headed 'An Essex Mystery.'"

Enid felt as if all the blood in her body was flowing towards her face. She congratulated herself that she was sitting with her back to the light. These remarks, these questions made her feel sick and faint. Yet she answered, composedly: — "Both the Coroner and the jury felt *sure* he had taken it on purpose. Poor Cecil had never been like himself since the unlucky day, for us, that the War ended!" And then to Miss Crofton's surprise and discomfiture Enid burst into tears.

The older lady got up and put her hand very kindly on the younger one's shoulder: — "I'm sorry I said anything, my dear," she exclaimed; "I'm afraid you went through a much worse time than you let me know."

"I did! I did!" sobbed Enid. "I cannot tell you how terrible it was, Alice."

Then she made a determined effort over herself, ashamed of her own emotion. Still neither hostess nor guest was sorry when there came a knock at the door, followed a moment later by the entry into the room of a stranger who was announced by the maid as "Miss Pendarth."

Enid Crofton got up, and as she shook hands with the newcomer she tried to remember what it was that Godfrey Radmore had said of her old-fashioned looking visitor. That she was a good friend but a bad enemy? Yes, that had been it. Then she remembered something else — the few kind words scribbled on a visiting card which had been left at The Trellis House a day or two ago.

She turned to her sister-in-law: — "I think Miss Pendarth knew poor Cecil years and years ago," she said softly.

"Are you — you must be Olivia Pendarth?" There was a touch of emotion in Alice Crofton's level voice.

"Yes, I am Olivia Pendarth."

Enid was surprised — not over pleased by the revelation that these two knew one another.

"I suppose it's a long time since you met?" she said pleasantly.

"Miss Crofton and I have never met before," said Miss Pendarth quietly. "But I knew your husband very well in India, when he and I were both young. My brother was in his regiment."

"The dear old regiment!" exclaimed Miss Crofton.

Enid Crofton smiled a little to herself. It amused her to see that these two old things — for so she described them to herself — had so quickly become friends. "The Regiment!" How sick she had got of those two words during her second married life! She was sorry that Alice, whom she liked, should be so queerly like Cecil. Even their voices were alike, and she had uttered the two words with that peculiar intonation her husband always used when speaking of any of his old comrades-in-arms.

All the same Miss Pendarth's sudden appearance had been a godsend. Enid hated going back to the dreadful time of her husband's death.

And then, when everything seemed going so pleasantly, and when Enid Crofton was still feeling a glow of joy at the thought of the check for £100, one of those things happened which seem sometimes to occur in life as if to remind us poor mortals that Fate is ever crouching round the corner, ready to spring. The door opened, and the buxom little maid brought in two letters on the salver she had just been taught to use.

One of the envelopes was addressed in a clear, ordinary lady's hand; the other, cheap and poor in quality, was in a firm, and yet unformed, handwriting.

Enid glanced at the two elder ladies; they were talking together eagerly. She walked over to the bow-shaped window, and opened the commoner envelope:

Dear Madam,

I hope you will excuse me writing to tell you that my husband has had to leave Mr. Winter's situation. Piper considers he has been treated shameful, and that if he chose he could get the law on Mr. Winter. I am writing to you unknown to Piper. If you could see me I think I could explain exactly what it is I want Piper to get. There do seem a difficulty now in getting jobs of Piper's sort, but from what he has told me there were one or two other jobs you heard of that might have suited him.

Yours respectfully,
AMELIA PIPER

Enid Crofton stared down at the signature with a sensation of puzzled dismay. *Piper married?* This was indeed a complication, and a complication which in her most anxious communings she had never thought of.

The man had always behaved like a bachelor — for instance he had always made love to the maids. There also came back to her the memory of something her husband had once said, with one of his grimly humorous looks: — "Piper's a regular dog! If he'd been born in a different class of life he'd have been a real Don Juan." She now asked herself very anxiously how far a married Don Juan of any class confides in his wife? Does he tell her his real secrets, or does he keep them to himself? Judging by her own experience the average man who loves a woman is only too apt to tell her not only his own, but other people's secrets.

Slowly she put the letter back in its envelope. She had gone to a great deal of trouble, and even to some little expense, over procuring Piper a really good situation. She had seen not only his new employer, but also what she liked doing far less, his new employer's wife; and she had got him extraordinarily good wages, even for these days. It was too bad that he should worry her, after all she had done for him. As for his wife — nothing would induce her to see Mrs. Piper. Neither did she wish Piper to come down to Beechfield. She was particularly anxious that the man should not learn of Godfrey Radmore's return to England. Unfortunately Radmore was on the lookout for a good manservant.

She took up the other letter. It was a nice, prosperous-looking, well addressed envelope, very different from the other. Perhaps this second letter would contain something that would cheer her up. But alas! when she opened it, she found it was from Mrs. Winter, Piper's late employer's wife.

Poor Enid Crofton! As she stood there reading it, she turned a little sick. Piper had got drunk the very first day he had been in his new situation. While drunk he had tried to kiss a virtuous young housemaid. There had been a regular scene, which had ended in the lady of the house being sent for. There and then Piper had been turned out neck and crop.

It was not only a justifiably angry letter, it was a very disagreeable letter, the writer saying plainly that Mrs. Crofton had been very much to blame for recommending such a man. . . .

Feeling very much disturbed she turned and came back towards her two visitors. They were now deep in talk, having evidently found a host of common associations: "I find I ought to answer one of my letters at once," she said. "Will you forgive me for a few moments?"

They both looked up, and smiled at her. She looked so pretty, so fragile, so young, in her widow's mourning.

She went through into the dining room. There was a writing-table in the window, and there she sat down and put her head in her hands; she felt unutterably forlorn, frightened too — she hardly knew of what. It had given her such a horrible shock to learn that Piper was married. . . .

Taking up a pen, she held it for a while poised in the air, staring out of the window at the attractive though rather neglected old garden, in which only this morning she had spent more than an hour with Jack Tosswill.

Then, at last, she dipped her pen in the ink, and after making two rough drafts, she decided on the following form of answer to Mrs. Piper, telling herself that it might be read as addressed to either husband or wife: —

Mrs. Crofton is very sorry to hear that Piper has lost his good situation. She will try and hear of something that will suit him. Mrs. Crofton cannot see Mrs. Piper for the present, as she is leaving home to start on a round of visits, but she will keep in touch with Mr. and Mrs. Piper and hopes to hear of something that may suit Piper very soon.

She began by writing "Mr. Piper," on one of her pretty black-edged mauve envelopes; then she altered the "Mr." to "Mrs." After all it was Piper's wife who had written to her, and she suddenly remembered with a slight feeling of apprehension, that Mrs. Piper, for some reason best known to herself, had not told Piper that she was writing. On the other hand it was quite possible that the husband and wife had concocted the letter between them.

Having addressed the envelope, she suddenly got up and ran up to her bedroom. There she opened her dressing-table drawer. Quite at the back lay an envelope containing four £5 notes. She took one of the notes, and running down again, slipped it in the envelope and added a postscript to her letter: —

Mrs. Crofton sends £5, which she hopes will be of use while Piper is out of a situation.

She went downstairs, giving her letter, on her way back to the drawing room, to the cook to take out to the post-box.

As she opened the drawing room door, something which struck her as a little odd happened. Her two visitors, the murmur of whose voices she had heard in deep, eager converse while she was stepping across her hall, abruptly stopped talking, and she wondered uneasily what they could have been saying that neither wished her to hear.

As a matter of fact that sudden silence was owing to a kindly, old-fashioned, wholly "ladylike" instinct, on the part of the two older women. Miss Crofton had been talking of her brother's death, confiding to Miss Pendarth her desire to learn something more as to how it had actually come about. With what was for her really eager sympathy, Miss Pendarth had offered to write to a friend in Essex, in order to discover the name of the local paper where, without doubt, a full account of the inquest on Colonel Crofton must have been published.

Chapter XIV

Saturday, Sunday, Monday, slipped away, and on Tuesday there seemed no reason why Godfrey Radmore should leave Old Place. And so he stayed on, nominally from day to day, settling down, as none of them would have thought possible that anyone now a stranger could settle down, to the daily round and common task of the life led by the Tosswill family. After two or three days he even began to take command of the younger ones, and Janet was secretly amused to see how he shamed both Rosamund and Dolly into doing something like their full share of the housework.

In relation to the two younger girls, his attitude was far more that of a good-natured, rather cynical, elder brother than was his attitude to Betty. Into her special department, the kitchen, he seldom intruded, though when he did so it was to real purpose. Thus, Dolly's twentieth birthday was made by him the excuse for ordering from a famous London caterer a hamper containing enough cold and half-cooked food to keep them junketing for two or three days. Janet was rather puzzled to note that Betty, alone of them all, seemed to look askance at the way Radmore spent his substance in showering fairy-godfatherlike gifts on the inmates of Old Place.

The happiest of them all was Timmy. Most men would have been bored by having so much of a child's company, but Radmore was touched and flattered by the boy's devotion, and that though there was a side of his godson which puzzled and disturbed him. Now and again Timmy would say something which made Radmore wonder for a moment if he had heard the words aright, but he followed the example silently set him by all the others of taking no notice of Timmy's claim both to see and foresee more than is vouchsafed to the ordinary mortal.

Miss Crofton had also stayed on in Beechfield, but only a day longer than she had intended to do – that is, till the Tuesday. She and Miss Pendarth had met more than once, striking up something like a real friendship. But this, instead of modifying, had intensified Miss Pendarth's growing prejudice against the new tenant of The Trellis House. She felt convinced that the pretty young widow had made her kind sister-in-law believe that she was far poorer, and more to be pitied, than she really was.

Life in an English village is in some ways like a quiet pool – and, just as the throwing of a pebble into such a pool causes what appears to create an extraordinary amount of commotion on the surface of the water, so the advent of any human being who happens to be a little out of the common produces an amount of discussion, public and private, which might well seem to those outside the circle of gossip, extravagant, as well as unnecessary.

The general verdict on Mrs. Crofton had begun by being favorable. Both with gentle and simple her appealing beauty told in her favor, and very soon the village people smiled, and looked knowingly at one another, as they noted the perpetual coming and going of Jack Tosswill to The Trellis House. No day went by without the young man making some more or less plausible excuse to call there once, twice, and sometimes thrice.

It was noticed, too, by those interested in such matters – and in Beechfield they were in the majority – that Mr. Godfrey Radmore, whose return to Old Place had naturally caused a good deal of talk and speculation – was also a frequent visitor at The Trellis House. Now and again he would call there in his car, and take Mrs. Crofton for a long drive; but they never went out alone – either Dolly or Rosamund, and invariably Timmy, would be of the party.

As the days went on, each member of the Tosswill family began to have a definite and, so to speak, crystallized view of Enid Crofton. Rosamund had become her champion, thus earning for the first time in her life the warm approval of her brother Jack; but Dolly and Tom grew rather jealous of their sister's absorption in the stranger. Rosamund was so very often at The Trellis House. In fact, when Jack was not to be found there, Rosamund generally was. But she had soon discovered that her new friend preferred to see her visitors singly. Betty kept her thoughts as to Mrs. Crofton to herself — for one thing the two very seldom met. But Janet Tosswill was more frank. With her, tepid liking had turned into dislike, and when she alluded to the pretty widow, which was not often, she would tersely describe her as "second-rate."

Now there is no word in the English language more deadly in its vague import than that apparently harmless adjective. As applied to a human being, it generally conveys every kind of odious significance, and curiously enough it is seldom applied without good reason.

Mrs. Crofton had gentle, pretty manners, but her manner lacked sincerity. She was not content to leave her real beauty of coloring and feature to take care of itself; her eye-brows were "touched up," and when she fancied herself to be "off color" she would put on a suspicion of rouge. But what perhaps unduly irritated the mistress of Old Place were Mrs. Crofton's clothes! To such shrewd, feminine eyes as were Janet Tosswill's, it was plain that the new tenant of The Trellis House had taken as much pains over her widow's mourning as a coquettish bride takes over her trousseau.

Janet Tosswill was far too busy a woman to indulge in the village game of constant informal calls on her neighbors. She left all that sort of thing to her younger step-daughters; and as Mrs. Crofton never came to Old Place — making her nervous fear of the dogs the excuse — Janet only saw the new tenant of The Trellis House when she happened to be walking about the village or at church.

But for a while, at any rate, an untoward event drove the thoughts of most of the inmates of Old Place far from Mrs. Crofton and her peculiarities, attractive or other.

*O*ne day, when Radmore had already been at Beechfield for close on a fortnight, Timmy drew him aside, and said mysteriously: "Godfrey, I want to tell you something."

Radmore looked down and said pleasantly, though with a queer inward foreboding in his mind: "Go ahead, boy — I'm listening."

"Something's going to happen to someone here. I saw Dr. O'Farrell last night, I mean in a dream. You were driving him in your car through our gate. Last time I dreamt about him Dolly had measles; she was awfully ill; she nearly died."

As he spoke, Timmy kept looking round, as if afraid of being overheard. "I don't mean to tell anyone else," he added confidentially.

"You see it upsets Mum, and makes the others cross, if I say things like that. But still, I just thought I'd tell *you.*"

Radmore was impressed, disagreeably so, in spite of himself; but: "Look here, Timmy," he said chaffingly. "The Greeks have a proverb about the bearer of ill-tidings; don't let yourself ever become that, old man! Have you ever heard, by the by, about 'the long arm of coincidence'?"

Timmy nodded.

"Don't you think it possible that your having dreamt about Dr. O'Farrell just before Dolly was taken ill may have been that long arm of coincidence — and nothing more? I can't help thinking that probably your mother said something about sending for Dr. O'Farrell — for people don't get measles in a minute, you know; they are seedy for some days beforehand — and that made you dream of him. Eh?"

But Timmy answered obliquely, as was rather his way when brought to book by some older person than himself. "I think this time it's going to be an accident," he said thoughtfully.

And an accident it was! Old Nanna, who, in spite of her age, had become the corner-stone of the household as regarded its material well-being, slipped on the back staircase, and sprained her leg, and of course it was Radmore who went off in his car to fetch and bring back Dr. O'Farrell.

A slight alleviation to their troubles was brought about by Miss Pendarth, who was going off on a visit the very day the accident happened, and who practically compelled Janet to accept the temporary service of her own excellent servant. It was her readiness to give that sort of quick, kindly, decisive help which made so many of those who had the privilege of her acquaintance regard Miss Pendarth with the solid liking which is founded on gratitude.

But the help, offered and accepted in the same spirit, could not go on for long, for Miss Pendarth came home after a four days' absence; and, for the first time in many months, Janet Tosswill made time to pay a formal call at Rose Cottage in order that she might thank her old friend. She intended to stay only the time that strict civility enjoined, and she would have been surprised indeed had she been able to foresee what a pregnant and, to her, personally, painful train of events were to follow as a result of the quarter of an hour she spent in Miss Pendarth's old-fashioned upstairs sitting room where only privileged visitors were ever made welcome.

"Will you come upstairs today, Janet? I have something about which I want to consult you."

And then, when they had sat down, Miss Pendarth said abruptly: "While I was in Essex I came across some people who had been acquainted with Mrs. Crofton and her husband."

Janet looked across at the speaker with some surprise. "What an odd thing!" she exclaimed, and she did think it rather odd.

But Olivia Pendarth was a very honest woman — too honest, some people might have said. "It was not exactly odd," she said quickly, "for, to tell you the truth, I made it my business while there to make certain enquiries about the Croftons. In fact, I partly went to Essex for that purpose, though I did not tell my friends so."

The visitor felt rather shocked, as well as surprised. Surely Olivia Pendarth's interest in her neighbors' concerns was, to say the least of it, excessive. But the other's next words modified her censorious thoughts.

"Colonel Crofton and one of my brothers were in the same regiment together. I knew him quite well when he and I were both young, and when Miss Crofton came to see her sister-in-law a fortnight ago, I offered to make certain enquiries for her."

There was a touch of mystery, of hesitation in the older lady's voice, and Janet Tosswill "rose" as she was perhaps meant to do. "What sort of enquiries?" she asked. "I thought Miss Crofton was on the best of terms with her sister-in-law."

"So she is; but she wanted to know more than Mrs. Crofton was inclined to tell her about the circumstances — the really extraordinary circumstances, Janet — concerning Colonel Crofton's death. And now I'm rather in a quandary as to whether I ought to tell her what I heard, and indeed as to whether I ought even to send her the report of the inquest which appeared in a local paper, and which I at last managed to secure."

"Of course I know that Colonel Crofton committed suicide." Janet Tosswill lowered her voice instinctively. "That poor, second-rate little woman seems to have told Rosamund as much, and Godfrey Radmore confirmed it."

"Yes, I suppose one ought to say that there is no real doubt that he committed suicide." Yet Miss Pendarth's voice seemed to imply that there was some doubt.

She went on: "It was suggested at the inquest that the chemist who made up a certain heart tonic Colonel Crofton had been in the habit of taking for some time, had put in a far larger dose of strychnine than was right."

Janet Tosswill repeated in a startled tone: "Strychnine! You don't mean to say the poor man committed suicide with that horrible poison?"

Miss Pendarth looked up, and Janet was struck by her pallor and look of pain. "Yes, Janet; he died of a big dose of strychnine, and the medical evidence given at the inquest makes most painful reading."

"It *must* have been a mistake on the part of the chemist. No sane man would take strychnine in order to commit suicide. Besides, how could he have got it?"

"There was strychnine in the house," said Miss Pendarth slowly. "When Mrs. Crofton was in Egypt it was prescribed for her. You know how people take it by the drop? A chemist out there seems to have given her a much greater quantity than was needed, and in an ordinary, unlabeled medicine bottle, too." The speaker waited a moment, then went on: "Though she brought it back to England with her, she seems to have quite forgotten that she had it. But *he* must have known it was there, for after his death the bottle was found in his dressing room."

"What a dreadful thing! And how painful it must have been for her!"

"Yes, I think she did go through a very dreadful time. But, Janet, what impressed me most painfully, and what I am sure would much distress Miss Crofton were I to tell her even only a part of what I heard, was the fact that the husband and wife were on very bad terms. This was testified to, and very strongly, by the only woman servant they had at the time of his death."

"I never believe servants' evidence," observed Janet Tosswill dryly.

"The Coroner, who I suppose naturally wished to spare Mrs. Crofton's feelings, told the jury that it was plain that Colonel Crofton was a very bad-tempered man. But the people with whom I was staying, and who drove me over to look at the God-forsaken old house where the Croftons lived, said that local feeling was very much against her. It was thought that she really caused him to take his life by her neglect and unkindness."

"What a terrible idea!"

"I fear it's true. And now comes the question — ought I to tell his sister this? Some of the gossip I heard was very unpleasant."

"Do you mean that there was another man?"

"Other men — rather than another man. She was always going up to London to enjoy herself with the various men friends she had made during the War, and the only guests they ever entertained were young men who were more or less in love with her."

Janet smiled a little wryly. "There's safety in numbers, and after all she's extraordinarily attractive to men."

"Yes," said Miss Pendarth, "there *is* safety in numbers, and it's said that Colonel Crofton was almost insanely jealous. They seem to have led a miserable existence, constantly quarreling about money, too, and often changing their servants. On at least one occasion Mrs. Crofton went away, leaving him quite alone, with only their odd man to look after him, for something like a fortnight. Colonel Crofton's only interest in life was the terriers which he apparently bred with a view to increasing his income."

"They can't have been so very poor," said Janet abruptly. "Look at the way she's living now."

"I feel sure she's living on capital," said Miss Pendarth slowly, "and I think — forgive me for saying so — that she hopes to marry Godfrey Radmore. I'm sure that's why she came to Beechfield."

"You're wrong there! She settled to come here before Godfrey came home."

"I'm convinced that she knew he was coming home soon."

Janet got up. "I must be going now," she exclaimed. "There's a great deal to do, and only Betty and I to do it."

"I suppose Godfrey Radmore will be leaving now?"

"I hope not, for he's a help rather than a hindrance. He takes Timmy off our hands —"

"— And he's so much at The Trellis House. I hear he dined there last night."

"Yes, with Rosamund," answered Janet shortly.

Miss Pendarth accompanied her visitor down and out to the wrought-iron gate. There the two lingered for a moment, and than Janet Tosswill received one of the real surprises of her life.

"Colonel Crofton and I were once engaged. I went out to India to stay with my brother, and it happened there. *Now* we should have married. But things were very different *then*. When my father found Captain Crofton was not in a position to make what was then regarded as a proper settlement, he declared the engagement at an end."

Janet felt touched. There was such a depth of restrained feeling in her old friend's voice. Somehow it had never occurred to her that Olivia Pendarth could ever have been in love!

"It must be very painful for you to have her here," she said involuntarily.

"In a way, yes. But I suspected she was his widow from the first."

"I think that, if I were you, I would say nothing to his sister," observed Janet.

"Very well. I will take your advice."

She changed the subject abruptly. "Let me know if Kate can be of anymore use. She's quite anxious to go on helping you all. She's got so fond of Betty: she says she'd do anything for her."

"We're managing all right now, and Godfrey really is a help, instead of a hindrance. He actually suggested that he should do the washing-up this morning!"

"That's the best thing I've ever heard of Godfrey Radmore," exclaimed Miss Pendarth. "I sincerely hope — forgive me for saying so, Janet — that there's really nothing between him and Enid Crofton. I should be sorry for my worst enemy to marry that woman, if the things I was told about her were true."

"I don't believe that he is thinking of her, consciously —" Janet Tosswill spoke slowly, choosing her words.

"Of course she's making a dead set at him. But there's safety in numbers, even here," observed the other, grimly. "I hear that your Jack simply lives at The Trellis House. The whole village is talking about it."

Jack? Janet Tosswill felt vexed by what she considered a bit of stupid, vulgar, village gossip. "Jack's the most level-headed young man about women I've ever known," she said, trying to speak pleasantly. "If anyone has fallen in love with Mrs. Crofton, it's our silly little Rosamund!"

Chapter XV

*T*he morning after Janet Tosswill's call at Rose Cottage, Rosamund followed her step-mother into the drawing room immediately after breakfast, and observed plaintively that it did seem strange that "Enid" was never asked to Old Place. "We take anything from her, and never give anything back," she said.

Janet, who had a certain tenderness for the pretty black sheep of the family, checked the sharp retort which trembled on her lips. Still, it was quite true that Rosamund had more than once been kept to lunch at The Trellis House, and that on the day of Nanna's accident Mrs. Crofton had issued a sort of general invitation to supper to the young people of Old Place — an invitation finally accepted, at Betty's suggestion, by Godfrey Radmore and Rosamund.

Janet admitted to herself that they did owe Mrs. Crofton some civility. If the thing had to be done, it might as well be done at once, and so, when Rosamund had reluctantly gone upstairs to do her share of the household work, his mother beckoned Timmy into the drawing room, and told him that she would have a note ready for him to take to The Trellis House in a few minutes.

"Oh, Mum, do let Jack take it!" the boy exclaimed. "I can't go to The Trellis House with Flick, and it's such a bore to shut him up."

"Why can't Flick go with you?"

"Mum! Don't you remember? Mrs. Crofton is *terrified* of dogs. Do let Jack take it!"

"But are you sure Jack is going there this morning?" she asked, and then she remembered Miss Pendarth's ill-natured remark.

"He goes there every morning," said Timmy positively, "and this morning he's going there extra early, as he's lending Mrs. Crofton our best preserving pan. She wants to make some blackberry jam."

And then there occurred one of those odd incidents which were always happening in connection with Timmy and with which his mother never knew quite how to deal. He screwed up his queer little face for a moment, shaded his eyes with his hand, and said quietly: "I think Jack is just starting down the drive now. You'll catch him if you'll open the window and shout to him, Mum — it's no good my going after him — he wouldn't come back for *me.*"

Janet Tosswill got up from her writing-table. She opened the nearest window and, stepping out, looked to her right. Yes, there was Jack's neat, compact figure sprinting down the long, straight avenue towards the gate. He was holding a queer-looking, badly done up parcel in his hands.

"Jack! Jack! Come here for a minute — I want you," she called out in her clear, rather high-pitched voice.

He slackened, and it was as if she could see him hesitating, wondering whether he dare pretend he had not heard her. Then he turned and ran back down the drive and across the wide lawn to the window.

"What is it?" he asked breathlessly. "I'm late as it is! I'm taking one of our preserving pans to The Trellis House. The fruit was all picked yesterday."

"I won't be a moment. I want you to take a letter for me to Mrs. Crofton. I'm asking her to come in to dinner tonight."

She turned back into the room and, sitting down, took up her pen: "Timmy? Go into the scullery, and help Betty for a bit."

After her little son had left the room, she called out to Jack, "Do come inside; it fidgets me to feel that you're standing out there."

After what seemed to Jack Tosswill a long time, though it was only three minutes, his step-mother turned, and held out her note: "She needn't write — a verbal answer will do. If she can't come we shall have done the civil thing."

And then, thinking aloud, she went on: "Somehow I don't expect her to stay long in Beechfield. She's too much of a London bird."

"I don't suppose she would have come at all if she had known what a beastly, inhospitable place Beechfield is," said Jack sharply. Though he was in such a hurry to be off, he waited in order to add: "She's been here nearly a month, and you've never called on her yet — it's too bad!"

Janet Tosswill flushed deeply. Jack had not spoken to her in such a tone since he was fifteen.

"What nonsense! She must be indeed silly and affected," she exclaimed, "if she expected me to pay her a formal call, especially as we had her in to supper the very first day she was here! I might retort by saying that she might have sent or called to know how poor old Nanna was! Everyone in the village has done so — but then your friend, Jack, is not what my father used to call '18 carat'!"

"I think it's we who are not '18 carat,'" he answered furiously. "We have shown Mrs. Crofton the grossest discourtesy, and I happen to know that she feels it very much."

Janet Tosswill looked at her elder stepson with a feeling of blank amazement. It had often astonished her to notice how completely Jack had his emotions and temper under control. Yet here he was, his face aglow with anger, his voice trembling with rage.

Poor Janet! She had had long days of fatigue and worry since the old nurse's accident, and suddenly she completely lost her temper. "I don't want to say anything unkind about the little woman, but I do think her both silly and second-rate. I took a dislike to her when she behaved in such a ridiculous manner over Flick."

"You were almost as frightened as she was," said Jack roughly.

"It's quite true that I was frightened for a moment, but only because I was afraid for Timmy."

"I can tell you one thing — she won't come here again to supper unless I can give her my word that all our dogs are really shut up. And I fear I must ask you to undertake to see that Timmy does not let Flick out after I *have* shut him up."

Janet Tosswill held out her hand. "I think you'd better give me that note back," she said curtly. "We certainly don't want anyone here of the kind you have just described. From something Godfrey said to me it's clear that Mrs. Crofton's horror of dogs is just a pose she thinks makes her interesting. Why, her husband bred terriers; Flick actually came from there! And Godfrey says that she herself had a little dog called by the absurd name of 'Boo-boo' to which she was devoted."

"'Boo-boo' was the exception that proves the rule," answered Jack hotly. "As for Colonel Crofton, it was beastly of him to breed terriers, knowing how his wife felt about dogs! She told me herself she would never have married him if she had known there was any likelihood of that coming to pass. She feels about dogs as some people feel about cats."

"I never heard such nonsense!"

"Nonsense?" he repeated in an enraged tone. "It isn't nonsense! The best proof that that horror of dogs is instinctive with her is the effect that she herself has on every dog she comes across. That was shown the evening she was here."

"Really, Jack, that's utterly absurd! Flick was not thinking of her at all. Something in the garden had frightened him. Your father feels sure that it was a snake which he himself killed the next morning." And then, for she was most painfully disturbed by this scene between herself and Jack, she said quietly: "I'm sorry that Mrs. Crofton ever came to Beechfield. I didn't think there was anyone in the world who would make you speak to me as you have spoken to me now."

"I hate injustice!" he exclaimed, a little shamefacedly. "I can't think why you've turned against her, Janet. It's so mean as well as so unkind! She has hardly any friends in the world, and she thought by the account Godfrey gave of us that *we* should become her friends."

"It's always a woman's own fault if she has no friends, especially when she's such an attractive woman as Mrs. Crofton," said Janet shortly. She hesitated, and then added something for which she was sorry immediately afterwards: "I happen to know rather more about Mrs. Crofton than most of the people in Beechfield do."

She spoke with that touch of mysterious finality which is always so irritating to a listener who is in indifferent sympathy with a speaker.

"What d'you mean?" cried Jack fiercely. "I insist on your telling me what you mean!"

Janet Tosswill told herself with Scotch directness that she had been a fool. But if Jack was — she hardly knew how to put it to herself — so — so bewitched by Mrs. Crofton as he seemed to be, then perhaps, as they had got to this point, he had better hear the truth:

"Mrs. Crofton made herself very much talked about in the neighborhood of the place where she and her husband settled after the War. She was so actively unkind, and made him so wretched, that at last he committed suicide. At least that is what is believed by everyone who knew them in Essex."

"I suppose a woman told you all this?" he said in a dangerously calm voice.

"Yes, it was a woman, Jack."

"Of course it was! Every woman, young or old, is jealous of her because she's so pretty and — so — so feminine, and because she has nothing about her of the clever, hard woman who is the fashion nowadays! The only person who does her justice in this place is Rosamund."

"I disapprove very much of Rosamund's silly, schoolgirlish, adoration of her," said Janet sharply.

She was just going to add something more when she saw Timmy slipping quietly back into the room. And all at once she felt sorry — deeply sorry — that this rather absurd scene had taken place between herself and Jack. She blamed herself for having let it come to this pass.

"I daresay I'm prejudiced," she exclaimed. "Take this note, Jack, and tell Mrs. Crofton that Flick shall be securely shut up."

"All right." Jack shrugged his shoulders rather ostentatiously, and disappeared through the window, while Janet, with a half-humorous sigh, told herself that perhaps he was justified in condemning in his own mind, as he was certainly doing now, the extraordinary vagaries of womankind. She turned back to her writing-table again. However disturbed and worried she might feel, there were the weekly books to be gone through, and this time without Nanna's shrewd, kindly help.

Suddenly she started, for Timmy's clawlike little hand was on her arm: "Mum," he said earnestly, "do tell me what Colonel Crofton was really like? Did that lady — you know, I mean the person Jack thinks is jealous of Mrs. Crofton — tell you what he was like?"

"No — yes — oh, Timmy! I'm afraid you must have been listening at the door just now?"

"I didn't like to come in," he said, wriggling uneasily. "I've never heard Jack speak in such an angry way before. He was in a wax, wasn't he? But, Mum, do tell me what Colonel Crofton looked like — I do *so* want to know."

She put down her pen, and turning, gazed down into the child's eager, inquisitive little face.

"Why should you wish to know, Timmy?" She spoke rather coldly and sternly.

She was sorry indeed now that she had been tempted to repeat what was perhaps after all only the outcome of Miss Pendarth's unconscious jealousy of the woman who had made a fool of the man she had loved as a girl. It was unfortunately true that Olivia Pendarth had an unconscious prejudice against all young and pretty women.

"I want to know," mumbled Timmy, "because I think I do know what he was like."

"If you know what he was like, then there is nothing more to say."

"I want to be sure," he repeated obstinately.

"But how absurd, Timmy! Why should you want to know about a poor old gentleman who is dead, and of whom you are not likely ever to hear anything? I have often told you how horrid it is to be inquisitive."

Timmy paused over that remark. "I want to know," he said in a low mumbling voice, "because I think I have seen him." He did not look up at his mother as he spoke. With the forefinger of his right hand he began tracing an imaginary pattern on the blue serge skirt which covered her knee.

She looked around apprehensively. Yes, the door was shut. She remembered that Dr. O'Farrell had told her never to encourage the child's confidences, but, on the other hand, never to check them.

"I first saw him the evening she came to supper," Timmy mumbled. "They were walking together down the avenue. I thought he was a real old gentleman. There was a dog with him, a terrier exactly like Flick, only a little bigger. Of course I thought it was a real dog too. But now I know that it wasn't. I know now that it was a ghost-dog. It is *that* dog, Mum, that frightens the other dogs who meet them — not herself, as she's come to think."

"Oh, Timmy," — Janet felt acutely uncomfortable — "you know I cannot bear to think that such things really happen to you. If you really think them I'd rather know, but I'd so much rather, dear boy, that you didn't think them."

But Timmy was absorbed in what he was saying. "I know now that it was Colonel Crofton," he went on, "because I've seen an old photograph of him, Mum. Mrs. Crofton brought a tin box full of papers with her, and there were some old photographs in it. There was one of an officer in uniform, and it had written across it, 'Yours sincerely, Cecil Crofton.' She tore it up the day after she came here, and threw it in the waste-paper basket, but her cook took it out of the dustbin, and that's how I saw it."

"How disgusting!" exclaimed his mother, feeling herself now on firm ground. "How often have I had to tell you, Timmy, not to go into other people's kitchens and sculleries? No nice boy, no little gentleman, would do such a thing. Of course it was seeing that photograph made you believe you saw Colonel Crofton's —"

She stopped abruptly, for she never, if she could help it, used the word "ghost," or "spirit," to the child.

"Up to now I've always supposed that animals had no souls, Mum, but now I know they have. I know another thing, too," but there was a doubtful note in his voice. "I suppose that ghost-dog hates Mrs. Crofton because she was so unkind to his master. That's why he makes the other dogs fly at her, I expect — or d'you think it's just because they're frightened that they do it?"

Janet Tosswill was an unconventional woman, also she was on terms of very close kinship with her strange little son. Still, she reddened as she drew him closer to her and said: "Look here, Timmy, I want to tell you something. I'm sorry now I said what I did say to Jack about Mrs. Crofton. I ought not to have said it — I'm ashamed of having said it! It was told me by someone who is rather fond of repeating disagreeable, sometimes even untrue, things."

Timmy had also grown very red while his mother was making her little confession. He took up her hand and squeezed it impulsively, as an older person might have done.

"I think I know who you mean," he said. "You mean Miss Pendarth?"

"Yes," said his mother steadily, "I do mean Miss Pendarth. I think it quite possible that poor little Mrs. Crofton was never really unkind to Colonel Crofton at all."

"But you wouldn't like Jack to marry her, Mum, would you?"

Janet felt a shock of dismay go through her. There flashed into her mind that sometimes most disturbing text — "Out of the mouths of babes and sucklings. . . ."

"I shouldn't like it at all," she exclaimed, "and I think you're old enough to understand that such a thing would be impossible. Jack won't make enough money to keep a wife for years and years." She hesitated, and then added, speaking to herself rather than to Timmy, "Still, I hope with all my heart that he won't get foolish about her."

"He *is* foolish about her," said Timmy positively. "Even Nanna thinks" — he waited a moment, then said carefully — "that he is past praying for. She said yesterday to Betty that there were some things prayers didn't help in at all, and that love was one of them. She says that Jack's heart has gone out of his own keeping. Isn't that a funny idea, Mum?"

"It is a terrible idea," and, a little to her own surprise, tears rose to Janet Tosswill's eyes. Timmy, looking up into her face, felt his heart swell with anger against the person who was causing his mother to look as she was looking now.

He moved away a little bit, as if aware that what he was going to say would not meet with her approval, and then he said in a peculiar voice, a defiant, obstinate voice which she knew well: "I do wish that Mrs. Crofton would die — I do hate her so!"

Janet Tosswill looked straight into her little son's face. She felt that she had perhaps made a mistake in treating Timmy as if he were grown up. "My dear," she said very gravely, "remember the Bible says — 'Thou shalt not kill.'"

"Of course I know *that*," — he spoke with a good deal of scorn. "Of course I want her to die a *natural* death."

Chapter XVI

"No, you mustn't come in; I'm tired. Besides, I've got someone coming to tea."

The ready lie slipped easily off Enid Crofton's tongue, as Jack Tosswill looked down into her face with a strained, pleading look. They were standing in the deserted road close to the outside door set in the lichen-covered wall of The Trellis House. It was already getting dusk, for they had been for a long walk.

"I shall never, never forget today!" He gripped her hand hard as he spoke, and she looked up and down the empty road a little apprehensively. But no one was coming or going, and the group of little old cottages opposite The Trellis House held as yet no twinkling lights.

"I shall never forget it, either," she said softly. "But I really *must* go in now — you know we are meeting this evening?"

"May I come and fetch you?" he asked.

"No, I'd rather you didn't do that — if you don't mind," and then, seeing his look of deep disappointment, she added, "Perhaps you will walk back with me after dinner?"

"Of course I will, but I'm afraid Radmore or one of the girls will want to come too."

As he gazed down into her face there was a look of infinite longing in his eyes, and even she felt a certain touch of genuine emotion sweep over her. It is so very, very delicious to be loved.

"Good-bye, darling," he whispered huskily; and, before she had time to stop him, he had taken her in his arms and kissed her, passionately, lingeringly. Then, with no other word, he released her and went off quickly down the road.

*A*fter Enid Crofton had shut the heavy door in the wall behind her, she did not go straight along the path which led to her front door. Instead, she turned in the gathering darkness to the left, and started walking round the garden which in daylight looked so different, now that Jack Tosswill had put in so many hard mornings' work at it.

She felt more surprised and moved by what had happened this afternoon than she would have thought possible. Poor Jack! Poor, foolish, adoring, priggish boy!

When he had come in this morning, bringing the note of invitation from his step-mother, he had seemed excited and ill at ease. She had felt vexed at his coming so early, as she was anxious to superintend the jam-making herself. Enid Crofton had a very practical side to her character, and she was the last person to risk the wasting of good sugar and good fruit through the stupidity of an inexperienced cook.

While Jack was still there one of her new acquaintances had come in for a moment, for she had already made herself well liked in the neighborhood, and after the visitor had gone, Jack, exclaiming angrily that they were never left in peace together, had begged her to go for a walk with him that afternoon. This she had consented to do, after discovering that Godfrey Radmore had gone up to London for the day.

And then, during their walk, Jack had suddenly made her a pompous offer of marriage!

No wonder she smiled mischievously to herself, when pacing slowly up and down the path between a row of espaliered apple trees.

She told herself that in a sense it had been her fault. They were sitting on a fallen tree trunk, in a lonely little wood, Jack, as he seldom was, tongue-tied and dull. Piqued, she had twitted him on his silence. And then, all at once, he had turned and, seizing her roughly, had kissed her with the pent-up passion of a man in love who till now has never kissed a woman.

Pacing slowly in her dark garden, Enid Crofton's pulse quickened at the recollection of those maladroit, hungry kisses. Something — a mere glancing streak of the great shaft of ecstasy which enveloped Jack Tosswill's whole being had touched her senses into what had seemed to him marvelous response.

When at last he had released her, and in words of at once triumphant and humble adoration, had made her an offer of marriage, she had felt it an absurd anti-climax to a very delicious and, even in her well-stored memory, a unique experience.

And now she remembered the last time a man had kissed her. It was quite a little while ago, on the day she had taken possession of The Trellis House. Of course Captain Tremaine had tipped the guard so that they should have a carriage to themselves. But she had been uncomfortably aware that he was half-ashamed of himself — that he remembered, all the time, that she was a newly-made widow.

Somehow Jack Tosswill hadn't remembered that. Jack hadn't thought of it. But oh! how absurd he had been when his first rapture was over. Without even waiting for an answer to his proposal, he had coolly suggested they should wait till he had made a start at the Bar! At last she had managed to make him listen to her plea that, till a year had elapsed, she could not think of re-marriage. And he had believed her!

All at once she told herself, a little ruefully, that she had perhaps been foolish; that this affair, slight and altogether unimportant as it was, might become a tiresome complication. Of course she could keep him in order, but she was well aware that when a man had kissed her once, he generally wanted to kiss her again, and very soon.

In principle, she had no objection to Jack Tosswill's kisses. There was something fresh, alluring, wholly delightful, even to so hardened a flirt as was Enid Crofton, in being the object of a youth's first love. But she told herself, almost fiercely, that she must make him understand very, very clearly that, though they might sometimes kiss, they must never be caught. Fortunately Jack was curiously cautious for so young a man. That had been one of the reasons why she had been tempted to — well — to make him lose his head.

And then another figure, one of far greater importance and moment to herself than poor Jack Tosswill, came and challenged Enid Crofton to anxious attention. How did she stand with regard to Godfrey Radmore?

She stopped in her pacing, and stared straight before her. For the first time in her life she was quite at a loss as to what a man, of whom she was seeing a great deal, really felt about her.

Rosamund Tosswill was very young, and Enid secretly thought her very stupid, but there could be no doubt as to her essential truthfulness. Now, a day or two ago, Rosamund had said: "Isn't it funny of Godfrey?

He told Janet when he first came here that he had made up his mind to remain a bachelor!"

And yet they two, she, Enid, and Godfrey, had had something tantamount to an emotional little scene the first time he had come to see her at The Trellis House. True, it had only lasted two or three seconds, but while it lasted it had been intense. Had Timmy Tosswill not burst into the room in that stupid, inopportune way, Radmore would have certainly taken her in his arms. Though Radmore was no innocent, high-principled boy, even one kiss between them would have altered their whole attitude, the one to the other. She would have seen to that. In her heart she had cursed Timmy for his idiotic intrusion, and now she cursed him again.

Lately she had thought Radmore was becoming aware of Jack Tosswill's growing absorption in her, and she had suspected, as well as hoped, that he was a trifle jealous. Now jealousy, as Enid knew well, is a potent quickener of feeling between a man and a woman. It was unfortunate that Radmore seemed to regard Jack Tosswill as a mere boy — a rather tiresome, priggish boy. Still, that had its good side. Jack was only a very slight complication after all!

Again she cast a fleeting thought to Tremaine. In a sense he was her real mate, her real soul, and, yes, body mate. If only he wasn't so poor! She felt for a moment tempted to throw up everything — to do what he had so urged her to do, what he was always writing and begging her to do. That was to marry him quickly just before the end of his leave, and go out to India with him. He wrote to her every day, and his last letter was in the little silk bag now hanging on her arm.

It was the kind of love-letter that Enid understood, and enjoyed receiving: full of ardent, if rather commonplace, expressions, and of comparisons, very pleasant to her vanity, between her pretty self and the stupid, ugly women he said he was now meeting. He had been with his people in Cornwall — but for that he would of course have come down to see how she was getting on. In this particular letter he announced that he was going to be in London very soon, and might he run down for a day? He had added a question, chaffingly worded, and yet, as she well knew, seriously intended. Did she think it would be improper for him to come and spend two or three days with her? And now she told herself, very decidedly, that of course she couldn't have him here — in stupid, old-fashioned Beechfield. It would be a tiresome, useless complication. But why shouldn't she go up to London for three or four days and have a good time with him there?

Enid was well aware that absence frequently makes the heart grow fonder, and that distance does lend enchantment to the view. But she would not have put it in those exact words.

At last she began walking towards the house, telling herself that she felt oddly tired, and that it would be very pleasant, for once, to have a solitary cup of tea. Her house-parlor maid was shaping very nicely. Thus the girl had evidently brought the lamps into the sitting room, though she had forgotten to draw the curtains.

Enid knocked and rang. She had a theory that the possession of a latchkey by their mistress makes servants slow to answer the door.

"There's a person waiting for you in the drawing room, ma'am. She says she's come down on purpose from London to see you. She came just after you went out first."

There swept over Enid Crofton a strong, sudden premonition of evil. She realized that for the last ten days she had been secretly dreading that this would happen to her. She blamed herself sharply, now that it was too late, for having done nothing further to help the Pipers; but she had hoped the five pounds would have kept them quiet.

"I'll go upstairs and take off my things," she said wearily. "Bring me a cup of tea in my bedroom — I don't want anything to eat — and then I'll come down and see this person." She forced herself to add, "I suppose it's a Mrs. Piper?"

The girl answered at once, "She didn't give her name, ma'am. She just said that she wanted to see you, and that it was urgent. She's not got very long; she wants to catch the six o'clock train from Telford. She wouldn't believe at first that you wasn't in."

Enid found some comfort in those words, and she made up her mind that she would linger upstairs as long as she possibly could, so as to cut short her coming interview with the tiresome young woman. After all there was very little to say. She had behaved in a kind and generous manner to her late husband's servant, and she had already said she would do her best to help him again.

When she got upstairs she lit the two high brass candlesticks on the dressing-table, and then, after she had taken off her hat and long black woolen coat, she sat down in her easy chair by the wood fire. Soon there came a familiar rap and a welcome cup of tea.

She was sipping it, luxuriously, when there suddenly came a very different kind of rap on the door. It was a sharp, insistent knock, and before she could call out "Come in," the door opened, and a singular-looking figure advanced into the luxurious-looking, low-ceilinged bedroom.

"Excuse me coming up like this, Modam. But I'm afraid of losing my train."

The speaker was small and stout, with a sallow face which might once have held a certain gypsylike charm, for, in the candlelight, the luminous dark eyes were by far its most arresting feature. She wore a small, old-fashioned-looking, red velvet bonnet perched on her elaborately dressed hair.

Enid Crofton looked at her odd-looking visitor with astonishment. Who on earth could this be? Certainly not Piper's wife. A feeling of intense relief came over her when the strange-looking woman came towards her with a soft, gliding step, and handed her a card on which was written:

Madame Flora
    Ladies' wardrobes, gold teeth, and old jewelry purchased at the
    highest prices known in the trade

"I do 'ope you will excuse me coming up like this," she said again, and her queer Cockney voice sounded quite pleasantly in Enid Crofton's ears. "I've not got very long, and I've been 'ere since four o'clock."

As she spoke she did not look at the pretty young lady sitting by the fire. Her dark eyes were glancing furtively round the attractively furnished bedroom, as if appraising everything that was there, from the uncommon-looking high brass candlesticks on the dressing-table to the pink silk covered eiderdown and drawn linen coverlid on the bed.

Perhaps because she was so extraordinarily relieved, Enid Crofton spoke to this somewhat impudent old-clothes woman very graciously.

"I'm sorry," she began, "but I've nothing in the least suitable for you, Madame Flora. It's a pity you wasted your time waiting for me. There are several other people in Beechfield with whom I expect you might have done business." She smiled as she spoke.

"I wish I'd thought of that, Modam." The woman spoke with a touch of regret. "But your maids expected you might be back any minute, and I did want to meet you, for Piper's that down on 'is luck, I sometimes don't know what to do with 'im! Instead of wanting to employ ex-soldiers, as in course they ought ter, people seem just to avoid them —"

"Piper?" repeated Enid Crofton in a low, hesitating voice. "Then are you Mrs. Piper?"

Was it conceivable that this strange-looking old thing was Piper's wife?

"I've been Mrs. Piper eighteen years," replied Madame Flora composedly, "but I've always kep' on my business, Modam. It's not much of a business now, worse luck! Ladies won't part with their clothes, not when they're dropping off them. In old days, if Piper was down, I was up, so we was all right. But we've both struck a streak of bad luck."

For a few moments neither of them spoke. Mrs. Crofton was staring, astonished, at her visitor, and through her shallow mind there ran the new thought of how very, very little any of us know of other people's lives. After her first shock of dismayed surprise to find that Piper was married at all, she had imagined Piper's wife as something young and, of course, in a way, attractive and easily managed.

"Did you ever come down to my house in Essex?" she asked, still trying to speak pleasantly.

"No, Modam, I never was there. Piper and I 'as always kep' clear of each other's jobs, and I wouldn't be interfering *now*, but that the matter's becoming serious. Piper's worse than no good when 'e's idle." She hesitated, then went on, "If 'e's to keep off 'is failing, 'e must be working."

There was a pause, and then Enid Crofton spoke, in a low, uncertain tone. "Believe me, Mrs. Piper, when I say that I really will do all I can for him. But it's not easy now to hear of good jobs, and Piper doesn't seem easy to suit."

"You wouldn't care to take my 'usband on again yourself, Modam?"

Again there followed that curious pause which somehow filled Enid with a vague fear.

"I wish I could," she said at last, "but I can't afford it, Mrs. Piper. As a matter of fact, I've done a foolish thing in coming here, to Beechfield, at all. Only the other day one of my husband's relations advised me to let the house."

"Piper thinks, Modam, as how you might 'elp 'im to a job with Major Radmore." The name tripped quickly off the speaker's tongue, as if she was quite used to the sound.

Enid felt a throb of dismay. Did the Pipers know Godfrey Radmore was back?

"We was wondering," said the woman, "if you would give us the major's address?"

Then they didn't know he was back — or did they?

"I don't know it."

Enid Crofton was one of those women — there are more than a truthful world suspects — who actually find it easier to lie than to tell the truth. But she saw the look of incredulity which flashed over the sallow face of her unwelcome visitor.

"Mr. Radmore," she went on hastily, "is taking a motor tour. But he'll be back in London soon, and I'll let you know the moment I know he's settled down."

"I should 'ave thought," said the woman, "that the Major would 'ave 'ad a club where Piper could 'ave written."

"If he has, I don't know it."

And then, all at once, Enid Crofton pulled herself together. After all the interview was going quite smoothly. Nothing — well, disagreeable — had been said.

She got up from her chair. "I hope you'll forgive me, Mrs. Piper, for saying that Piper will never keep any job if he behaves as he did with these last people — I had a very disagreeable letter from the lady."

Mrs. Piper, alias Madame Flora, grew darkly red.

"Piper 'ad a shock this last July," she said, moving a little farther into the room, and so nearer to Enid Crofton. "The thing's been a-weighing on 'is mind for a long time. It's something 'e won't exactly explain. But it's on 'is conscience. Only yesterday 'e says to me, 'e says, 'If I'm drinking, my dear, it's to drown care; I ought to have spoken up very differently to what I done at the poor Colonel's inquest.'"

The terrible little woman again took a step or two forward, and then she waited, as if she expected the lady to say something. But Enid, though she opened her lips, found that she could not speak. Hardly knowing what she was doing, she sat down again. And, after what seemed to the owner of the attractive, candle-lit room an awful silence, Mrs. Piper went on, speaking now in quite a different tone — easy, confidential, and with a touch of wheedling good nature in it.

"Thanks to your late gentleman, Piper knows all about dogs, and all 'e requires, Modam, to set 'im up as a dog fancier, so to speak, is a moderate bit o' money. As 'e says 'imself, five hundred pound would do it easy. If I may make so bold, that's what reely brought me 'ere, Mrs. Crofton. It do seem to us both, that, under the circumstances, you might feel disposed to find the money?"

Enid looked down as she answered, falteringly: "I told Piper some time ago that it was quite impossible for me to do anything of the kind."

In her fear and distress she uttered the words more loudly than she was aware, and the woman looked round at the closed door with an apprehensive look: "Don't speak so loud. We don't want to tell everyone our business," she said sharply.

Now she came quite close up to her victim, for by now Enid Crofton knew that she was in very truth this woman's victim.

"You think it over," whispered Madame Flora. "We're not in a 'urry to a day or two. And look here, Modam, I'll be open with you! If you'll do that for Piper, it'll be in full discharge of anything you owe 'im — d'you take my meaning?"

Enid Crofton got up slowly from her chair almost as an automaton might have done. She wanted to say that she did not in the least know what Mrs. Piper *did* mean. But somehow her lips refused to form the words. She was afraid even to shake her head.

"I told you a fib just now" — Mrs. Piper's voice again dropped to a whisper. "Piper's made a clean breast o' the matter to me, and I do think as what it's common justice to admit that my 'usband's evidence at that inquest was worth more than twenty-five pound to you. It wasn't what Piper said; *it was what 'e didn't say that mattered,* Mrs. Crofton. It's been on 'is mind awful — I'll take my Bible oath on that. But 'live and let live,' that's my motter. We don't want to do anything unkind, but we're in a fix ourselves —"

"I haven't got five hundred pounds," said Enid Crofton desperately; "that's God's truth, Mrs. Piper."

To that assertion Madame Flora made no direct answer; she only observed, in a quiet conversational tone, and speaking no longer in a whisper. "The insurance gent told Piper as what 'e was not entirely satisfied, and 'e said as 'e'd be pleased to see Piper anytime if anything 'appened as could throw further light on the Colonel's death. 'An extraordinary occurrence' — that's what the insurance people's gentleman called it, Mrs. Crofton — 'an extraordinary occurrence.'"

And then Enid was stung into saying a very unwise thing. "The Coroner did not think it an extraordinary occurrence," she said quietly.

"'E says sometimes as what 'e ought to give 'imself up and say what 'e saw," went on Mrs. Piper with seeming irrelevance.

There was another brief pause: "If you 'aven't got five hundred pounds, Modam, I take it the insurance money has not yet been paid, for it was a matter of two thousand pounds — or so Piper understood from that party what came down to make enquiries."

Enid Crofton looked at her torturer dumbly. She did not know what to say — what to admit, and what to deny.

"Think it over," said the terrible little woman. "We're not in a 'urry to a day or two. We'll give you a fortnight to find the money."

She put her hand, fat, yet clawlike, on Mrs. Crofton's shoulder. "There's nothing to look so frightened about," she said a little gruffly. "Piper and me aren't blackmailers. But we've got to look out for ourselves, same as everybody else does. It's Piper's idea — that five hundred pounds is. 'E says 'twould ease 'is conscience to carry on the pore old Colonel's dog-breeding. As for me, I'd just as lief 'ave 'im in a good job — what gentlefolk call 'a cushy job' — with a gentleman like this Major Radmore seems to be. But there! Piper's just set on them nasty dogs, and 'e's planned it all out."

"Five hundred pounds is a great deal of money." Enid Crofton spoke in a dull, preoccupied tone.

"Not so much as it used to be, not by any manner of means," said Mrs. Piper shrewdly. "Think it over, Mrs. Crofton — and let us know what you *can* do. Perhaps it needn't be paid all in one; but best to write to Piper next time. 'E says 'e'd like to feel you and 'im were partnerslike. I'll tell 'im I arranged for you to 'ave ten days to a fortnight to think it over."

"Thinking won't make money," said Enid in a low voice.

"Such a beautiful young lady as yourself, Modam, can't find it difficult to put 'er 'and on five hundred pounds," murmured Mrs. Piper, and as she said the words there came a leering smile over her small, pursed-up mouth.

And then, turning, she glided across the candle-lit room, and noiselessly opening the door, she slid through it.

Enid Crofton sank farther back into her chintz-covered easy chair. She was trembling all over, and her hands were shaking. She had not felt so frightened as she felt now, even during the terrible moments which had preceded her being put in the witness-box at the inquest held on her husband's body; and with a feeling of acute, unreasoning terror, she asked herself how she could cope with this new, dreadful situation.

What, for instance, did that allusion to the insurance company mean? She had had the two thousand pounds, and she had spent about a quarter of it paying bills of which her husband had known nothing. Then the settling in at The Trellis House had cost a great deal more than she had expected. Of course she had some left, but five hundred pounds would make a hideous hole in her little store.

What could the Pipers do to her? Could they do anything? The sinister woman's repetition of Piper's curious remark, "'E says sometimes as what 'e ought to give 'imself up, and say what 'e saw," came back to her with sickening vividness.

She looked round her, timorously. The candles on her dressing-table gave such a poor light. How stupid of a village like Beechfield not to have electric light! She stood up and rang for a hot-water bottle. At any rate she might as well try to get a little beauty sleep before dressing to go to the Tosswills.

Chapter XVII

*A*lthough no definite suggestion or order had been issued by Janet Tosswill, it was understood by everyone in Old Place that special honor was to be paid to Mrs. Crofton this evening.

Janet, when giving Betty a slight but vigorous sketch of the scene which had taken place between herself and Jack, observed, "If she's *that* sort of woman I think we ought to give her a proper dinner, don't you?" And Betty heartily agreed.

This was the reason why Betty herself, Tom, who acted as butler, and Timmy, who was supposed to help generally both in the kitchen and in the dining room, did not sit down to table with the others.

Mrs. Tosswill's sarcastic observation was so far justified in that Enid Crofton did feel vaguely gratified to find herself treated tonight far more as a guest of honor than she had been on the first occasion when she had come to the house. The guest herself had done honor to the feast by putting on the most becoming of her diaphanous black evening dresses, and, as she sat to the right of her host, each of her three feminine critics admitted to their secret selves that she was that rather rare thing, a genuinely pretty woman. Features, coloring, hair, were all as near perfection as they well could be, while her slight, rounded figure was singularly graceful.

How fortunate it is that we poor mortals cannot see into each other's hearts and minds! Who, looking at Jack Tosswill's composed, secretive, self-satisfied face, could have divined, even obscurely, his state of mingled pride, ecstasy, and humble astonishment at his own good fortune? To him the lovely young woman sitting next his father was as much his own as though they had already been through the marriage ceremony, and he felt awed and uplifted as well as triumphantly glad.

As for Godfrey Radmore, he also was affected rather more than he would have cared to admit even to himself by the presence of Enid Crofton this evening.

She had become to him something of a mystery, and there is always something alluring in a mystery, especially if the mystery be young, and endowed with that touch of pathos which makes feminine beauty always a touch more attractive to the masculine heart. He was aware that she preferred to see him alone, and this flattered him. While he was able to assure himself confidently that he was in no sense in love with her, his heart certainly beat a little quicker on the comparatively few occasions when he went over into her garden, or, better still, into her little sitting room, and found her by herself. He also thought it very good-natured, if a little tiresome, of her, to put up with so much of the company of a prig like Jack, and of a selfish girl like Rosamund.

Tonight Radmore wondered, not for the first time, why Janet Tosswill did not like Enid Crofton, for he felt, somehow, that there was no love lost between them. He told himself that he must ask Betty to try to become friends with her. Instinctively he relied on Betty's judgment, and that though he saw very little of her, considering what very old friends he and she were. And then, when he was thinking these secret, idle thoughts, he became suddenly conscious that Betty was not among those sitting at the full dining-table.

When Tom came in, bearing a huge soup tureen, and looking, it must be confessed, very red and embarrassed, Janet observed composedly that the person on whom they had relied to help them tonight had failed them at the last moment, and they had decided that it would be simpler for them to wait on themselves.

Radmore muttered to his neighbor, Rosamund, "Where's Betty?"

"In the kitchen. She's the only one of us who knows how to cook. She *loves* cooking. She'll come into the drawing room later if she's not too tired."

Radmore felt indignant. It was too bad that Betty, whom he vividly remembered as the petted darling of the house, should now have become — to put it in a poetical way — the family Cinderella! But as the dinner went on, and as the soup was succeeded by some excellent fish, as well as by roast chicken, a particularly delicious blackberry fool, and a subtly composed savory, he began to wonder whether some good professional cook had not been got in after all. He could hardly believe that Betty had cooked and dished up this really excellent dinner.

All through the meal Timmy flitted in and out, bringing round and removing the plates, but it was Tom who did most of the waiting.

At last Janet, catching Enid Crofton's eye, got up and delivered as parting injunction, "Please don't stay too long behind us, gentlemen — we're going to have coffee in the drawing room."

Jack Tosswill sprang to the door, and tried to catch Mrs. Crofton's eye as she passed out first, but of course he failed, and as he came back to the table, he observed: "I do hope Betty won't be too tired to come into the drawing room. Mrs. Crofton was saying the other day that she wished she knew her better." He was in a softened mood, the kind of mood which makes a man not only say, but think, pleasant things.

And then Mr. Tosswill made one of his rare practical remarks. "I have always thought that every woman ought to be taught cooking," he said musingly. "We have certainly just had a very good dinner; I must remember to tell Betty how much I enjoyed that savory."

"Did Betty cook it all?" asked Radmore.

It was Jack who answered, "Yes, of course she did. Early in the War there was a great shortage of cooks in some of the country hospitals, and so Betty asked a friend of ours to allow her to spend a few weeks in her kitchen. So now we have the benefit of all she learnt there."

Five minutes later the three men stood at the open door of the drawing room, and at once Radmore saw that Betty was not there. That was really too bad! What selfish girls her sisters were!

Acting on an impulse he could not have analyzed, he stepped back into the corridor and walked quickly towards the green baize door which led to the kitchen quarters. Just as he reached it, the door burst open, and Tom, rushing through, almost knocked him over.

"Hullo! Steady there! Where are you going?"

"I'm so sorry, Godfrey, but I'm in the devil of a hurry, for I've got to clear the dining room. Once that's done, my work's over, and I can go into the drawing room." Tom was grinning good-humoredly. "I say, Mrs. Crofton does look a peach tonight, doesn't she?"

Even as he spoke, he was hooking the door back. Then he hurried into the dining room without waiting for an answer.

Godfrey went on with rather hesitating steps down the broad, stone-flagged passage. According to tradition, this part of Old Place was mediæval, and it was certainly quite different from the rest of the house. He felt a little awkward for he knew he had no business there, and when he got to the big, vaulted kitchen, he stopped and looked round him dubiously. The fire in the old-fashioned, wasteful range had been allowed to die down, and on the round wooden table in the middle of the room were heaped up the dinner plates and dishes.

Suddenly he noticed that the door which led into the scullery was ajar, and he heard Betty's clear, even voice saying: "When you've tidied yourself up a bit, run down and let me see how you look. I'm afraid they're not likely to play any games this evening. It's a real, proper dinner-party, you know, Timmy."

Then he heard his godson's eager voice. "Oh, Betty, do come too! Mrs. Jones can do the washing-up tomorrow morning. If you want to dress I'll hook you up."

"I'm too tired to go up and dress," and Betty's voice did sound very weary. There was a despondent note in it, too, which surprised the man standing in the kitchen. Excepting during the few moments, to him intensely moving and solemn moments, when they had spoken of George within a day or two of his return to Beechfield, he had always seen Betty extraordinarily cheerful.

"You can go just as you are," he heard Timmy say eagerly. "You could pretend you'd just been to a fancy ball as a cook!" He added, patronizingly, "If you put on a clean apron, you'll look quite nice."

Radmore did not catch the answer, but he gathered that it was again in the negative, and a moment later Timmy's little feet scampered up the uncarpeted flight of stairs which led into the upper part of the house.

Walking forward, he quietly pushed open the scullery door, and for some seconds he stood unseen, taking in the far from unattractive scene before him.

The scullery of Old Place was a glorified kind of scullery, for, just before the War, Janet had spent a little of her own money on "doing it up." Since then she had often congratulated herself on the fact that in the days when the process was comparatively cheap, she had had the scullery walls lined five feet up with black and white tiles matching the linoleum which covered the stone floor.

Against this background Betty Tosswill was now standing, a trim, neat figure, in her pink cotton gown and big white apron. She was engaged in washing, drying, and polishing the fine old table glass which had been used that evening.

It was such a relief to her to be alone at last! For one thing, though Timmy and Tom both loved her dearly, their love never suggested to them that it must be disagreeable to her to hear them constantly bickering the one with the other, and they would have been surprised indeed had they known how their teasing squabbles had added to the strain and fatigue of serving the elaborate dinner she had just cooked.

She felt spent, in body and in mind, and in the mood when a woman craves, above all things, for solitude.

"Look here, Betty, can't I do anything to help?"

She started violently, and gave a little cry, while the stem of the wine-glass she held in her hand snapped in two. But Radmore, to her relief, did not notice the little accident.

"There isn't anything to do, thank you." She tried to speak composedly and pleasantly. "I'm going to leave most of the washing-up to the woman who comes in every morning to help us."

"Then why don't you come into the drawing room now? I heard what Timmy said — and it's quite true!"

"What Timmy said just now?" She turned and looked at him, puzzled.

Godfrey Radmore, in his well-cut dress clothes and the small, but perfect, pearl studs in the shirt of which she had heard Jack openly envy the make and cut, seemed an incongruous figure in the Old Place scullery.

He blundered on. "Timmy said that you look as if you had been at a fancy dress ball as a cook. He ought to have said 'cordon bleu,' for I've never eaten a better dinner!"

And then to his aghast surprise, Betty sat down on one of the wooden chairs near the table where she had been standing and burst into tears. "I don't want to be a 'cordon bleu,'" she sobbed. "I *hate* cooking — and everything connected with cooking." Then, feeling ashamed of herself, she pulled a clean handkerchief out of her apron pocket, and dabbed her eyes. "I'm just tired out, that's what it is!" she exclaimed, trying to smile. "We had a worrying half-hour, thinking the fish was not going to arrive. You see, Janet dislikes poor Mrs. Crofton so much that she suddenly made up her mind that it was her duty to kill the fatted calf, and in such a case I have to do the killing!"

"It's such a waste for you to be doing the things you are doing now." He spoke with a touch of anger in his voice. "Why, you and I hardly ever see one another! After all, even if you've forgotten the old times, *I* often remember them — I mean the times when you and I and George were so much together and such good pals. I love every brick of Old Place because of those days." He was speaking with deep feeling now. "Sometimes I feel as if I should like to run away — it's all so different here from what it used to be."

He saw a kind, moved, understanding look come over her eyes, and firm, generous mouth, and quickly, manlike, he pressed his advantage.

"Look here," he said coaxingly, "don't you think we might hit on some kind of compromise? Won't you allow me just to get some sort of temporary housekeeper who can look after things while poor Nanna is laid up?"

She shook her head. "I don't think any of us would like that," she said. "But I daresay I have become too much of a Martha."

She got up, feeling painfully afraid that she was going to cry again. "I don't see why I shouldn't do as Timmy said — change my apron, I mean, and go into the drawing room. For one thing, I should like to see Mrs. Crofton's dress. Tom says she looks a regular peach! That's his highest form of praise, you know."

Radmore suddenly resolved to say something which had been on his mind of late. "Don't you think that Jack's making rather a fool of himself over that pretty little lady?"

Betty looked across at him with the frank, direct gaze that he remembered so well. "I'm afraid he is," she answered. "He and Janet had quite a row about her this morning. He seemed to think we had been rude to her; he was most awfully huffy about it. But I suppose saying anything only makes things worse in such a case, doesn't it?"

"I don't see why I shouldn't speak to *her*. She and I know each other pretty well. She was a desperate little flirt when I first knew her in Egypt." And then, as he saw a look cross her face to which he had no clue, he added hastily: — "She's quite all right, Betty. She's quite a straight little woman."

"I'm sure she is," said Betty cordially.

She was wondering, wondering, wondering what Godfrey really thought of Enid Crofton? Whether or no there had been a touch of jealousy in what he had said about Jack just now? He had said the words about Jack's making a fool of himself very lightly. Still there had been a peculiar expression on his face.

During the last fortnight, while doing the hundred and one things which fell to her share, Betty had given the subject of Enid Crofton and Godfrey Radmore a good deal of thought, while telling herself all the time that, after all, it was none of her business — now.

All at once she became aware that Radmore was looking hard at her. "Look here," he exclaimed, coming up close to where she was again engaged in drying and polishing the heavy old crystal goblets. "I want to ask you a favor, Betty. It's absurd that I should be here, with far more money than I know what to do with, while the only people in the world I care for, are all worried, anxious, and overworking themselves. Janet says it's impossible to get a cook. What I want to do if you'll let me —" he looked at her pleadingly, and Betty's heart began to beat: thus was he wont to look at her in the old days, when he wanted to wheedle something out of her.

"What I want to do," he went on eagerly, "is to go up to London tomorrow morning and bring back a cook in triumph! Life has taught me *one* thing, — that is that money can procure anything." As she remained silent, he added in a tone of relief, "There, that's settled! You go up to bed now. I'll be off early in the morning, and we'll have a cook back by lunch-time."

"Indeed you won't!" She faced him squarely. "I know you mean very kindly, Godfrey — I know exactly how you feel. I've often felt like that myself; you feel that

"'Sympathy without relief
Is like mustard without beef.'

"That's the organ-grinder's motto, and a very good motto, too. But we're the exception which proves the rule. We're grateful for your sympathy, but we don't want your relief."

As he gazed at her, both dismayed and very exasperated, she went on, speaking a little wildly: — "Mustard's a very good thing. I think I needed a little mustard just now to binge me up!"

"But that's perfectly absurd!" he exclaimed. "Why not have the beef as well as the mustard? And look here. I don't think it's fair to me." He stood, looking straight at her, his face aglow with feeling. And again it was as if the old Godfrey of long ago, the Godfrey that had been impetuous, hot-tempered, unreasonable, and yet so infinitely dear to her, who stood there, so near to her that had she moved, he must have touched her. She sat down, and unseen by him, she put her two hands on the edge of the well-scrubbed table, and pressed her fingers down tightly. Then she smiled up at him, and shook her head.

"You're treating me like a stranger," he protested doggedly; "however badly I've behaved, I've not deserved that."

He was looking down at her hair, the lovely fair hair which had always been her greatest beauty — the one beauty she now shared with Rosamund. He wondered if it would ever grow long again. And yet now he told himself that he did not want to see her different from what she had become.

"Treating you like a stranger? You're the first visitor we've had to stay at Old Place since the Armistice."

As he said nothing, she went on, a little breathlessly, "D'you remember what a lot of people used to come and go in the old days? That was one of the nice things about Janet. She loved to entertain our friends, even our acquaintances. But now we never have anybody. It shows how we feel about you that we are having you here, like this. But we can only do it if you'll take us as we are."

"Of course I take you as you are," he said aggrieved, "but I don't see why I shouldn't do my little bit, when it's so easy for me to do it. People talk such rot about money! They'll take anything in the world but money from those who —" he hesitated, and then boldly brought out the word — "love them."

"And yet," said Betty quietly, "you yourself contemptuously rejected the money that father wanted to give you when he could well afford it — the day you left Beechfield nine years ago."

He hesitated, unutterably astonished, and yes, very much moved, too, at this, her first reference to their joint past.

"I know I did," he said at last, "and I was a fool to do it. That check of Mr. Tosswill's would have made all the difference to me during certain awful weeks in Australia when I didn't know where to turn for a shilling. I've been right up against it — the reality of things, I mean — and I know both how much and how little money counts in life. It counts a lot, Betty."

"I've been up against the reality of things, too," said Betty slowly, "and I've learnt how very little money counts. You'd have known that, if you'd been with the French Army. That was the difference between the French and the English. The French *poilu* had no money at all, and the English Tommy had plenty. But it made no difference in the big things."

Chapter XVIII

Meanwhile Timmy, upstairs, had performed what was for him quite an elaborate toilet. He possessed a new Eton suit of which he was secretly proud, for in this as in so many things unlike most little boys, he took great care of his clothes, and had an almost finicking dislike to what was rough or untidy. His two younger sisters' untidiness was a perpetual annoyance to him, and he still felt sore and angry at the way Rosamund had upset his toy-box when looking for that old prescription.

Tonight he felt queerly excited and above himself. After-dinner coffee had been made in a way Betty had learnt in France, and she had foolishly allowed him to drink a cup of the strong, potent, delicious fluid. This had had a curious effect on him, intensifying his already acute perceptions, and making him feel both brave and bold as well as wary — wary Timmy Tosswill always was.

And now he was eagerly debating within himself whether he could carry out an experiment he had an eager wish to try. It had filled his mind, subconsciously, ever since he had slipped quickly in front of his brother Jack to open the front door to Mrs. Crofton, a couple of hours ago.

Mrs. Crofton was very much of a town lady, and she had actually been accompanied, during her short progress through the dark village, by her parlor maid. When Timmy opened the front door, she had been engaged in giving the girl a few last directions as to how a lighted candle was to be left out for her in her hall, for she had brought her latchkey with her. After ringing the bell, the lady and her maid had moved away from the door a little way, and Timmy, staring out at the two figures, who stood illumined by the hall light out on the gravel carriage drive, had seen Something Else.

He did not invariably see Mrs. Crofton accompanied or companioned by that of which he had spoken to his mother. Sometimes days would go by and he would see nothing, though he was a constant, if never a welcome, visitor at The Trellis House.

Then all at once, sometimes when she was in the garden, at other times in the charming little parlor, Timmy would see the wraith of Colonel Crofton, and the wraith of Colonel Crofton's terrier, Dandy, looking as real as the flesh-and-blood woman beside whom they seemed to stand. Sometimes they appeared, as it were, intermittently, but now and again they would stay quite a long time.

As long as he could remember, Timmy had been aware of what Nanna expressed by the phrase "things that were not there," and he was so accustomed to the phenomena that it did not impress his own mind as anything very much out of the way, or strange.

Dr. O'Farrell had always shown a keen interest in Timmy's alleged visions and presentiments. Like so many country doctors of the old school, he was a man not only of great natural shrewdness, but of considerable intellectual curiosity, and, from his point of view, by far the most inexplicable of the little boy's assertions had concerned a long vanished building which had stood, for something like three centuries, close to the parish church, right on the main street of the village.

One Easter Sunday, Timmy, coming out of church, had excitedly exclaimed that he saw to his right a house where no house had been up to yesterday. His sisters had laughed at him and his mother had snubbed him. But when Janet had told Dr. O'Farrell of her little boy's latest and most peculiar claim to having seen something which was not there, the doctor had gone home and looked up an old county history, to find that up to Waterloo year there had still been standing in the pretty little hamlet of Beechfield, a small Elizabethan manor-house which had figured in the Titus Oates conspiracy.

*B*ut to return to the evening of Mrs. Crofton's second visit to Old Place.

Timmy had given his mother his word of honor that Flick should not be released from the stable till their visitor had left. But no casuist ever realized more clearly than did Timothy Tosswill, the delicate distinctions which spread, weblike, between the spirit, and the letter, of a law. And while he moved nimbly about his bedroom, the plan, or rather the plot he had formed, took formal shape.

Josephine, Timmy's white Angora cat, was now established in a comfortable basket in a corner of the scullery. There she lay, looking like a ball of ermine, with her two ten-days old kittens snuggling up close to her. Josephine was a nervous, fussy mother, but she was devoted to her master, and he could do with her anything he liked.

Very softly he crept past Nanna's door, and as he started walking down the back staircase, he heard voices.

Then Betty and Godfrey were still in the scullery? That was certainly a bit of bad luck, for though he thought he could manage his godfather, he knew he couldn't deceive Betty. Betty somehow seemed to know by instinct when he, Timmy, was bent on some pleasant little bit of mischief.

He need not have been afraid, for as he slowly opened the door at the bottom of the stairs, Betty exclaimed, "I'm going into the drawing room after all! But first I must run upstairs and make myself tidy. You two go on, and I'll follow as soon as I can."

She ran past Timmy, and at once the boy said firmly to Radmore, "I'm going to take my cat, Josephine, into the drawing room. Ladies who hate dogs nearly always like cats."

"I don't think Mrs. Crofton cares for cats," answered Radmore carelessly.

"Oh, yes, she does — and the other day she said The Trellis House was overrun with mice. Betty thinks it would be a very good home for one of Josephine's new kittens."

Even while he was speaking, the big white cat had left her basket and was walking round her master, purring. He stooped down and lifted her up.

"If Mrs. Crofton sees Josephine, she will simply long to have one of her kittens! Will you bring along the white one, Godfrey — the one we call Puff? We do so want to find him a good home."

Radmore walked across to where the big basket stood on the floor, and peered into it dubiously: "Why, Timmy, they're tiny! Poor little wretches! I wouldn't dream of bringing one of them along — it would

be sheer cruelty. Of course you can bring the cat if you feel like it, but
I shouldn't if I were you."

"I'll only take her in for a minute."

Timmy felt just a little sorry Radmore had refused to bring Puff along,
for he was well aware that a cat is never so fierce as when she imagines
she is defending her young.

They went off together, Radmore in front, Timmy, hugging
Josephine, behind. Just outside the drawing room door the boy stopped
for a moment, and shifted the cat's weight from one arm to the other.
There had come over him a rather uncomfortable premonition of evil,
but he now felt strung up to go through with his experiment.

From within the drawing room there came the sound of laughter and
talking. It was evident that the party was going well, and that everyone
in there was merry and at their ease.

"Would you mind opening the door, Godfrey?" There was a slight
quiver of apprehension in Timmy's voice.

Radmore opened the door, and for a fleeting moment he saw an
attractive, placid scene spread out before him.

The two girls, in their pretty light dresses, were standing by the wood
fire. On the sofa, to their left, with the light from one of the lamps
focused full on her, sat Mrs. Crofton, her bare left arm hanging over
the side of the low couch. Jack, perched on the arm of a big chair, was
looking at her, all his soul in his eyes. Mr. Tosswill sat some way off
under a shaded reading lamp; his wife, knitting, not far from him. Tom
was surreptitiously reading a book in a corner behind the sofa.

And then, all at once, Radmore found himself whirled into an
unutterable scene of confusion and terror.

As Timmy walked through the open door Josephine had leapt out of
his arms on to the floor. For a flashing second the cat stood on the
carpet, her white fur all abristle, her back arched, and her tail lashing
furiously in the air. Then, uttering a hoarse cry of rage and fear, she
sprang towards Mrs. Crofton, and dug first her claws, and then her teeth,
into the white arm that hung over the side of the couch. . . . Josephine's
terrified victim gave a fearful cry, everyone in the room got up and
rushed forward, and at that exact instant Betty came into the drawing
room. Sweeping a piece of embroidery off the piano, she threw it over
the cat's head, took up the now struggling, helpless bundle, and rushed
out of the room with it.

Then followed a scene of appalling confusion. Enid, completely
losing control of herself, screamed and screamed and screamed.

Few people, fortunately for themselves, have ever heard a woman
scream, and some of those present felt they would never forget the

sound. In the minds of most of the grown-up people there was the same unspoken question — had the cat suddenly gone mad? Had she got hydrophobia?

They all crowded round their unfortunate guest — all but Timmy, who stood aside with a look in which remorse, fear, and triumph struggled for mastery on his queer little face.

And then at last, when Mrs. Crofton lay back, moaning, on the sofa, surrounded by her distracted and horrified hosts, somebody suggested that Dr. O'Farrell should be sent for, and Jack rushed into the hall to find Betty already at the telephone.

Meanwhile Janet Tosswill was doing her best to persuade the victim of Josephine's savage aggression to come upstairs and await the doctor there; but, shudderingly, Enid Crofton refused to stir.

A slight diversion was created when Betty came in with a basin of warm water, soap, and a sponge. Again everyone crowded round the sofa, and Jack and Radmore both felt alarm, as well as horror, when they saw the wounds made by the cat's claws and the cat's teeth.

While her arm was being bathed, Mrs. Crofton grew so pale that Janet feared she was going to faint, and Rosamund was sent flying up to the medicine cupboard to get some brandy.

Dr. O'Farrell was at home when telephoned for, but the quarter of an hour which elapsed before he reached Old Place seemed very long to some of the people waiting there. The doctor came in smiling, but his face altered and grew very grave when he saw Mrs. Crofton's arm, and heard the confused, excited account of what had happened.

To the patient he made light of the whole matter, but while someone was putting on Mrs. Crofton's overshoes and while her evening cloak was being brought in he moved a little aside with Jack, Mr. Tosswill, and Radmore. None of them noticed that Timmy was hovering on the outskirts of the group.

"I want to say," he began in a low voice, "that of course that cat will have to be kept under observation, or else she'll have to be destroyed and her body sent up to town to make sure of — you know what! Meanwhile, no one must go near her. Where is she now?"

Mr. Tosswill looked vaguely round. "I think Betty took her into the kitchen," he said slowly, and then he called out, "Betty?"

The girl came up. "Yes, father?"

"What did you do with Timmy's cat?"

"I put her back in the scullery, with her kittens. They only opened their eyes yesterday. Of course Timmy ought never to have brought her into the drawing room."

Dr. O'Farrell looked much relieved. He turned round: "Oh, she's just had kittens, has she? That probably accounts for the whole thing."

Mrs. Crofton roused herself. "I do hope that horrible cat will be killed at once," she cried hysterically. "I can't stay in Beechfield if she's left alive."

Dr. O'Farrell answered soothingly, "Don't you fret, Mrs. Crofton. She's a vicious brute, and shot she shall be."

No one noticed that Timmy had heard every word of this conversation; no one noticed the expression on his face.

It had been arranged that the doctor should take Mrs. Crofton home in his car, and that only when she was comfortably in bed should those ugly little wounds be properly dressed.

As the doctor was hurrying down the passage into the hall, he was surprised to see Timmy at his elbow and to hear the boy's voice pipe up: "If my cat's not mad, she won't have to be killed, doctor, will she?" He asked the question in a quiet, matter-of-fact tone.

"Yes, my little friend, mad or not mad, she's deserved death — and no one must go near her till the fell deed is done!" And then, as he suddenly caught sight of Timmy's strained, agonized face, he added kindly: "She'll be in the cats' heaven before she knows she's touched. I'll come down in the morning and I'll shoot her through the window myself — I'm a dead shot, Timmy, my boy."

As Janet came along, Timmy burst out crying, and his mother, distracted, turned to Radmore. "Oh, Godfrey, do get him away upstairs! He's tired out, that's what it is. Unfortunately the cat belongs to him, and he's very fond of her — he's almost as fond of Josephine as he is of Flick."

Radmore put his hand on his godson's shoulder. "Come, Timmy, don't cry. It's unmanly."

But Timmy, instead of making an effort to control himself, wrenched himself away and ran down the long corridor towards the kitchen. Even as a tiny child he had hated to be caught crying.

There followed an absurd scene at the front door, Jack and Rosamund almost quarreling as to which of them should accompany Mrs. Crofton home. In the end they had both gone, and Janet, ordering everyone else to bed, sat up, wearily awaiting their return, for neither of them had thought of taking a latchkey.

Poor Janet! Her thoughts were sad and worried thoughts, as she waited, trying to read, in the drawing room. At the very last, Betty had lingered for a moment after the others, and she had noticed that the girl's eyes were full of tears.

"Why, Betty, what's the matter? I don't think we need really worry over Mrs. Crofton."

"I'm not thinking of Mrs. Crofton. I can't bear the thought of poor Josephine being shot tomorrow morning."

"Oh, my dear, don't *you* turn sentimental! I never did like that poor cat; to me there's always been something queer and uncanny about her."

"You've never liked cats," Betty answered, rather aggressively. "Timmy and I are devoted to Josephine — so is Nanna."

Janet had checked the contemptuous words trembling on her lips. Abruptly she had changed the subject: "I want to tell you, Betty, how splendidly the dinner went off tonight. Your cooking was first chop!"

Betty at once softened. But all she said was: "I would give anything for Mrs. Crofton to leave Beechfield, Janet. Did you see Jack's face?"

"Yes, and I do feel worried about it. Yet one can't do anything."

"I suppose one can't. But it's too bad of her. I think her a horrid woman. Jack is just a scalp to her. I don't mind her flirtation with Godfrey — that's much more reasonable!"

Then she had hurried off upstairs without waiting for an answer, and her step-mother, looking back, rather wondered that Betty had said that.

Chapter XIX

*T*wo hours later Janet Tosswill, after having tried in vain to read herself to sleep, got out of bed and put on her dressing gown. Somehow she felt anxious about Timmy. She had gone to his room on her way up to bed; but, hearing no sound, she had crept away, hoping that he had already cried himself to sleep.

All sorts of curious theories and suspicions drifted through her mind as she lay, tossing this way and that, trying to fall asleep. She wondered uneasily why Timmy had brought Josephine at all into the drawing room. Of course there had been nothing exactly wrong in his doing so, though, as Betty had justly remarked, it was a stupid thing to do so soon after the birth of the cat's kittens. And Timmy was not stupid.

Janet told herself crossly that it was almost as if Mrs. Crofton had the evil eye, as far as animals were concerned! There had come back to her the unpleasant scene which had occurred on the first evening their late guest had come to Old Place, when Flick, most cheerful and happy-minded of terriers, had behaved in such an extraordinary fashion. But disagreeable as that affair had been, it was nothing to what had happened tonight.

She felt she would never forget the scene which had followed on the white cat's attack on Mrs. Crofton. And yet, while concerned and sorry, she had been shocked at the poor young woman's utter lack of self-control.

It was quite true, as Betty had somewhat bitterly remarked, that she, Janet Tosswill, did not care for cats. Unfortunately there was a certain sentimental interest attached to Josephine, for she had been brought from France as a kitten, a present from Betty to Timmy, by an officer who had been George's closest pal. She was also ruefully aware that old Nanna would very much resent the disappearance of "French pussy," as she had always called Josephine. As for Timmy, Janet had never seen her boy look as he had looked tonight since the dreadful day that they had received the War Office telegram about George.

Leaving her room, she walked along the corridor till she came to Timmy's door. She tried the handle, and, finding with relief that the door was unlocked, walked in. At once there came a voice across the room, "Is that you, Mum?"

"Yes, Timmy, it's Mum."

Shutting the door, she felt her way across the room and came and sat down on Timmy's bed. He was sitting up, wide awake.

She put her arms round him. "I'm so sorry," she said feelingly; "so sorry, Timmy, about your poor cat! But you know, my dear, that if — if she were left alive, we could never feel comfortable for a single moment. You see, when an animal has done that sort of thing once, it may do it again."

"Josephine would never do it again," said Timmy obstinately, and he caught his breath with a sob.

"You can't possibly know that, my dear. She would of course have other kittens, and then some day, when some perfectly harmless person happened to come anywhere near her, she would fly at him or her, just as she did at Mrs. Crofton."

"No, she wouldn't — she didn't do anything like that when she had her last kittens."

"I know that, Timmy. But you heard what Dr. O'Farrell said."

"Dr. O'Farrell isn't God," said Timmy scornfully.

"No, my dear, Dr. O'Farrell is certainly not God; but he is a very sensible, humane human being — and the last man to condemn even an animal to death, without good reason."

There was a rather painful pause. Janet Tosswill felt as if the child were withdrawing himself from her, both in a physical and in a mental sense.

"Mum?" he said in a low, heart-broken voice.

"Yes, my dear?"

"I want to tell you something."

"Yes, Timmy?"

"It's I who ought to be shot, not Josephine. It was all my fault. It had nothing to do with her."

"I don't know what you mean, Timmy. You mustn't talk in that exaggerated way. Of course it was foolish of you to bring the cat into the drawing room, but still, you couldn't possibly have known that she would fly at Mrs. Crofton, or you wouldn't have done it."

"I *did* think she'd fly at Mrs. Crofton," he whispered.

Janet felt disagreeably startled. "What d'you mean, Timmy? D'you mean that you saw the cat fly at her before it happened?"

She had known the boy to have such strange, vivid premonitions of events which had come to pass.

But Timmy answered slowly: "No, I don't mean that. I mean, Mum, that I wanted to try an experiment. I wanted to see if Josephine would see what Flick saw — I mean if she'd see the ghost of Colonel Crofton's dog. She did, for the dog was close to Mrs. Crofton's arm — the arm hanging over the side of the sofa, you know."

"Oh, Timmy! How very, very wrong of you to do such a thing!"

"I know it was wrong." Timmy twisted himself about. "But it's no good you saying that to me now — it only makes me more miserable."

"But I *have* to say so, my boy." Janet was not a Scotch mother for nothing. "I have to say so, Timmy, and I shall not be sorry this happened, if it makes you behave in a different way — as I hope it will — the whole of your life long."

"It won't — I won't let it — if anything is done to Josephine!"

But she went on, a little desperately, yet speaking in a quiet, collected way: "I believe the things you say, Timmy. I believe you do see things which other people are not allowed to see. But that ought to make you far, far more careful — not less careful. Try to be an instrument for good, not for evil, my dear, dear child."

Timmy did not answer at once, but at last he said in a queer, muffled voice: "If I were to tell Dr. O'Farrell what I did, do you think it would make any difference? Do you think that he'd let Josephine go on being alive?"

"No," his mother answered, sadly, "I don't think it would make any difference."

"I thought by what the doctor said at first that they were going to take Josephine somewhere to see if she was really mad," said Timmy in a choking voice, "just as they did to Captain Berner's dog last year."

Janet Tosswill got up from her little boy's bed. She lit a candle. Poor Timmy! She had never seen the boy looking as he was looking now; he seemed utterly spent with misery.

"I'll tell you what I'll do, my dear. I'll speak to Dr. O'Farrell myself in the morning, and I'll ask him whether something can't be done in the way of a reprieve. I'll tell him we don't mind paying for Josephine to be sent away for a bit to a vet."

Hope, ecstatic hope, flashed into Timmy's tear-stained face. "You mean to a man like Trotman?"

"Yes, that's what I do mean. But I mustn't raise false hopes. I fear Dr. O'Farrell has made up his mind; he promised Mrs. Crofton the cat should be shot. Still, I'll do my *very* best."

Timmy put his skinny arms round his mother's neck.

"I'm glad you're my mother, Mum," he muttered, "and not my step-mother."

She smiled for the first time. "That's rather a double-edged compliment, if I may say so! But I suppose it's true that I would do a good deal more for you than I would for any of the others."

"I didn't mean *that*," exclaimed Timmy, shocked. "I only meant that I wouldn't love you as well. I don't mean ever to be a step-father — I shall start a lot of boys and girls of my own."

"All right," she said soothingly, "I'm sure you will. Lie down now, and try to go to sleep." She hoped with all her heart that the boy would sleep late the next morning, as he very often did when tired out, and that the execution, if execution there must be, would be over by the time he woke.

She bent down, tucked him up, kissed him, blew out the candle, and then went quickly out of the room.

*A*s soon as his mother had shut the door, Timmy sat up in bed, and then he gave a smothered cry. It was as if he had seen flash out into the darkness his beloved cat's wistful face, her beautiful, big, china-blue eyes, gazing confidently at him, as if to say, "You'll save me, Master, won't you?"

He listened intently for a few minutes, then he slipped down and felt his way to the door. He opened it; but there came no sound from the sleeping house. Closing the door very, very softly, he lit his candle and rapidly dressed himself in his day clothes, finally putting on a thick pair of walking shoes, and over them galoshes. Timmy hated galoshes, and never wore them if he could help it, but he had read in some detective story that they deadened sound.

Then he blew his candle out, and again he went across to the door and listened. Opening it at last, he slithered along the familiar corridor till he reached the three shallow steps which led up to the comparatively new part of Old Place. There he felt his way with his fingers along the wall to the room which had always been called, as long as he could remember, "George's room." Turning the handle of the door slowly, he saw, to his great surprise and gladness, that his godfather was not asleep.

Radmore was sitting up in bed, reading luxuriously by the light of four candles which he had placed on a table by his bedside.

"Hello!" he exclaimed, as his godson's odd-looking little figure shuffled across the room. "Why, what's the matter?" He spoke very kindly, for Timmy's face was scared, his eyes red-rimmed with crying.

"Come to have a chat, old boy? Why, Timmy —" as he suddenly realized the boy was fully dressed, "whatever have you been doing? I thought you'd gone to bed ever so long ago!"

"I've been in bed a long time," answered Timmy, sidling up close to his bed, "but I've just had a talk with Mum. I've come to ask you, Godfrey, if you'll help me with something very important." He added: "Even if you won't help me, I trust you to keep my secret."

"Of course I'll keep your secret, old son."

"I'm going to take Josephine and her kittens to Trotman," Timmy announced solemnly. "I've been wondering, coming along the passage, if you would take us there in your motor. But if you don't feel you want to do that, I'm going to walk. It's not very far, only seven miles if one goes by footpaths, and I could get a lift back."

"Trotman?" repeated Radmore. "Who's Trotman?"

It was Timmy's turn to be surprised. "I thought everyone — I mean every man — in the world, knew about Trotman! Why, there was an account of him once in the *London Magazine*. He's the famous vet — he lives at Epsom."

Radmore lay back, and whistled thoughtfully.

Timmy went on eagerly. "Last year there was a man near here who thought he had a mad dog — and he took *him* to Trotman. Trotman kept him forever so long, and it turned out that the dog was not mad at all. I *know* that Josephine isn't mad."

"I don't think she's mad," said Radmore frankly, "but she's a pretty vicious brute, Timmy. Is this the first time she's ever flown at anyone?" He looked searchingly at his godson.

"The very first time of all," answered the boy passionately. "I know why Josephine flew at Mrs. Crofton — at least she didn't fly at her — at Mrs. Crofton. She flew at the dog Mrs. Crofton always has with her."

Radmore gave the child a long, steady look.

"Come, Timmy, you know as well as I do that Mrs. Crofton had no dog with her."

"She had a dog with her," repeated Timmy obstinately. "It's not a dog *you* can see, but I see him and Flick sees him. I wanted to see if Josephine would see him too. That's why I took her in there. So if she's shot it will be all my fault." His voice broke, and, covering his face with his hands, he turned his back on the bed and its occupant.

Radmore stared at the small heaving back. There could be no doubt that Timmy was speaking the truth *now*. "All right," he said quickly. "I'll do what you want, Timmy. So cheer up! I suppose you've got a big basket in which you can put your cat and her kittens? While I put on some clothes, you can go and get her ready. But I advise you for your own sake to be quiet. Our game will be all up, if your mother wakes. I simply shouldn't dare to disobey *her,* you know." He smiled quizzically at the child, and, as he mentioned Janet, he lowered his voice instinctively.

Chapter XX

However long Radmore lives, he will never forget that strange drive through the autumn night. Fortunately, from the two conspirators' point of view, there were only old-fashioned stables at Old Place, and Radmore's car was kept in the village in a barn which had been cleverly transformed by the blacksmith into a rough garage.

While he dressed, and, indeed, after he joined the boy downstairs, he had puzzled over Timmy — over the mixture of cruelty and kindness the child had shown that evening. He could not but recall, with a feeling of discomfort, the simple, innocent way in which the boy had explained why he wanted to take his cat, Josephine, into the drawing room — really to do a kindness to the mistress of The Trellis House! It was somewhat disagreeable to reflect how he, Radmore, who rather prided himself on his knowledge of human nature, had been taken in.

Off the two started at last, creeping out of one of the back doors. But in his agitation over the business of getting the cat and her kittens safely out of Old Place, Timmy had forgotten to put on a coat. They were halfway down the avenue before Radmore noticed that the boy was shivering, and then, mindful of Janet, he ordered him to go back and get the warmest coat he could.

And then, while he waited impatiently in the avenue, Radmore visualized the extraordinary scene which had taken place in the drawing room last evening. Had the cat really seen anything of a supernatural nature? Or was it only that she had been frightened by being suddenly brought into a room full of people? If so, it was perhaps natural that she had blindly flown at the one stranger there.

At last Timmy returned, and they started off, neither speaking a word until they were clear of the village. Radmore thought he knew every inch of the way, for he and Betty had once cycled together all over the countryside. He checked a sigh as he thought of those days — how happy he had been, with that simple, unquestioning happiness which belongs only to extreme youth. He wondered if Betty ever remembered those far-off days. They had come very near, the one to the other, last evening, and yet, from his point of view, theirs was an unsatisfactory kind of friendship. It was as if she was always holding something back from him. And then, while he was thinking of Betty, the little boy sitting by his side suddenly observed:

"Perhaps we might tell Betty — I mean when we get back again — where Josephine and her kittens are? She was awfully upset last night; almost as upset as I was. You see, Josephine's a French cat. She was brought home — I mean to England, you know — by the officer who now wants to marry Betty." Timmy uttered these words in a very matter-of-fact voice. Then, for a moment, he forgot Betty, for the car swerved suddenly.

"The officer who wants to marry Betty?" repeated Radmore. "I didn't know there was an officer who wanted to marry Betty."

"Nobody's supposed to know," said Timmy composedly. "But Mum and I, as well as father, know. Only a very vulgar sort of girl lets anyone know when someone wants to marry her. Mr. Barton is so ridiculous about Dolly, following her about and always looking at her, that we all know it, though Mum wonders sometimes if he knows it himself. But neither Dolly nor Rosamund knows about Betty's man. Luckily, they were away when he last came here and saw father. The first time Betty meant him to send the kitten in a basket from London. She even gave him the money for Josephine's fare, but he *would* give it back to father. He brought her himself because he wanted to see father, and talk to him about Betty and George."

"Then he knew George, too?"

"Yes, that's how he got to know Betty, when she was in France, you know, and why she gave him the kitten to bring home on leave. He knew all about *us*, and when father called me into the study to take Josephine, he said: 'Is this Timmy?' And then after that he just went straight on about Betty, as if I wasn't there. He said that if he got through, he meant to wait — he didn't mind how long, if only Betty would say 'Yes' in the end."

"Has he been here since Betty came home?" asked Radmore abruptly.

Somehow this revelation astonished and discomfited him very much. It had never occurred to him that Betty might marry.

"No," said Timmy. "He has never come again, for he's in Mesopotamia; but he writes to Betty, and then she writes back to him. You see he was a friend of George's — that makes her like him, I suppose."

They drove on for a while in silence, and then Timmy enquired, rather anxiously: "You won't tell Betty I've told you, will you, Godfrey? I don't think she wants anyone to know. He sent me a lovely picture postcard once — it was to Timmy Tosswill, Esq. — and then I asked Betty whether she meant to marry him, as he was such a nice sort of man. She was awfully angry with me for knowing about it, and she began to cry. So you won't say anything to her, will you?"

"No, of course I won't," said Radmore hastily.

They were now emerging on the wide sweep of down commanding the little old country town which stands to the whole world as the racing capital of England. To their left, huge and gaunt against the night sky, rose the Grand Stand.

"Where does Trotman hang out?" asked Radmore. "Shan't we have a devil of a difficulty in knocking him up?"

"I don't think we shall," said his small companion, confidently. "You see there must always be some sick animal for someone to sit up with. I'd rather be nurse to a dog than to a woman, wouldn't you?"

They turned into the steep road leading into the town, flashing past shuttered villas set in gardens, till they reached a labyrinth of quaint, narrow, walled thoroughfares dating from the 18th century.

"We're very near now," said Timmy. "Isn't it funny, Godfrey, to feel that everybody's asleep but us?" They had come to a corner where high walls enclosed what might once have been the kitchen garden of a Georgian manor-house.

"Here it is!" cried the boy.

Radmore stopped the car and then he jumped out and struck a match. Over a door, set in the wall, stood out in clear lettering the words, "John Trotman, Veterinary Surgeon." Feeling a little doubtful of what their reception would be like, he pulled the bell. There was a pause, a long pause, and then they heard the sound of light, quick footsteps, and the door was unlocked.

"Who's there? What is it?" came in a woman's voice, and a quaint figure, dressed in a short, dark dressing gown, and looking not unlike Noah's wife, appeared holding a lantern in her hand. She had a kindly, shrewd face, and when Radmore said apologetically, "I'm sorry to disturb you, but the matter is really urgent, and we've brought a sick animal many miles in order that it may benefit by Mr. Trotman's skill," her face cleared, and she said cordially: "All right, sir, come right in."

As they walked along through a curious kind of trellised tunnel, Timmy carrying Josephine and her kittens, there arose an extraordinary chorus of sounds in which furious barking predominated.

"You have a regular menagerie here," said Radmore, smiling.

"Why, yes, sir," she answered simply, "but they'll all quiet down after a bit. They're startled like, hearing strange footsteps."

She led them into the house, and so through into a pleasant little parlor, full of the good 18th Century furniture which may still be found in the older houses of an English country town. Sporting prints – some of considerable value – hung on the walls. There was still a little fire alight in the deep grate, throwing out a warmth that was comforting to both the man and the boy.

"If you'll wait here, I'll get my husband."

While Mrs. Trotman had left the room, Radmore remarked: "I've made up my mind what to say to Trotman, so please don't interrupt."

And Timmy listened silently to the explanation his godfather gave of Josephine's strange behavior of the night before. It was an explanation that squared with the facts – at any rate, according to the speaker's point of view — for Radmore told the famous vet that the cat, upset by the sight of a strange dog, had flown at a lady and bitten her. He added frankly that the doctor had suggested that the animal should be kept under observation, and then he managed to convey that money was no object, as the cat was a cherished pet sent from France during the War.

Everything was soon arranged, for Mr. Trotman was a man of few words. Radmore gave his own name and the address of Old Place, and then, just before leaving the house, he put down a £5 note on the table.

The sturdy, grizzled old man took up the note and held it out to his new client. "I'd rather not take this, sir, if you don't mind," he said a little gruffly. "We'll send you in a proper bill in due course. You needn't be afraid. The cat shall have every care, and of course, if things should go wrong — you know what I mean — I'll at once give you a telephone call. But, as far as I can tell, you're right, and it was just fear for her young made her behave so." He turned to his wife. "Now then, mother, you just get back to bed! I'll see to these gentlemen, and to poor pussy."

They shook hands with Mrs. Trotman, and then the famous vet took them down the trellised path and stood in the doorway till they got into the car.

"I'm glad to have met you, Mr. Trotman," Radmore called out heartily. "I'd like to come over here one day, and go over your place."

As they raced up towards the Downs, Radmore suddenly turned to Timmy: "The more time goes on, the more it's borne in on me that there's nothing like the old people of the old country." And as the boy, surprised, said nothing for once, he went on, "I hope that the stock won't ever give out."

"How d'you mean?"

"Well, take those two people, that man and woman. We get them out of their warm, comfortable bed in the middle of the night, they knowing nothing about us, except that we bring a cat which may be mad; and yet they take it all in the day's work; they're civil, kindly, obliging — and the man won't take money he hasn't earned! I call that splendid, Timmy. You might almost go the world over before you'd find a couple like that — anywhere but in England."

*T*hey drove on and on, and then all at once, Radmore, glancing down to his left, saw that Timmy had fallen asleep. Now Timmy, asleep, looked like an angelic cherub, and so very different from his usual alert, inquisitive, little awake self. And there welled up in Radmore's heart the strangest feeling of tenderness — not only for Timmy but for the whole of the Tosswill family — not only for the Tosswill family, but for the whole of this sturdy, quiet, apparently unemotional world of England to which he had come back.

The human mind and brain work in mysterious ways. Radmore will never know, to the day of his death, the effect that this curious night drive had on the whole of his future life. He was not a man to quote poetry, even to himself, but tonight there came into his mind some words he had heard muttered by a corporal in Gallipoli:

"What do they know of England
  Who only England know?"

When he had left his homeland, now nearly ten years ago, he had been in a bitter mood. It had seemed to him that his own country was rejecting him with scorn. But now his heart swelled proudly at the thought of the old country — of all that she had endured since then. He had thought England altered and very much for the worse, when he was in London on his two brief "leaves" during the War, but now he knew how unchanged his country was — in the things that really matter. . . .

When he had come back for good, this summer, he had looked forward to an easy, selfish life — the sort of life certain men whom he had envied as a boy used to lead before the war.

Radmore knew, as every man who has lived to the age of thirty-two must know, that marriage brings with it certain cares, responsibilities, and troubles, and so he had deliberately made up his mind to avoid marriage, though he had been conscious the while that if he fell violently in love, then, perhaps, half knowing all the time that he was a fool, he might find himself pushed into marriage with some foolish girl, or what was perchance more likely, with a pretty widow.

Tonight he realized with a sort of shame that there were moments — he was glad that they were only moments — when he felt uneasily yet strongly attracted to Enid Crofton, and that though he knew how selfish, how self-absorbed and, yes, how cruel she could be. For well he knew she had been cruel to her elderly husband. He was sorry now that she had come to Beechfield. She had become an irritating, disturbing element in his life.

Radmore had looked at every eligible property within a radius of twenty miles of Old Place, but though some of them did not fall far short of the ideal he had in his mind, he hadn't felt as if he wanted any of them. They were too trim, too new — in a word, too suburban. Even the very old houses had been transformed by their owners much as The Trellis House had been transformed, into something to suit modern taste. He told himself that he must begin looking again — looking in real dead earnest, going farther afield.

Absorbed in his thoughts, he had driven on and on, almost mechanically, till suddenly they came to four cross-roads. He drew up under a sign-post, jumped out and struck a match, and as he read the painted words he realized, with vexation, that he had gone a good bit out of his way. There was nothing for it now but to go on till they struck the Portsmouth Road. It was the quietest hour of the twenty-four, and it was very unlikely they would meet with anyone who could put them right.

And then, while going up a lane, which he knew to be at any rate in the right direction, he came to a park gate. Just within was a lodge, and in one of the windows of the lodge there shone a light. Again Radmore stopped the car and jumped out, Timmy still heavily asleep.

He went up to the door of the lodge and rapped with his knuckles. It opened and revealed a young woman, fully dressed. "What do you want?" she exclaimed, in a frightened voice.

"I've lost my way," he said, "and seeing a light in your window, I ventured to knock. I've no idea where I am — I want to get to Beechfield."

"Beechfield? Why, you're nigh forty miles from there," she said, surprised.

"Can you tell me how I can get on to the Portsmouth Road?"

"Aye, I think I could do that; but stop your engine, please — I've a little girl in here as is very ill."

He ran out and did what she asked. Then he came back, and as she took him into her tiny living room, he saw that there were tears rolling down her tired face.

"Is your child very ill?" he asked.

She nodded. "Doctor says if she can get through the next two days she may be all right."

"Is your husband with you?"

She shook her head. "I'm a widow, sir; my husband was killed in the War. I'm only caretaking here. When the house up there is sold, they'll turn me out."

"I'm looking for a country house. Perhaps I'll come over and see it one day. Is it an old house?"

"Well," she said vaguely, "it isn't a new house, sir. It's a mighty fine place, and they do say it's going dirt cheap." And then she added slowly, "There's a map hanging in the kitchen. It was hanging up yonder in the servants' hall but I brought it down here, as so many people asks the way."

It was an old-fashioned country road map, and Radmore, bending down, saw in a moment where he was, and the best way home; and then feeling in a queer kind of mood, a mood in which a man may do a strange and unexpected thing, he took out of his pocket the £5 he had offered to Mr. Trotman.

"Look here," he said, "I'd like you just to take this and get your little girl whatever you think necessary when she's on the mend. She'll want a lot of care, eh?"

Twice the woman opened her mouth, and found she couldn't speak.

He held out his hand, and she squeezed it with her thin, work-worn fingers. "I do hope God will bless you, sir!" she said. And he went back to the car, feeling oddly cheered.

*I*t was past five when Radmore and Timmy crept like burglars through one of the back doors of Old Place. He sent the boy straight up to bed, but he himself felt hopelessly wide awake, so he went out of doors again, into Janet's delightful scented garden, and tramped up and down a bit to get warm. Suddenly he knew that he was hungry. Why shouldn't he go into the scullery and brew himself a cup of tea?

As he went into the kitchen, he saw on the table a kettle, a spirit stove, a cup and saucer, tea caddy and teapot, even a thermos full of hot water — everything ready to make an early cup of tea. He left the thermos alone, and filled up the kettle at the scullery sink.

Radmore was still very much of an old campaigner. Still it was a long time since he had made himself a cup of tea, and he became a little impatient for the cold water took a long time to boil.

The kettle was just beginning to sing, when the door which led to the flight of stairs connecting the scullery with the upper floors of the house opened quietly, and Betty appeared — Betty, in a becoming blue dressing gown, which intensified the peachy clearness of her skin, and the glint of pale gold in the shadowed fairness of her hair. Morning was Betty's hour. As the day wore on, she was apt to become fagged and worried, especially since Nanna's accident.

Just for a moment she looked very much taken aback, then she smiled, "I've come down to make a cup of tea for Nanna."

"So I suppose, but *you* must have a cup first. See, I'm making some for you."

"Are you?" She tried not to show the surprise she felt.

"While you're having it, we'll make Nanna a cup of tea with the water in the thermos there. But where's the milk?"

He saw her face from merry become sad. "I always save some milk for Josephine," she said. "I'll go and get it now. But we mustn't use it all; I must save some for that poor cat."

"You'll have to go a long way to give milk to Josephine," he observed.

She looked at him, startled, and going to the scullery door, glanced quickly at the corner where stood the now empty basket.

"Where is she?" she exclaimed — and her whole face lightened. "Oh, Godfrey, have you managed to hide her away?"

He nodded. "Yes, ever so many miles away, where no one will find her."

"What do you mean?" She could not conceal her astonishment — her astonishment and her intense relief.

"Timmy and I spirited her away," he went on, "to a cat's paradise where she's going to be kept under observation."

"Won't Dr. O'Farrell be very angry?"

"I don't think he'll mind as much as he'll pretend to. The moment he was told about her kittens he knew that the cat wasn't mad at all."

"The person who will be angry," exclaimed Betty, "is Mrs. Crofton! I thought it horribly cruel of her to say what she did last night."

"It was rather vindictive," he said reflectively. "On the other hand, you must remember that she'd had an awful shock. I don't wonder she felt angry with Josephine, eh?" He looked a little quizzically, a little deprecatingly, over at Betty.

"Still it seemed so — so unnecessary that she should *ask* for the cat to be killed." Betty was now bustling about the kitchen with a heightened color.

Radmore poured out a cup of tea. "Now then," he said, "do come and sit down quietly, and take your tea, Betty." Rather to his surprise, she meekly obeyed.

Presently she asked him, "But why have you got up so early?"

And then he told her the story of his and Timmy's night expedition, ending up with: "I intend going round to Dr. O'Farrell's house about eight o'clock. It wouldn't be fair to let the old fellow come down here to indulge his sporting instincts, eh?"

To that Betty made no answer, and as the water was now boiling she went across to the dresser and brought a clean cup and saucer. "Now then, Godfrey, this cup is for you. Nanna can wait a little longer for hers."

He sat down opposite to her, and into both their minds there came the thought that if they had married and gone out to Australia they would have often sat thus together in the early morning.

And then, when Nanna's cup of tea was at last ready, together with some nice thin bread and butter cut, he asked, "Can't I carry the tray up for you?"

She shook her head, smiling.

"I suppose you'll be down again soon? Isn't there anything else I can help you with?"

But this time Betty shook her head even more decidedly than before.

"Oh, no!" she exclaimed. "I've got to make Nanna comfortable for the day, and it's a long business, for she's dreadfully particular. As a matter of fact, Rosamund and Dolly will be down before I am. They'll start everything going for breakfast. They've been very good lately, you know! Perhaps you'd like to give *them* a hand?"

He looked at her hard. There was just the flicker of a mischievous smile on her face.

"I suppose I ought to help them," he said without enthusiasm. "But I'll go and have a bath now. You'll let me be your scullion when you're getting lunch ready, eh, Betty?" He added hastily, "I think Timmy ought to stay in bed all day today. You *will* let me take the place of Timmy, won't you, Betty?"

"That will be very kind of you," she replied demurely. And then, before she could say a word of protest, he had taken the heavy tray out of her hands. "You'll find me much more useful than Timmy," he said, with a touch of his old masterfulness. "Now you lead the way up, and I'll hand you over the tray at Nanna's door."

Chapter XXI

Some three or four hours later, Miss Pendarth, attired in a queer kind of brown smock which fell in long folds about her tall, still elegant figure, and with a gardening basket slung over her arm, stood by the glass door giving into her garden, when suddenly she heard a loud double knock on her stout, early Victorian knocker.

She turned quickly into her morning room. Who could it be? She knew the knock and ring of each of her neighbors, and this was none of them.

Her maid hurried out of the kitchen, and a moment later she heard a man's voice exclaim: "Will you kindly give this note to Miss Pendarth? I will return for the answer in about an hour."

Miss Pendarth knew the voice, and, stepping out of her morning room, she called out: "Come in just for a few minutes, Mr. Radmore."

In the old days she had always called him "Godfrey," but when Timmy had brought him to call within a day or two of his return to Beechfield, she had used the formal mode of address.

Radmore had to obey her, willy-nilly, and as he came down the hall towards her, she was struck by the keenness and intelligence of his dark face. She told herself grudgingly that he had certainly improved amazingly, at any rate in outward appearance, during the last ten years.

"Do let us go into your garden," he said courteously. "I hear that you are still Mrs. Tosswill's only rival!"

She softened, in spite of herself. The Godfrey Radmore of ten years ago would not have thought of saying such a civil, pleasant thing.

They walked through the glass door, and proceeded in silence down the path. The herbaceous borders were in fuller beauty than anything the Old Place garden could now show, but Radmore paid no further compliment, and it was she who broke the silence.

"You must see amazing changes at Old Place," she said musingly. "The rest of Beechfield has altered comparatively little, but Old Place is very different, with George gone, and all those young people who were children when you went away, grown up. As for Timmy, he was little more than a baby ten years ago."

"Timmy is my godson," said Radmore quickly. Her allusion to George had cut him.

Miss Pendarth turned on him rather sharply. "Of course I know that! I remember his christening as if it was yesterday. It must be twelve or thirteen years ago. I can see you and Betty standing by the font —" and then she stopped abruptly, while Radmore blushed hotly under his tan.

He said hastily: "Timmy's a dear little chap, but I confess I can't make him out sometimes."

Miss Pendarth turned and looked at him. She knew everything there was to know about Timmy Tosswill. His mother had early confided in her, and she never spoke of the child to other people. Like so many gossips, when really trusted with a secret, Miss Pendarth could keep a confidence — none better.

But she felt that Godfrey Radmore was entitled to know the little she could tell him, so "Timmy is a very queer child," she said slowly, "but I can't help thinking, Mr. Radmore —"

"Do call me Godfrey," he exclaimed, and at once she went on:

"Well, Godfrey, I think a certain amount of his oddity is owing to the fact that he's never been to school or mixed with other boys. I'm told he's a good scholar, but he's a shocking speller! Where's the good of knowing Latin and Greek if you can't spell such a simple word as chocolate — he spells it 'chockolit.' Still, I'm bound to admit the child sees and foresees more than most human beings are allowed to see and foresee."

And then, as Radmore remained silent, she went on: "Do you yourself believe in all that sort of thing, Godfrey — I mean second sight, and so on?"

Radmore answered frankly: "Yes, I think I do. I didn't before the War — I never gave any thought to any of these subjects. But during the War things happened to me and to some of my chums which made me believe, in a way I never had believed till then, in the reality of another state of being — I mean a world quite near to this world, one full of spirits, good and evil, who exercise a certain influence on the living."

They had come to a circular stone seat which was much older even than this old garden, and Miss Pendarth motioned her visitor to sit down.

"It isn't a new thing with Timmy," she said. "As a matter of fact, even before you left Beechfield, Dr. O'Farrell regarded the child as being in some way abnormal."

"D'you mean while he was still a baby?" asked Radmore.

"Well, when he had just emerged from babyhood. But I doubt if anyone knew it but Timmy's parents, the doctor, myself, and yes, I mustn't forget Nanna. He was a very extraordinary little child. He spoke so very early, you know."

"I do remember that."

"Unfortunately," went on Miss Pendarth, "it's difficult to know when Timmy is telling the truth, or what he believes to be the truth, about his gift. I think that often — and I know that Betty agrees with me — the boy invents all kinds of fantastic tales in order to impress the people about him."

"As far as I can make out," said Radmore slowly, "he's always told *me* the truth."

"I'll tell you something curious that happened — let me see, about seven years ago. You remember an old man we used to call Gaffer John? He had Wood Cottage, and lived in a very comfortable sort of way."

"Of course I remember Gaffer John! He was well over ninety when I left Beechfield, and he had been valet years ago to one of Queen Victoria's cousins."

"Yes, that's the man I mean. At last he was found dead in his chair. He had what was by way of being rather a grand funeral. Timmy, for some reason or other (I think he had a cold), wasn't allowed to attend the funeral, and as he was set on seeing it, Janet said that he might come and see it from one of my windows. Well, after the funeral was over, he stayed on with me for a few minutes, and suddenly he exclaimed: 'Gaffer John isn't dead at all, Miss Pendarth.' I naturally answered, 'Of course he is, Timmy. Why, we've just seen him buried.' And then he said: 'Don't you see him walking out there, along the road, quite plainly? He's behind an old gentleman dressed up for a fancy ball.' Then, Godfrey, the child went on to describe the kind of uniform which would have been worn seventy years ago by a staff officer. I couldn't help being impressed, in spite of myself, for I'd never given Timmy the slightest encouragement to talk in that sort of way, and it's the only time he's ever done it, with me."

"What does his mother really think of this queer power of his?" asked Radmore. "I've never liked to talk to her about it."

"It's difficult to say. In some ways Janet Tosswill's a very reserved woman. But I'll tell you another curious thing about the child." Instinctively she lowered her voice.

"The day before poor George was killed, Timmy cried and cried and cried. It was impossible to comfort him — and he wouldn't give any reason for his grief. Both Janet and Betty were dreadfully upset. They thought he had some pain that he wouldn't tell them of, and they would have sent for Dr. O'Farrell, but they knew he was away, some miles off, at a very difficult case. Betty actually came in and asked if *I* would try to make him say what was the matter! But of course I could do nothing with him. I think you know that he was passionately fond of George."

"What does Dr. O'Farrell think of it all?"

"He's convinced that Timmy has got a kind of peculiar, rare, thought-reading gift. He won't hear of its being in any sense supernatural. I haven't spoken to him about it lately, but the last time he mentioned the child, he told me he was sure that what he called the boy's 'subconscious self' would in time sink into its proper place."

"I wonder if it will?" exclaimed Radmore. "I don't see why it should."

"No, nor do I, excepting that, as time goes on, Timmy has become much more like a normal boy than he used to be. I'm convinced that very often he pretends to see things that he doesn't see. He loves frightening the village people, for instance, and some of them are really afraid of him. They think he can heal certain simple ailments, and they're absolutely certain that he can what they call 'blight' them!"

"What a very convenient gift," observed Radmore dryly. "I've known a good many people in my time I should have liked to 'blight'!"

Even as he spoke, an unpleasant question was obtruding itself. Was it possible that Timmy had a "scunner" against poor little Enid Crofton?

"D'you think the child has a jealous disposition?" he asked abruptly.

Miss Pendarth looked round at him, rather surprised by the question. "He's never any occasion to be jealous," she said shortly. "Betty and Janet both worship him, and so does his old nurse. I don't think he cares for anyone else in the world excepting these three. Perhaps I ought to make an exception in *your* favor — from what I'm told he cherishes a romantic affection for *you.*"

Miss Pendarth went on: "Mind you — I think there's often a touch of malice about the boy! Timmy wouldn't be at all averse to doing mischief to anyone he didn't like, or whom he thought ill of."

"There are a good many grown-up people of whom one can say that," observed Radmore.

And then, almost as if the other had seen into his mind, Miss Pendarth, with a touch of significance in her voice, observed musingly: "I fancy Timmy doesn't much like the pretty young widow who has taken The Trellis House. The first evening Mrs. Crofton came to see the Tosswills, she got an awful fright. Timmy's dog, Flick, rushed into the room and began snarling and growling at her. There was a most disagreeable scene, and from what one of the girls said the other day, it seems to have prejudiced the boy against her."

Radmore looked straight into Miss Pendarth's face. Then she hadn't yet heard about last night?

There was a slight pause.

"Yes," said Radmore at last. "I'm afraid that Timmy does dislike Mrs. Crofton."

"Perhaps," said Miss Pendarth slowly, "the boy has more reason to dislike her than we know." As Radmore said nothing, she went on: "Mrs. Crofton is behaving in a very wrong, as well as in a very unladylike, way with Jack Tosswill."

Radmore moved uneasily in his seat. It was time for him to escape. This was the Miss Pendarth of long ago — noted for the spiteful, dangerous things she sometimes said.

He got up. "Jack certainly goes to see her very often," he said, "but I don't think that's her fault. Forgive me for saying so, Miss Pendarth, but you know what village gossip is?"

"I'm afraid that she's giving Jack a great deal of deliberate encouragement. Even her servants believe that he regards himself as engaged to her."

"What absolute nonsense!" exclaimed Radmore vigorously. "Why, if it comes to that, Rosamund's quite as much at The Trellis House as Jack is, and even *I* go there very often!"

"Yes, I know you do; at one time you were first favorite," said Miss Pendarth coolly.

She had never been lacking in courage.

"And yet I can assure you," he exclaimed in a challenging tone, "that I, at any rate, am not at all in love with Mrs. Crofton."

"Sit down, Godfrey. There's something I want to ask you."

Unwillingly he obeyed.

"I think you knew Colonel Crofton?"

"Yes, and I liked him very much."

"I'm afraid from what I've heard that she wasn't a particularly good wife to him." Radmore was surprised at the feeling in her voice, but he asked himself irritably how the devil had Miss Pendarth heard anything of the Croftons and their private affairs?

He got up again, feeling vexed with himself for having come in to Rose Cottage.

She also rose from the stone seat.

"Stop just one moment, Godfrey. I didn't realize that you knew Mrs. Crofton as well as you seem to do. I do beg of you to convey to her that she ought to be more prudent. I'm quite serious as to the talk about Jack Tosswill. They seem to have gone on a walk together yesterday afternoon, and the girl at the post office, who is often sent long distances with telegrams and messages, saw them in the North Wood kissing one another."

Godfrey uttered an exclamation of surprise and disgust.

How extraordinary that a woman of Miss Pendarth's birth and breeding should listen to, and believe, low village gossip!

"Really," he said at last, "that's too bad! I can't understand, Miss Pendarth, how you can believe such a story —" He nearly added, "or allow it to be told you!"

"I wouldn't believe everybody," she said in a low voice, "but I do believe Jane Nichol. She's a sensible, quiet, reserved girl. She seems to have passed quite close to them, but they were so absorbed in themselves that they didn't see her. She told no one but her aunt, and her aunt told me. I'm sorry to say I do believe the story, and I think you will agree that what may be sport to your pretty friend might mean lifelong bitterness to such a boy as Jack Tosswill." She added earnestly, "Can't you say just a word to her?"

"Well, no, I don't see how I can! Still I promise you to try to do it if I get the chance."

He felt sharply disturbed and annoyed, and yet he didn't believe a word of that vulgar story! Of course it was foolish of Enid Crofton to go for a long walk alone with Jack Tosswill. That sort of thing was bound to make talk. What would the village people think if they knew how often he, Radmore, and Mrs. Crofton had dined and lunched together during the three weeks that he had been there? Thank Heaven, they didn't know, and never would.

"Did you ever read the report of the inquest on Colonel Crofton?" asked Miss Pendarth meaningly.

"I hadn't the chance. I was still in Australia," he said shortly.

"If you'll wait a moment I'll bring it to you," was the, to him, astonishing reply.

Miss Pendarth walked off with her quick, light footsteps towards the house, and Radmore, gazing after her, told himself that she was indeed a strange woman. In some ways he had liked her far better today than he had ever liked her before, but the low, silly bit of gossip she had just told him filled him with disgust.

Very soon she was back, holding in her hand a newspaper.

An inquest of the kind that was held on Colonel Crofton is a godsend to any local sheet, and Radmore saw at a glance that this county paper had made the most of it.

"Will you read it here, if you're not in a hurry? I don't want it taken away; so while you're reading it, I'll go and do some potting over there."

She disappeared into a glass-house built across a corner of her garden, and he settled down to read the long newspaper columns.

Soon his feeling quickened into intense interest. The local Essex reporter had a turn for descriptive writing, and, as he read, Godfrey Radmore saw the scene described rise vividly before him. He seemed to visualize the intensely crowded little court-house, the kindly coroner, the twelve good men and true, and the motley gathering of small town and country folk drawn together in the hope of hearing something startling.

Yet the facts were simple enough. Colonel Crofton had died from either an accidental, or a deliberate, overdose of strychnine. And his death had been a terrible one.

The outstanding points of interrogation were: Had he consciously added to a tonic which he was taking an ounce or more of the deadly drug? Or, as some people were inclined to believe, had the local chemist by some mistake or gross piece of carelessness, put a murderous amount of strychnine into a mixture which had been prescribed for his customer about a fortnight before?

But for the fact that a bottle of nux vomica had been actually found on the ledge of the dead man's dressing-room window, it would have gone hard with the chemist. But there the bottle had been found, and in her evidence, evidently given very clearly and simply, Mrs. Crofton had explained that, during the war, while in Egypt, she had palpitations of the heart, and so many drops of diluted strychnine had been ordered her.

When asked why there was so large a bottle full of the deadly stuff, she had answered that it had come from the Army Stores, where they always did things in a big and generous way. At that there had been laughter in Court.

Mrs. Crofton had further explained that, as a matter of fact, she had brought the bottle back to England without really knowing that she had done so; and that she had never given it a thought till it had been found, as described, after her husband's death, by the doctor who had been called in to attend Colonel Crofton in his agonizing seizure.

One thing stated by Mrs. Crofton much surprised Radmore. She had asserted, quite definitely, that her husband had suffered from shell-shock. That Radmore believed to be quite untrue.

With quickened, painful interest he read her account of how odd and how cranky Colonel Crofton had become when wholly absorbed in his hobby of breeding wire-haired terriers. How, when one of his dogs had failed to win a prize, he would go about muttering to himself, and visiting his annoyance and disappointment on those about him.

She had drawn a sad picture of the last long months of their joint life together and Radmore began to feel very, very sorry for her. . . . What an awful ordeal the poor little woman had gone through!

The doctor's evidence made painful reading, but what had really clinched the matter was the evidence of one Piper, the Croftons' general odd man and trusted servant. He had been Colonel Crofton's batman during part of the war, and was evidently much attached to him. When Piper repeated the words in which his master had once or twice threatened to take his own life, his evidence had obviously made a strong impression on both coroner and jury.

Radmore remembered Piper with a faint feeling of dislike. It was Piper who had prepared the puppy, Flick, for the cross-country journey to Beechfield, and Radmore had given the man a handsome tip for all the trouble he had taken.

Yes, he had not liked Piper; so much he remembered. He had thought the man self-assertive, over self-confident, while disagreeably cringing in manner.

He read through the coroner's charge, which was given fully, very attentively. It was quite clear that the coroner was strongly biased, if one could put it that way, in Mrs. Crofton's favor. He had spoken touchingly of the difficult time the poor young lady had had with her husband. Then he had recalled that the Colonel's own favorite terrier, Dandy, on which he had built great hopes, had only been commended, instead of winning, as he had hoped, the first prize at an important show, and that had thoroughly upset him. Indeed, according to Piper's evidence, he had used the exaggerated phrase, "My life is no longer worth living." Finally the coroner had touched lightly, but severely, on evidence tendered by a spiteful ex-woman-servant of the Croftons who had drawn a very unpleasant picture of the relations existing between the husband and wife.

Yet when the verdict of *felo de se* had been returned, there had been murmurs in Court, at once sharply checked by the coroner.

Radmore felt surprised. Surely everyone present should have rejoiced from every point of view. Had a different verdict been returned, it would have put the unfortunate chemist in a very difficult position, and might easily have ruined his business.

Though Radmore was grateful to Miss Pendarth for allowing him to read the report, it had an effect very different from that she had intended, for it made him pity Mrs. Crofton intensely. Somehow he had never realized what a terrible ordeal the poor little woman had been through.

Chapter XXII

A week later Enid Crofton lay in her drawing room on the one couch which The Trellis House contained. She looked very charming in her new guise of invalid.

Several people had already called to know how she was, including Jack Tosswill and his father, but no visitor had yet been admitted. Now it was past four, and she was expecting the doctor — also, she hoped, in due course, Godfrey Radmore. That was why she had come downstairs, after having had an early cup of tea in her bedroom, and lain herself on the sofa.

The door opened, and as his burly form came through the door, Dr. O'Farrell told himself that he had seldom if ever attended such an attractive looking patient! She was still very pale, for the shock had been great; but today, for the first time since her widowhood, she had put on a pink silk jacket, and it supplied the touch of color which was needed by her white cheeks. She had made up her mind that even a little rouge would be injudicious, but she had just used her lip-stick. It was pleasant to know that she had every right to be an interesting invalid with all an interesting invalid's privileges.

And yet, well acquainted as she was with the turns and twists of masculine human nature, Mrs. Crofton would have been surprised to know how suddenly repelled was the genial Irishman when she exclaimed eagerly: — "I do hope that horrible cat has been killed! Didn't I hear you say that you meant to shoot her yourself?"

It was not without a touch of sly satisfaction that Dr. O'Farrell answered: — "That was my intention certainly, Mrs. Crofton. But I was frustrated. The cat and her kittens vanished — just entirely away!"

"Vanished?" she exclaimed. "Then perhaps someone else has killed her?"

"Bless you, no. I'm afraid that the brute has still got her nine lives before her! She was spirited away by that broth of a boy. Timmy Tosswill's a good hater and a good lover, and that's the truth of it! I wasn't a bit surprised when I got the news that my services wouldn't be wanted — that the cat wasn't any longer at Old Place."

"D'you mean you don't know what's happened to the horrible creature?" she exclaimed vexedly.

"That's just what I do mean, Mrs. Crofton. That smart little fellow just spirited the creature away."

As he spoke, sitting with his back to the window, he was observing his pretty patient very closely. She had reddened angrily and was biting her lips. What a little vixen *she* was, to be sure! And suddenly she saw what he was thinking.

"I'd like to put a question to you, Mrs. Crofton."

"Do!" she insisted, but his question, when it came, displeased her.

"Is it true that that wasn't the first time you'd had an unpleasant experience with an animal at Old Place?"

Dr. O'Farrell had not meant to ask his patient this question today, but he really felt curious to know the truth concerning something Godfrey Radmore had told him that morning.

"Yes," she answered, slowly, "the first time I was in Old Place, Timmy Tosswill's dog frightened me out of my wits."

"That's very strange," said the doctor, "Flick's such a mild-mannered dog."

Enid Crofton lifted herself up from her reclining position. "Dr. O'Farrell! I wouldn't say so to anyone but you, but don't you think there's something uncanny about Timmy Tosswill? My little maid told me last night that the village people think he's a kind of — well, I don't know what to call it! — a kind of boy-witch. She says they're awfully afraid of him, that they think he can do a mischief to people he doesn't like." As he said nothing for a moment, she added rather defiantly: — "I daresay you think it is absurd that I should listen to village gossip, but the truth is, I've a kind of horror of the child. He terrifies me!"

Dr. O'Farrell looked round the room as if he feared eavesdroppers. He even got up and went to see if the door was really shut. "That's very curious," he said thoughtfully. "Very curious indeed. But no, I'm not thinking you absurd, Mrs. Crofton. The child's a very peculiar child. Have you ever heard of thought transference?"

She looked at him, astonished. "No," she answered, rather bewildered, "I haven't an idea what you mean by that."

"Well, you've heard of hypnotism?"

"Oh, yes, but I've never believed in it!"

To that remark he made no answer, and he went on, more as if speaking to himself than to her: — "We needn't consider what the village people say. Timmy just tries to frighten them — like all boys he's fond of his practical joke, and of course it's a temptation to him to work on their fears. But the little lad certainly presents a curious natural phenomenon, if I may so express myself."

She looked at him puzzled. She had no idea what he meant.

"If that child wasn't the child of sensible people, he'd have become famous — he'd be what silly people call a medium."

"Would he?" she said. "Do you mean that he can turn tables and do that sort of thing?"

The doctor shook his head. "What I mean is that in some way as yet unexplained by science, he can create simulacra of what people are thinking about, or of what may simply be hidden far away in the recesses of their memory. In a sort of way Timmy Tosswill can make things seem to appear which, as a matter of fact, are not there. But how he does it? Well, I can't tell you *that.*"

Enid Crofton stared at Dr. O'Farrell. It was as if he were speaking to her in a foreign language, and yet his words made her feel vaguely apprehensive. Surely Timmy could not divine the hidden thoughts of the people about him? She grew hot with dismay at the idea.

The doctor bent forward, and looked at her keenly: "I should like to ask you another question, Mrs. Crofton. Have you in your past life ever had some very painful association with a dog — I mean any very peculiar experience with a terrier?"

The color receded from her face. She was so surprised that she hardly knew what to answer.

"I don't think so. My first experience of a really disagreeable kind was when that boy's terrier flew at me. It's true that I've always had a peculiar dislike to dogs — at least for a long time," she corrected herself hastily. She added after a moment's pause, "I expect you know that Colonel Crofton bred dogs?"

"Aye, and that very dog, Flick, was bred by your husband — isn't that so?"

"I believe he was."

She was wondering anxiously why he asked her this question, and her mind all at once flew off to Piper and Mrs. Piper, and she felt sick with fear.

"I ask you these questions," said the doctor very deliberately, "because, according to Mrs. Tosswill, Timmy thinks, or says he thinks, that you are always accompanied by — well, how can I put it? — by a phantom dog."

"A phantom dog?"

She stared at him with her large dark eyes, and then, all at once, she remembered Dandy, her husband's terrier, who, after his master's tragic death, had refused all food, and had howled so long and so dismally that, in a fit of temper, she had herself ordered him to be destroyed.

She lay back on her pretty, frilled pillow, and covered her face with the hand belonging to the arm that was uninjured.

"Oh," she gasped out, "I see now. What a horrible idea!"

"Then you have no painful associations with any one particular terrier apart from Flick?" persisted Dr. O'Farrell.

He really wanted to know. According to his theory, Timmy's subconscious self could in some utterly inexplicable way build up an image of what was in the minds of those about him.

"Perhaps I have," she confessed in a very low voice. "My husband had a favorite terrier called Dandy, Flick's father in fact. The poor brute got into such a state after his master's death that he had to be sent to one of those lethal chambers in London. The whole thing was a great trouble, and a great pain to me."

Dr. O'Farrell felt a thrill of exultation run through him. To find his theory thus miraculously confirmed was very gratifying.

"That's most interesting!" he exclaimed, "for Timmy, even the very first time he saw you walking down the avenue towards the front door of Old Place, thought you were followed by a dog uncommonly like his terrier, Flick. His theory seemed to be that both Flick and the cat did not fly at *you*, but at your invisible companion."

"My invisible companion?"

He saw the color again receding from her face. "Don't for a moment believe *I* think there is any phantom dog there," he said soothingly. "All I believe — and what you have told me confirmed my theory — is that Timmy Tosswill can not only see what's in your subconscious mind, but that he can build up a kind of image of it and produce what is called, I believe, in the East, collective hypnotism. I should never be surprised, for instance, if someone else thought they saw you with a dog — that is as long as that boy was present. It's a most interesting and curious case."

"It's a very horrible case," said Enid faintly.

She felt as if she were moving in a terrible nightmare world, unsuspected, unrealized by her till then.

"All abnormality is unpleasant," said the doctor cheerfully, "I always thought the boy would grow out of it, and, to a certain extent, he *has* grown out of it. You'll hardly believe me, Mrs. Crofton, when I tell you that, as a little child, Timmy actually declared he could see fairies and gnomes, 'the little people' as we call them in my country! I think that's what first started this queer reputation of his among the village folk. I tell you he's anything but a welcome guest in the cottages — people with evil consciences, you know!" The doctor laughed. "They're afraid of Master Timmy, that's what the bad folks in Beechfield are — they think he can 'blight' them, bring ill-luck on them. Well, well, I mustn't stop, gossiping here with you, though it's very pleasant. By the way, I'll ask you to keep all I've said to you to yourself — not but what the boy's parents know quite well what I think about him!"

Then followed a few professional questions and answers, and then the doctor went off, well satisfied with his visit.

After Dr. O'Farrell had gone, Enid Crofton lay back and shut her eyes. Her nerves had by no means recovered from the horrible experience, and she felt a sort of utter distaste to Beechfield and to everybody there — with the one exception of Godfrey Radmore. She promised herself fiercely that if Radmore did what she was always telling herself secretly he would surely end by doing, then she would make it her business to see that they never, either of them, came back to this horrible place anymore.

Apart from anything else, Jack Tosswill was already beginning to be more of a complication than was pleasant to one in her weak, excited state. He had left a letter when he called that morning – an eager, ardent love-letter, entirely assuming that they were engaged to be married.

She took it out of the pretty fancy bag, which lay on her pale blue silk eiderdown, and read it through again with a mixture of amusement and irritation. It was a long letter, written on the cheap, grey Old Place notepaper, very unlike another love-letter she had had today, written on nice, thick, highly-glazed letter-paper which had a small coronet embossed above the address. In that letter Captain Tremaine urgently asked to be allowed to come down for the next weekend. He pointed out that his leave was drawing to a close, and that they had a lot of things to discuss. He, too, considered himself engaged to her, but somehow she didn't mind that. She told herself pettishly that Providence has a way of managing things very badly. If only Tremaine had Radmore's money, even only a portion of his money, how gladly she would leave England behind her, and start a new, free, delightful life in India! Tremaine knew the kind of grand, smart people she longed to know. He was staying with some of them now.

Just as this thought was drifting through her mind, the door opened and she hurriedly stuffed Jack's letter beneath her silk quilt. Radmore walked in, and his face softened as he looked down on the pale, fragile-looking girl – for she did look very much like a girl – lying on the sofa.

"I've brought you a lot of messages from Old Place," he began. "They really are most awfully miserable about you!"

"I'm glad the cat hasn't been killed after all," she said weakly.

She had at last seen the look of recoil on Dr. O'Farrell's face, and she was now trimming her sails accordingly.

"That's very magnanimous of you." Radmore smiled. He was surprised, and a little touched, too. "May I sit down?"

He drew up a chair, and then he touched the hand belonging to the bandaged arm. "I do hope you are fairly free from pain?" he said solicitously.

"It does hurt a good deal."

There was a pause; his hand was still lying protectingly over her hand.

She lay quite still – a vision of lovely Paris frocks, a Rolls-Royce running smoothly by a deep blue sea, a long rope of pearls, flashed before her inner consciousness. Then she was awakened from this dream of bliss by Radmore's next words: — "My godson's going to write you a letter of apology," he said.

And then, to her chagrin, he took his hand away; it was as though Timmy's malign influence had fallen between them. His very tone changed; it was no longer tender, solicitous — only kindly.

"Mr. Radmore, I want to tell you something. I'm horribly afraid of Timmy!"

There was an accent of absolute sincerity in her low voice. She went on: — "Dr. O'Farrell has been talking to me about him. He seems a most strange, unnatural child. The village people believe that he has supernatural powers. Do you believe that?"

"I don't quite know what I think about Timmy," he answered hesitatingly. He felt acutely uncomfortable, also rather shocked that Dr. O'Farrell had said anything about a child who might, after all, be regarded as his patient. But Enid Crofton was looking at him very intently, and so he went on: —

"I've never spoken to any of them about it, but, yes, if you ask me for my honest opinion, I do think the child has very peculiar powers."

And then, all at once, Enid Crofton burst into tears. "Timmy terrifies me," she sobbed. "I wish he never came near me! He hates me — I feel it all the time. I'm sure he made that cat fly at me!"

Radmore remained silent — he didn't know what to say, what to admit. He wondered uncomfortably how she had come so near the truth.

"Come, come," he said, bending forward, "you mustn't feel like that. I don't think the child hates you, but I do think that he loves trying experiments with that queer power of his. I'm afraid he wanted to see whether the cat would behave as the dog had done."

"That's what I mean," she exclaimed, dabbing her eyes, "that's exactly what I mean! I don't want to hurt his feelings, or to make a fuss, but I should be so grateful if you could manage to prevent his coming here. I don't want to make you vain," she smiled, very winningly, "but sometimes I do feel that 'two's company.' Since I've been here I've hardly ever seen you alone. I used to enjoy our talks in London! I feel, I know that you're the only friend I've got in Beechfield."

"That's rather hard on Jack Tosswill," and though he smiled, he looked at her significantly.

Enid was so surprised that for a moment her composure gave way, and the color rushed into her pale face. Then she pulled herself together. "It really hasn't been my fault," she said plaintively.

"I'm sure it hasn't. But in a village one has to be careful. Would it surprise you to hear that as I came along this morning, one of the

inhabitants of Beechfield spoke to me of you and Jack, and suggested
— forgive me for saying so — not only that the boy was very much in
love with you but that you — well — encouraged him!"

Enid Crofton sat up. "I've always heard that villages were far more
wicked places than towns, and now I know it's true!"

"Steady on," he said smiling, "forgive me for having repeated a silly
bit of gossip. But, after all, what you said just now is quite true — I am
your oldest friend by a long way, and so I feel I ought to give you a
word of warning. I do think the poor boy *is* very fond of you, eh?"

Enid Crofton put out her hand and took his in hers. She squeezed
it convulsively. "I feel so miserable," she sobbed, "so miserable and
lonely!"

"Do you, dear —" And then they both started violently, and Radmore
moved his chair away with a quick movement, for the door behind them
had swung open, and Jack Tosswill, quite unaware of the other man's
presence, came through it, and at once began speaking eagerly, excitedly,
in a voice so unlike his usual "home" voice that Radmore hardly
recognized it: —

"I'm so glad you're downstairs. I came this morning I hope you got
my —" and then he saw the other man, and checked himself abruptly.

He had given the beloved woman he regarded as his future wife, his
most solemn word of honor that no one should suspect that they were
more than mere acquaintances. So, after a perceptible pause, he con-
cluded, lamely, "my step-mother's message."

"Yes, I did; thank you very much."

He saw that she had been crying, and his heart welled up with
tenderness, and with angry, impatient annoyance against Radmore's
presence.

Why didn't the stupid fellow go? Surely he must realize, surely there
must be something in the atmosphere, which must tell even the blindest
of onlookers, how things were between him, Jack Tosswill, and the
invalid?

But Radmore was quite impervious to the atmosphere of emotion
and strain — or so it seemed. On and on he sat, Enid Crofton languidly
making conversation with them both in turn, until at last Rosamund
came in, and both men rose to leave together.

And then something curious happened. Radmore, even while conscious that he was a fool, felt a violent desire to see Enid Crofton again
and very soon, alone. He was trying to make up a form of words to
convey this to her before the other two, when good fortune seemed to
favor him, for brother and sister began — as they were wont to do —
wrangling together.

Seeing his opportunity he bent down a little over Mrs. Crofton's couch in order to suggest to her that he should come again tomorrow. And then, in a flash, the whole expression of his face altered and stiffened. Half under the lace coverlet over the eiderdown a letter written on familiar looking pale grey notepaper was sticking out, and he couldn't help seeing the words: — "My own darling angel."

Straightening himself quickly and hardly knowing what he was saying, he exclaimed, "I do hope you'll soon feel all right again."

And then he saw that she was aware of what had happened for she became even whiter than she had been before. Every bit of color fled from her face — except for the unnaturally pink lips.

Chapter XXIII

*A*s he walked away from The Trellis House Radmore felt terribly disturbed, and maddened with himself for feeling so disturbed.

After all, Enid Crofton meant very little to him! He even told himself that he had never really liked, still less respected, her and yet there had been something that drove him on, that allured him, that made him feel as he had felt tonight. But for the accident of his having seen that letter from poor foolish Jack Tosswill he might, by this time tomorrow, have been in the position of Enid Crofton's future husband! The knowledge turned him sick.

Just now he felt that he never wished to see her again.

As he walked on, leaving the village behind him, and emerging on the great common which stretched between Beechfield and the nearest railway station — he asked himself whether or no it was possible that she had genuinely fallen in love with Jack Tosswill?

And then he stayed his steps suddenly. He had remembered the look of terror, the look of being "found out," which had crossed her face, when she had realized that he had seen that fatally revealing corner of her love-letter.

Why had she looked like that? And then, all at once, he knew. It was for him that Enid Crofton had come to Beechfield, for him, or rather for his money. He felt hideously disturbed as certain tiny past happenings crowded on his memory. He felt he would give half his possessions were it possible thereby to transplant The Trellis House hundreds of miles from Beechfield.

He threw a rueful thought to Jack Tosswill. Miss Pendarth had been right, after all. That sort of experience might well embitter the whole of the early life of such a priggish, self-centered youth; and while he was chewing the cud of these painful, troubling thoughts there came a woman's voice out of the darkness.

"Does this lead on into Beechfield, sir? I want to find The Trellis House. I've been there once before, but it was broad daylight then."

Radmore peered at the speaker: a thin, medium-sized woman she seemed to be; obviously not one of the country folk — by her accent a Londoner.

"Go straight on, and in about a quarter of an hour, you'll find The Trellis House on your right. But you'd better enquire as soon as you get into the village itself. Is it Mrs. Crofton's house that you want to find?"

"Yes, that's the place I'm bound for," said the woman.

"Look here," said Radmore good-naturedly. "I was only going for a walk. I'll take you along to The Trellis House. You might easily miss it."

He turned, and they began walking along the road side by side.

"I suppose Mrs. Crofton 'asn't gone away yet, I'm sure to find 'er there, sir?" There was a doubting, almost a resentful, tone in the mincing voice.

"I think she's at home. Isn't she expecting you?" Radmore had taken the woman for a superior servant.

"She's not expecting me exactly, but me and my 'usband have been 'oping for a letter from Mrs. Crofton. As nothing's come, I thought I'd just come down and see 'er. My 'usband asked 'er to get the address of a gentleman who 'e thinks might 'elp 'im — Major Radmore. I don't suppose as what you've ever 'eard of 'im, sir?"

Radmore said quietly, "I know Major Radmore rather well. May I ask your name?"

She hesitated, then answered: — "Mrs. Piper, sir. My 'usband was Colonel Crofton's dog-breeding assistant, and 'e's about to start for 'imself in the same line, if 'e can get the money that's been promised 'im. If 'e can't get that money — well, 'e'll have to go into service again, and 'e thought that Major Radmore, who's a kind, generous gentleman, might 'elp 'im to a job."

Radmore felt amused, interested, and, yes, a little touched. Evidently his distaste for Piper had not been reciprocal.

"I suppose to start dog-breeding requires a good bit of money," he said.

"Well, sir, it's this way. Fancy dogs fetch a good bit more money than they did. Such a lot o' breeding stopped during the War. But what with one thing and another, and prices 'aving gone up so, Piper says 'twould be no good going in for such a thing under a matter of £500. But we've got good hopes of getting the money," said the woman composedly.

"Have you indeed?"

Then he felt rather ashamed of the little game he was playing with this no doubt excellent woman.

"Look here, Mrs. Piper," he exclaimed, "perhaps I ought to tell you frankly that *my* name is Radmore. I no longer call myself 'Major Radmore.' My address for the present is Old Place, Beechfield. But Beechfield alone would find me, and I hope your husband will let me know if I can do anything for him."

"There now! Could one ever hope for such a thing coming to pass as my meeting you, sir, accidental like?"

Mrs. Piper was genuinely moved and excited. She felt that Providence, in whom she only believed when she was in trouble, had done her a good turn. For a moment or two she remained silent, thinking intently, wondering whether she dared take advantage of this extraordinary chance — a chance that might never occur again.

"I take it, sir," she said at last, "that you are a friend of Mrs. Crofton's?"

"Of course I am well acquainted with the lady you name." There came a tone of reserve, instantly detected by the woman's quick ear and quicker mind, into the speaker's voice. "And I had a great regard for your husband's late employer, Colonel Crofton," he added.

"Aye, 'e was a good gentleman and no mistake," said Mrs. Piper feelingly.

She was wondering how far she dare go. She knew the man walking by her side was very rich; Piper had called him a millionaire.

"I 'ope you won't think me troublesome, sir, if I tells you 'ow matters are between Mrs. Crofton and my 'usband?"

There came no immediate answer to her question. Still she decided to go on.

"Piper was with the Colonel a long time, sir. And after the poor gentleman's death Mrs. Crofton promised Piper that she'd oblige 'im in the matter of financing 'is new business."

Radmore was very much surprised. He felt certain that Enid Crofton had no money to spare, then he told himself that women are sometimes very foolish, especially if any matter of sentiment is in question. But somehow he would not have thought that particular woman would ever be tempted to show herself impulsively generous.

"You spoke just now, Mrs. Piper, as if there was some doubt about the money?"

"Did I, sir? Well, one can never tell in this world. But I think Mrs. Crofton *will* find the money." She added, almost in a whisper, "It's to 'er interest to do so, sir."

"To her interest?" repeated Radmore. "What exactly do you mean?"

"I don't quite understand it myself, sir." Mrs. Piper spoke with a touch of light indifference in her voice, "Piper don't tell me very much. I was in Islington, conducting a little business I've got, when Colonel Crofton came by 'is sad death. Mrs. Crofton spoke to Piper most feelingly, sir, about the service 'e'd done her by what 'e said at the inquest. I've always 'ad my belief, sir, that Piper might 'ave said something more and different that would have been, maybe, awkward for Mrs. Crofton." She waited a moment, realizing that she had burned her boats. "Do you take my meaning, sir?"

"No," said Radmore sternly, "I don't take your meaning at all, Mrs. Piper. I don't in the least understand what you meant to imply just now."

A most disturbing suspicion had begun to assail him. Was this woman, with her low, mincing voice, and carefully chosen words, something of a blackmailer?

They walked on in silence for a few minutes, and on her side, Mrs. Piper began to doubt very much whether she had acted for the best in being so honest — "honest" was the word she used to herself. But she told herself that now she had started, perhaps she had better go straight on with it.

"It's my belief that Piper did ask Mrs. Crofton to speak to you, sir, about the matter, and I thought, maybe, that she 'ad done so. 'Ave I your permission to say, sir, that I met you in the road, and that the subject cropped up as it were?"

"You can say anything you like," said Radmore coldly.

He could not ask this strange, sinister woman to remain silent, yet the thought that Enid Crofton was about to be told that he and this Mrs. Piper had discussed her affairs was very disagreeable to him.

Radmore was tempted for a moment to do a quixotic act, to say to the woman, "I will find this money for your husband; don't trouble Mrs. Crofton," and but for what had happened not an hour ago he would almost certainly have done so. But now he felt as if he never wanted to hear Enid Crofton's name mentioned again, and he would have given a good deal to obliterate her and her concerns entirely from his memory.

They were now, much to his relief, close to The Trellis House: "I will ring the bell for you," he said courteously, and then, without waiting for her thanks, he hurried off towards Old Place.

*T*he next evening Jack Tosswill drew Radmore aside. "Look here," he said awkwardly, "I wonder if you'd kindly wait a bit after the others have gone to bed? I want to ask you something, Godfrey."

"Of course I will, old chap." Radmore looked hard into the young man's moody, troubled face, and came to a certain conclusion. Doubtless Enid Crofton had given Jack his dismissal, and the foolish fellow was going to pour it all out. He felt he was in for a disagreeable, not to say painful, half hour. Few people of a kindly disposition even reach the age Radmore had reached without having had more than one such talk with a young man crossed in love.

As soon as they settled themselves down, each with his pipe, in front of the drawing room fire, Jack began, speaking obviously with a great effort, and yet with a directness and honesty which the older man admired: —

"Look here, Godfrey? It's no use beating about the bush. I want to know if you can lend me £500, and I want to say at once that I don't know when I shall be able to pay you back. Still, I shall be able to pay you interest. I suppose one pays the bank rate? I don't know anything about those things. Of course, you may ask why don't I go to my father, but —"

Radmore stopped him. "It's all right, old chap. I'll give you a check this evening before we go to bed."

"I say —" Jack turned round. "You're a good fellow, Radmore; I wouldn't do it, only — only —"

"I know," said Radmore coolly. "I quite realize it isn't for yourself. I suppose it's to oblige a pal. You needn't tell me anything more about it. As a matter of fact I meant to ask you whether you'd take a present from me of just that sum. I don't suppose you know how I feel about you all. George and I were just like brothers. He'd have given me anything."

"No, no! I want this to be a business transaction, Godfrey." He said the words just a little fiercely.

"So it shall be — if you want it that way. I'll go and get my checkbook now."

When he came back, the check made out in his hand, he said thoughtfully, "I hope your friend hasn't got into the sort of scrape which means that one has to pay money of a — well, of a blackmailing sort? There's no end to *that*, you know."

Jack Tosswill looked surprised. "Good Heavens, no! He's only being rushed over a bill — legal proceedings threatened — you know the sort of thing?"

"I've made out the check to self and endorsed it," observed Radmore.

"Thanks awfully. You *are* a good sort. I am far more grateful than I can say, far more than — than — if it was only for myself —"

He stopped abruptly, and there was an awkward pause. Then Jack, speaking rather breathlessly, asked an odd question: —

"You knew Crofton very well, didn't you, Godfrey? What kind of a chap was he?"

He brought out the question with an effort. But he did so want to know! For the first time in his self-confident, comfortable, young life Jack Tosswill was in love and full of painful, poignant, retrospective jealousy.

Radmore looked away, instinctively. "I liked Colonel Crofton, I always got on with him — but he was not popular. He was not at all happy when I knew him, and unhappy people are rarely popular."

He was wondering whether he had better say anything to Jack — whether the favor he had just done him gave him the right to speak.

"I suppose he was at least thirty years older than Mrs. Crofton?"

Radmore nodded, and then they neither spoke for a few moments. Each was waiting for the other to say something, and at last Jack asked another question.

"They didn't get on very well together, did they?"

"When I first knew them they seemed to be all right. But he was very jealous of her, and he had cause to be, for most of the fellows out there were in love with her, and well, not to put too fine a point on it, she liked it!" He hesitated. "She was rather too fond of telling people that her husband wasn't quite kind to her."

"I think that was very natural of her!" exclaimed Jack, and Radmore felt a surge of pity for the young fellow. Still he forced himself to go on: "It's no use pretending. She was — and still is — a tremendous flirt."

Jack made a restless movement.

"I'm afraid you think me rather a cad for saying that, and I wouldn't say it to anyone but you. She was bred in a bad school — brought up, so I understood from a man who had known her as a girl, in Southsea, by a widowed mother as pretty as herself. Her first husband —"

"But — but surely Colonel Crofton was her first husband?"

"No," again Radmore avoided looking at his companion, "she's been married twice. Her first husband, a good-looking young chap in the 11th Hussars, died quite soon after the marriage, the two of them having 'blued' all they had between them. I suppose she foolishly thought there was nothing left for it but for her to marry Colonel Crofton. And the real trouble was that Colonel Crofton was poor. I fancy they'd have got on perfectly well if he had had pots of money."

"I — I don't agree to that," Jack said hotly.

"I'm afraid it's true. But we really oughtn't to discuss a woman, even as we are doing now. The only excuse is that we're both so fond of her," said Radmore lightly.

But even as he spoke he felt heavy-hearted. Jack Tosswill had got it very badly, far worse than he had suspected, and somehow he didn't believe that the medicine he had just administered had done the young man any good.

Chapter XXIV

*T*wo days went by, and now Saturday had come round again.

In a sense nothing had happened during those two days, and to some of the inmates of Old Place the week had seemed extremely long and dull.

Mrs. Crofton had suddenly gone up to town for two nights, and both Jack and Rosamund, in their very different ways, felt depressed and lonely in consequence. But she was coming back today, and Rosamund was going to meet her at the station with the Old Place pony cart.

At breakfast Rosamund suggested that perhaps Godfrey might like to motor her there instead, but to her vexation he didn't "rise" at all. He simply observed, rather shortly, that he was going on a rather long business expedition: and Rosamund retorted, pertly, "Business on a Saturday? How strange!" to receive the dry reply: "Yes, it does seem strange, doesn't it?"

Half an hour later Betty and Timmy were busily engaged in washing up the breakfast things when Godfrey Radmore strolled into the scullery.

"I thought that I was always to be in on this act?" he exclaimed. And it was true that he had fallen into the way of helping to wash up, turning what had always been a very boresome task into what Timmy to himself called "great fun" for while Radmore washed and dried the plates and dishes, he told them funny things about some of his early experiences in Australia.

"We've done quite well without you. We're nearly through," said Betty merrily. Somehow she felt extraordinarily light-hearted today.

Her visitor — for very well she knew he was her visitor rather than Timmy's — came a little nearer, and shut the scullery door behind him.

"Look here," he said mysteriously, "I want just us three to take a secret expedition today. I think I've found my house of dreams! If you'll then both run upstairs and put on your things, we could go there and be back in quite good time for tea."

"For tea?" repeated Betty, startled. "But who would look after lunch?"

"There's plenty of delicious cold mutton in the house," said Radmore decidedly. He added with a certain touch of cunning: "I did ask your mother, Timmy, if she'd come too, but she can't leave the house this morning: she's expecting a very important telephone message — something to do with the garden. She'll see about lunch, for she's particularly anxious," — he turned to Betty, — "that *you* should have a good blow this time. We shall get a little lunch while we are out, and be home by four."

"Let's take lunch with us," broke in Timmy eagerly. "We can eat it anywhere." He had always had a passion for picnics.

Betty was the last human being to make any unnecessary fuss. Also, somehow, she felt as if today was not quite like other days. She could not have told why. "All right. I'll cut some sandwiches, and then I'll go and get ready," she said.

Janet was in the hall when Betty came down.

"That's right," she said heartily, "I'm glad you're going to have a real outing at last!"

She took the girl in her arms and kissed her, and Betty felt touched. Her step-mother was not given to affectionate demonstration. And then, all at once, Janet looked round and said in a low voice: "Betty, I'm dreadfully worried about Jack. D'you think it's conceivably possible that there's anything *serious* between him and Mrs. Crofton?"

Betty hardly knew what to answer. For some days past she had felt quite sure that there was something between those two. Jack had been so odd, so unlike himself, and once he had said to her, "Betty, I do wish you'd make friends with Mrs. Crofton. After all you're my sister . . ." and then they had been, perhaps fortunately, interrupted. But if there was anything between Jack and the fascinating widow, Rosamund, who was so devoted to Enid Crofton, knew nothing of it.

"I really can't say," she answered at last, "I've hardly ever felt so doubtful about anything in my life! Sometimes I think there is, and sometimes I think there isn't."

"I'm afraid there's no doubt as to what *he* feels. I happen to know she's just had a very good offer for The Trellis House — seven guineas a week for six months. But she seems to have settled in here for good and all, doesn't she?"

"I wonder if she really has," said Betty. And then she grew a little pink.

Deep in her heart she had felt quite convinced that Mrs. Crofton had come to Beechfield for Godfrey Radmore, and for no other reason. Now she wondered if she had been unjust.

"How I wish she'd stay away *now,* even for a few days longer!" exclaimed Janet.

At that moment Timmy rushed into the hall, Radmore drove up in his motor, and in a couple of minutes the three were off — Janet looking after them, a touch of wistful longing and anxiety in her kind heart.

She had hoped somehow, that Godfrey would persuade Betty to go alone with him today, and she was wondering now whether she could have said a word to Timmy. Her child was so unlike other little boys. If selfish, he was very understanding where the few people he cared for were concerned, and his mother had never known him to give her away.

But the harm, if harm there was, was done now, and for some things she was not sorry to get rid of Timmy for some hours. There had arisen between the boy and his eldest half-brother a disagreeable state of tension. Timmy seemed to take pleasure in teasing Jack, and Jack was not in the humor to bear even the smallest practical joke just now.

*O*n and on sped the party in the motor, Timmy sitting by his godfather in front, Betty, in lonely state, behind.

They hadn't gone very far before the countryside began to have all the charm of strangeness to Betty Tosswill, and she found herself enjoying the change of scene as only a person who has been cooped up in one familiar place for a considerable time can enjoy it.

"Why, we must be on the borders of Sussex!" she called out, at a point where Radmore, slowing down, was consulting a sign-post. He turned round and nodded.

They started again. And then something rather absurd happened. Betty's hat blew off! It was an ordinary, rather floppy hat, and she had tied it on, as she thought, securely with a veil under her chin.

Both Timmy and Radmore jumped out to pick the hat up, and as they came back towards the car, Timmy exclaimed: "It's a shame that Betty hasn't got a proper motor bonnet! Rosamund's got a lovely one."

"Why hasn't Betty got one?"

"Because they're so expensive," said Timmy simply. He went on, "When I've got lots of money, I shall give Betty heaps of beautiful clothes; but only one very plain dress apiece to Rosamund and Dolly."

"Betty! You ought to have a motor bonnet," called out Radmore as he came up to the car.

Her fair hair, blowing in the wind, formed an aureole round her face. She looked very, very different to the staid Betty of Old Place.

She answered merrily: "So I will when my ship comes home! I had one before the War, and I stupidly gave it away."

"Surely we might get one somewhere today," suggested Radmore.

"Get one today — what an extraordinary idea? Motor bonnets don't grow on hedges —"

But when they were going through — was it Horsham? — Radmore, alone of the three, espied a funny little shop. It was called "The Bandbox": its woodwork was painted bright green, and in the window were three hats.

"Now then," he exclaimed, slowing down, "this, I take it, is where motor bonnets grow. At any rate we'll get down and see."

"What a lark!" cried Timmy delightedly. "Please, *please* Betty, don't make yourself disagreeable — don't be a 'govvey'!"

And Betty, not wishing to be a "govvey," got out of the car.

"But I've no money with me," she began.

"I wouldn't let you pay for what's going to be a present," said Radmore shortly. "You're the only inhabitant of Old Place to whom I haven't given a present since I've been home."

Home? It gave Betty such pleasure to hear him call it that.

They all three marched into the tiny shop where the owner of "The Bandbox," described by Timmy to his mother, later, as a "rather spidery-looking, real lady," sat sewing.

She received them with a mixture of condescension and pleasure at the thought of a new customer, which diverted Radmore, who was new to the phenomenon of the lady shopkeeper. But when it came to business, she took a very great deal of trouble, bringing out what seemed, at the time, the whole of her considerable stock, for "The Bandbox" was cleverly lined with deep, dust-proof cupboards.

At last she produced a quaint-looking little blue and purple bonnet, with an exquisitely soft long motor veil of grey chiffon.

"My sister is at Monte Carlo," she observed, "and when she was passing through Paris she got me a dozen early autumn models. I have already copied this model in other colors, but this is the original motor bonnet. May I advise that you try it on?"

It was in its way a delightful bit of color, and Betty hardly knew herself when she looked in the glass and saw what a very pretty reflection was presented there. She was startled — but oh, how pleasantly startled — to see how young she still could look.

"Of course you must have that one," said Radmore, in a matter of fact tone, "and leave the horrid thing you wore coming here behind you." Then he turned to Timmy: — "Now then, don't you think *you* could choose something for your mother?"

The lady of the shop turned patronizingly towards the little boy. She went across to a corner cupboard and opened what appeared to be a rather secret receptacle. Though she had not been in business long, she already realized what an advantage it is to deal, as regards feminine fripperies, with a man-customer. Also, Radmore, almost in spite of himself, looked opulent.

"I think I have the very thing!" she explained. "It's a little on the fantastic side, and so only suits a certain type of face."

As she spoke she brought out a miniature brown poke bonnet which was wreathed with one uncurled ostrich feather of a peculiar powder blue tint. She put it deftly on Betty's head, then stepped back and gazed delightedly into the smiling face and dancing eyes of her new client.

"I have kept this back," she began, "hoping I should come across a bride-elect whom it might really suit, for it would make a perfect 'going-away' hat! But it is so extraordinarily becoming to *this* lady, that I feel I ought to let *her* have it!"

She turned appealingly to Radmore, but Timmy intervened: — "That's not my mother!" he cried, going off into fits of laughter. "We want a hat for my *mother*. That's only my sister!"

The shop-lady looked vexed, and Radmore felt awkward. He realized that he and Betty had been taken for husband and wife, Timmy for their spoilt little boy.

"I'm quite sure I could find something that would suit Janet," exclaimed Betty, hastily taking off the delightful bit of headgear.

She put on the motor bonnet again, and then she went over to where a black garden hat, with just one rose on the brim, and with long blue velvet strings, was lying on a table.

"I think Timmy's mother would look very nice in this," she said smiling.

The black hat was slipped into a big paper-bag, and handed to Timmy. Then Radmore exclaimed: "Now then, we've no time to lose! Help your sister into the car, Timmy, while I stop behind and pay the bill."

The bill did not take a minute to make out, and Radmore was rather surprised to find that the three hats — for he bought three — cost him not far short of fifteen pounds between them, though the lady observed pleasantly, "Of course I can afford to sell my hats at a *much* less price than London people charge."

To Betty's eyes, Godfrey looked rather funny when he came out of the gay little painted door with a flower-covered bandbox slung over his right arm.

She had thought it just a little mean that the shop-woman should give Timmy Janet's hat in a paper-bag. Though Betty would have been horrified indeed at the prices paid by Radmore, she yet suspected that "The Bandbox" lady asked quite enough for her pretty wares to be able to throw in a cardboard box, so "Is that for Janet's hat?" she called out.

"This," he said, looking up at her, "is that queer-looking brown thing with the blue feather that suited you so well. Of course I meant you to have it too."

Betty felt at once disturbed, and yet, absurdly pleased. "I'm afraid it was very expensive," she began. And then suddenly Radmore told himself that after all the poke bonnet had been cheap indeed if the thought of it could bring such a sparkle into Betty's eyes, and such a vivid while delicate color to her cheeks.

There came a day, as a matter of fact the day when Betty wore that quaint-looking bonnet for the first time, when she did venture to ask Godfrey what it had cost. He refused to tell her, simply saying that whatever he had paid he had had the best of the bargain as it had been worth its weight in gold. Even so it is very unlikely that she will ever know what that queer little bonnet, which she intends to keep as long as she lives, really meant to Godfrey Radmore — how it had suddenly made him feel that here was the young Betty of nine years ago come back, never to disappear into the mists of time again.

Something else happened in the High Street of that little Sussex town. Radmore decided that it was Timmy's turn to sit behind, and the boy gave in with a fairly good grace; though after they had left the houses behind them and were again moving swiftly between brown hedges, he called out patronizingly: — "The back of your head looks very nice now, Betty — quite different to what it looked in that horrid old hat you left in the shop."

At last the car slowed down in front of a gate, on one side of which was a big board. On this board was painted a statement to the effect that the historic estate of Doryford House was to be let or sold, furnished or unfurnished, "Apply to the principal London agents."

The finding of the place had not been quite easy, and Radmore drew a breath of relief as he helped Betty down.

"When Timmy and I were last here," he said hurriedly, "there was a child very ill at the lodge. So I think I'd better go and just find how things are."

He was hoping with all his heart that the news he would see on the mother's face would be good news. Somehow he felt that it would be of happy augury for himself.

As he rang the bell his heart was beating — a feeling of acute suspense had suddenly come over him, of which he was secretly ashamed, for it was almost entirely a selfish distress. And then, when the door opened, he saw that all was well, for the young woman's worn face was radiant.

"Is that you, sir? Oh, I did hope that you would come again!" she exclaimed, "The doctor says that my little girl's certain to get well. I was terrible anxious the day before yesterday, but now though she's weak and wan, you'd hardly know she'd been bad, sir."

"I wonder if you could give me the keys of Doryford House?" began Radmore. "I want to go over it, and we need not trouble you to come with us."

"I'm supposed always to go up with visitors," she said hesitatingly, "even if I leaves them there," but she looked troubled at the thought of leaving her child. Then, all at once, Radmore had a happy inspiration.

"Would you feel easier if we left the little boy we've brought with us in charge? He's very intelligent. He might sit in your kitchen."

She looked across to where Betty Tosswill and Timmy were standing. "Why, yes!" she exclaimed, relieved. "If the young gentleman don't mind, perhaps he would sit with Rosie. 'Tain't nothing infectious, you know, sir, and it would please her like to have a visitor. She's got a book in which there's a picture of a little sick girl and someone coming to see her. She said to me yesterday, 'No one comes to see me, mother, 'cepting doctor.'"

Radmore went off to the other two.

"The woman evidently feels that she ought to come up herself to the house. But she's nervous about leaving her little girl. I was wondering whether Timmy would mind staying and amusing the child? We might have our picnic in the house itself, if it's in any way possible."

"What sort of a little girl is she?" began Timmy, but his godfather cut him short.

"Never mind what sort of a little girl she is — she's longing for a visitor, and you will be the first one to see her since she's been ill."

He turned to Betty. "Perhaps you'd like to go in and see what sort of a place it is? Meanwhile I'll open the gate and get the car through."

Betty and Timmy followed the woman through the kitchen of the lodge to a bedroom, where lay a pale-faced little girl of six. On the patchwork counterpane were a pair of scissors and a big sheet of paper. It was evident that the child had been trying to amuse herself by cutting out patterns. As the visitors came in, she sat up, and her little face flushed with joy. Here was her dream come true! Here were some visitors — a beautiful lady in a peculiarly lovely blue bonnet, and a pleasant-looking young gentleman too!

Timmy, who was quite unshy, went up to her bedside. "Good-morning," he said in a polite, old-fashioned way. "I'm sorry you're ill, and I hope you'll soon be quite well. I've come to look after you while your mother goes up to the house with my godfather and my sister. If you like, I'll cut you some beautiful fairy figures out of that paper, and then we can pretend they're dancing."

He looked round and espied a chair, which he brought up close to the bed.

Rosie was far too excited and shy to speak.

"What's your name?" he began. "Mine is Timothy Godfrey Radmore Tosswill."

The little girl whispered "Rosamund."

"I've got a sister called Rosamund; now, isn't that curious?" cried Timmy.

He had already seized the scissors, and was engaged in cutting out some quaint, fantastic looking little figures.

After the others had left the room, Rosamund's mother turned to Betty. "I never saw such a nice, kind, young gentleman!" she exclaimed. "He fair took my breath away — a regular little doctor he'd make."

*H*ouses are like people — they have their day, their hour, even, one feels inclined to add, their moods of sadness and of joy, of brightness and of dullness.

Today the white Corinthian-looking building called Doryford House was at its best, in the soft lambent light of an autumn day. For a moment, when the long, pillared building first came into view, Radmore had felt a thrill of unreasonable disappointment. He had hoped, somehow, for a red-brick manor-house — a kind of glorified Old Place. But a few minutes later, when the mahogany front doors had been unlocked, and they passed into a light, circular hall and so into a delightful-looking sunny drawing room filled with enchanting examples of 18th century furniture, he began to think that this was, after all, a very attractive house.

"In what wonderful order everything seems to be!" he exclaimed. "Have the people to whom the place belongs only just left it?"

"It's this way, sir. The gentleman to whom it belongs has several other homes — he don't care for this place at all. But it's all kep' up proper — one of the gardeners sees to the furnace — and about all this here furniture, anybody who takes the house unfurnished, or buys the place, will be able to keep what they likes at a valuation. Perhaps you and your lady would like to go over the house by yourselves? People often do, I notice. If you'll excuse me, I'll just nip away. I wants to go to the village for a few minutes — that is if your little boy will be so kind as to stay with my Rosie till I'm back."

"I'm sure he will," said Radmore heartily. He told himself that it was very natural that everyone should think that he and Betty were married.

The front door shut behind the caretaker, and the two left behind began going through the ground floor of the great empty house. Their progress gave Betty an eerie feeling. She felt as if she was in a kind of dream; the more so that this was quite unlike any country house into which she had ever been.

They finally came to the last living room of all, and both exclaimed together: "This is the room I like best of all!"

It was an octagon library, lined with mahogany bookcases filled with bound books which looked as though they hadn't been disturbed for fifty years. The wide, fan-shaped window looked out on a formal rose garden.

And then, all at once, Radmore's quick eye detected a concealed door in the wall, on which there were encrusted the sham book titles often to be found on the doors of an old country home library. Quickly he went across and, opening it, found it gave straight on to a corkscrew staircase.

Filled with a queer sense of adventure, he motioned Betty to go up first, in front of him.

The staircase led up to a tiny lobby, into which opened a most beautiful bedchamber, a replica as to shape and size of the library beneath.

The furniture there interested Betty, for she had never seen anything like it, except once in a château near Arras. It was First Empire, and on the pincushion, lying on the ornate dressing-table, someone had written in a fine Italian hand on an envelope, the words: "This room was furnished from Paris in 1810. The bed is a replica of a bed made for the Empress Josephine."

They went on through many of the rooms on the upper floor, full today of still, sunny late autumn charm.

Radmore scarcely spoke at all during their curious progress through the empty house, and Betty still felt as if in a dream. She had asked herself again and again if he could really be thinking of buying this stately mansion.

The mere possibility of such a thing meant that he must be thinking of marrying Mrs. Crofton, and also that he must be much richer than any of them knew.

At last they came down a wide staircase which terminated in a corridor leading into the circular hall, and then it was Betty who broke what was becoming an oppressive silence:

"Shall we go on and see the kitchen and the servants' quarters, Godfrey?"

"No; they're sure to be all right."

Again came what seemed to Betty a long, unnatural silence.

"Do you really like the house?" he asked at last.

"I like it very much," she said frankly. "But wouldn't it cost a tremendous lot of money, Godfrey? It would be a pity not to buy it exactly as it stands. It all seems so — so —"

"I know! As if the furniture had grown there," he broke in.

"So beautiful and so — so unusual," Betty went on diffidently.

"I'm afraid I'm a commonplace person, Betty. I like a room to be beautiful, but I like comfort, and I think this is a very comfortable house. I feel, somehow, as if happy, good people had lived here. I like that, too."

He was standing by one of the round pillars which carried out the type of architecture which had been the fashion at the time Doryford was built; and he was gazing at her with what seemed to her a rather odd expression on his dark face. Was he going to tell her of his hopes or intention with regard to Mrs. Crofton?

Betty felt, for the first time that day, intensely shy. She walked away, towards the big half-moon window opposite the front door. A wide grass gallop, bordered with splendid old trees, stretched out as if illimitable, and she began gazing down it with unseeing eyes.

He came quickly across the hall, and stood by her. Then he said slowly, "I'm wondering, wondering, wondering if I shall ever be in this house again!"

"You must think it well over," she began.

But he cut her short. "It depends on *you* whether Doryford becomes my home or not."

"On me?" she repeated, troubled. "Don't trust to my taste as much as that, Godfrey."

"But you do like it?" he asked insistently.

"Of course I like it. If it comes to that, I don't know that I've ever been in so beautiful and perfect a house. And then, well perhaps because we've everything so shabby at Old Place, I do like to see everything in such apple-pie order!"

A little disappointed, he went on, "I fear it isn't your ideal house, Betty? Not your house of dreams?"

And then, all at once, she knew that she couldn't answer him, for tears had welled up in her eyes, and choked her speech.

Her house of dreams? Betty Tosswill's house of dreams had vanished, she thought, forever, so very long ago. Betty's house of dreams had been quite a small house — but such a cozy, happy place, full of the Godfrey of long ago, and of good, delicious dream children. . . .

She turned her head away.

"Well," he exclaimed, "that's that! We won't think about this house again. We'll go and look at another place tomorrow."

His matter-of-fact, rather cross, tone made her pull herself together. What a baby he was after all!

"Don't be absurd, Godfrey. I don't believe if we were to look England through, that I should see a house I thought more delightful than this house. I'm a little overawed by it, that's all! You see I've never dwelt in marble halls —"

"Oh, one gets used to that!"

"Yes, I expect one does."

"Whether I buy this place depends on you," he said obstinately.

"Well, then, if I'm to decide, I say buy it!" She turned and smiled at him a little tremulously, keeping her head well down — her face shadowed by the deep brim of her motor-bonnet.

More and more was this like a scene out of a dream to Betty Tosswill. In a way, it was, of course, natural that she and Godfrey should be alone, and that he should turn to her as his closest friend. And yet it seemed strange and unnatural, too. But Betty had a very generous nature — and to this man, who was looking at her with such an eager, searching look, she felt in a peculiar relation. So she repeated, with greater ease and lightness, "Let's settle, here and now, that this is to be the future residence of Godfrey Radmore, Esquire! Timmy's a little bit like a cat, you know. He'll simply adore this house. He'll love all the pretty things in it. Perhaps you'd run him up in the motor presently, while I stay with the little girl and that nice woman?"

And then all at once he took a step forward and roughly took her two hands in his: "Betty," he said, "don't you understand? I shall never enter this house again unless you're willing to come and share it with me. No place would be home to me without you in it. Why, Old Place is only home now because you're there."

She looked at him with a long, searching, measuring look; a look that was, unconsciously, full of questioning; but her hands remained in his strong grasp.

"Don't you know that I've always been yours?" he asked — "that I shall always be yours even if you won't have me — even if I end by marrying another woman, as I daresay I shall do if you won't have me, for I'm a lonely chap —" And then something in her face made him add: "Try to love me again, Betty. I want you to say to yourself — 'a poor thing but mine own.' Do, my dear."

And then Betty burst out crying, and found herself clasped in his arms, strained to his heart, while his lips sought and found her soft, tremulous mouth.

He was gentle with her, gentle and strangely restrained. And yet as the happy moments went by in that silent, sunny house, something deep in her still troubled heart told her that Radmore really loved her — loved her as perhaps he had not loved her ten years ago, in his hot, selfish, impulsive youth.

"We needn't tell anyone for a little while, need we?" she whispered at last.

She had shared her life, given her services to so many during the last nine years, and she longed to keep this strange new joy a secret for a while.

"If you like, we need never tell them at all," he answered. "We can just go out, find a church, and be married!"

"Oh, no; that wouldn't be fair to Janet." And yet the notion of doing this fascinated her.

Chapter XXV

*A*nd meanwhile what had been going on at Old Place? Outwardly very little, yet one long-expected, though when it happened, surprising, thing had occurred. Also Janet, as the day went on, felt more and more worried about Jack.

He wandered in and out of the house like an unhappy, unquiet spirit, for the sudden departure of Enid Crofton for London two days before had taken him utterly by surprise, the more so that she had left no address, and he was suspicious of — he knew not what! It was reasonable to suppose she had gone to pay the debt for which he had provided the money; but then why keep her address in town secret from him?

At last, this morning, there had come a postcard to Rosamund, asking to be met at the station, alone, with the Old Place pony-cart. It was a reasonable request, for the funny little vehicle only held two people and a minute quantity of luggage. Still Jack had felt annoyed she had not asked him to meet her. She seemed to him absurdly overcautious.

About ten minutes before the motoring party's return, Rosamund hurried in with a casual message that Enid was very tired, and so had gone straight to bed; that she hoped some of them would come in and see her on the morrow, Sunday. In any case they would all meet at church.

Jack was puzzled, hurt, and bitterly disappointed, and at once he went off to write a note which should be, while wildly loving, yet clear in its expressions of surprise that she had not sent him some sort of message appointing a time for their next meeting. He found the letter unexpectedly difficult to write, and he had already torn up two beginnings, when the door behind him burst open, and, turning round irritably, he saw Timmy rush across to a window and shout exultantly, "Mum? We're back! And we've brought Josephine and her kittens. Mr. Trotman said she'd be all right now."

Jack Tosswill jumped up from his chair. It was as if his pent-up feelings of anger had found a vent at last: "You have, have you?" he cried in an enraged voice. "Then I'll see to the shooting of the brute this very minute!"

Quick as thought, Timmy rushed back to the door and turned the key in the lock. Then he bounded again to the open window. "Mum!" he screamed at the top of his voice. "Come here — I'm frightened!"

Janet Tosswill, walking quickly across the lawn, was horrified at the look of angry despair on the child's face.

"What's happened?" she asked, and then, suddenly, she saw Jack's blazing eyes.

"J-Janet," he began, stuttering in his rage, "either that cat is shot today, or I leave this house forever."

Even in the midst of poor Janet's agitation, she could not help smiling at the melodramatic tone in which the usually self-contained Jack uttered his threat. Still —

"It was very, very wrong of you, Timmy, to bring back your cat today," she said sternly. "Had I known there was any idea of such a thing I should have absolutely forbidden it. Josephine is not fit to come back here yet; you know what Dr. O'Farrell said."

The color was coming back into Timmy's face. He had a touching belief in his mother's power of saving him from the consequences of his own naughty actions.

"I'm very sorry," he began whimperingly. "It was not my fault, Mum. Even Mr. Trotman said there was nothing the matter with her."

And now Jack was beginning to repent of his hasty, cruel words. He was as angry as ever with Timmy, but he was ashamed of having spoken as he had done to Janet — the woman who, as he knew deep in his heart, was not only the best of step-mothers, but the best of friends, to his sisters and himself.

"Of course I don't mind her being at Trotman's, but I do very much object to her being here," he said ungraciously.

"I'll see about her being sent back to Epsom today," said Janet quietly. She turned to her son: "Now then, Timmy, I'm afraid we shall have to ask poor Godfrey to start back at once after tea."

"Oh, I say," called out Jack awkwardly. "I don't want the cat to go as soon as that, Janet. Tomorrow will do all right. All I ask is that the brute shall be taken away before it has a chance of seeing Mrs. Crofton again."

"Very well; the cat shall go tomorrow."

Drawing her little boy quickly after her, Janet left the drawing room, crossed the corridor, walked into the empty schoolroom, and then, to Timmy's unutterable surprise, burst into bitter tears.

Now Timmy had never seen his mother cry — and she herself was very much taken aback. She would have given a great deal to have been left alone just then to have her cry out, but Timmy's scared little face touched her.

"I can't think why you did it," she sobbed. "I always thought you were such an intelligent boy. Oh, Timmy, surely you understood how angry it would make Jack and Rosamund if you brought Josephine back now, today?"

"I never thought of them," he said woefully. "We were so happy, Mum — Godfrey, Betty and I. Oh, why are people so horrid?"

"Why are people so selfish?" she asked sadly. "I'm surprised at Betty; I should have thought that she, at least, would have understood that the cat must stay away a little longer."

"It wasn't Betty's fault," said Timmy hastily. He waited a moment, then added cunningly, "It was really Mr. Trotman's fault; he said Josephine ought to come home."

But his mother went on a little wildly: "It isn't an easy job, taking over another woman's children — and doing the very best you can for them! Today, Timmy, you've made me feel as if I was sorry that I ever did it."

"Sorry that you married Daddy?" asked Timmy in an awe-struck voice.

Janet Tosswill nodded.

"Sorry that I was ever born?" cried Timmy. He flung his skinny arms round her bent neck.

She looked up and smiled wanly. "No, Timmy, I shall never be able to say that, however naughty you may be."

But Timmy was not to be let off yet.

"What happened today has hurt me very, very much," she went on. "It will be a long time before I shall feel on the old, happy terms with Jack again. Without knowing it, Timmy, you've pierced your mother's heart."

But even as she uttered these, to Timmy, dreadful words, Janet Tosswill got up, and dried her eyes. "Now then, we must go and see about Josephine being shut up in some place of safety, where she and her kittens will not offend the eyes of Jack and Rosamund. How about the old stable?"

She was her own calm, satirical, determined self again. But Timmy felt, perhaps for the first time in his life, deeply conscious of sin. His mother's phrase made him feel very uneasy. Had he really pierced her heart — could a mother's heart be permanently injured by a wicked child?

It was a very mournful, dejected, anxious boy who walked into the kitchen behind Janet Tosswill.

Timmy had a very vivid imagination, and during the drive back he had amused himself by visualizing the scene when he would place Josephine and her kittens in their own delightful, roomy basket in the scullery. It would be such fun, too, introducing Flick to the two kittens! At Betty's suggestion, Flick had been shut out from the scullery after Josephine's kittens were born, and that though the dog and the cat got on extremely well together. In fact, Flick was the only creature in the world with whom Josephine, since she had reached an approximately mature age, ever condescended to play.

And now poor Josephine and her kittens were to be banished to the old stable, and tomorrow driven back ignominiously to Epsom, all because of that tiresome, hateful Mrs. Crofton!

There was no one in the kitchen, and it did not look as tidy as it generally looked; though the luncheon things had been washed up, they had not been put away.

Mother and son walked on into the scullery to find Betty there, boiling some water over a spirit lamp. "Betty? How very delightful you look!" her step-mother exclaimed. "Just like an old picture, child! Wherever did you get that charming motor-bonnet?"

And then Timmy chipped in: "*I* thought of it," he said triumphantly; "it was *my* idea, Mum, but Godfrey paid for it. He said he hadn't given Betty a proper present yet, so he *had* to pay for it, and, and —"

Janet was just a little surprised. She was very old-fashioned in some ways, and she had brought up her step-daughters to be, as regarded money matters at any rate, as old-fashioned as herself. It seemed to her very strange that Betty had allowed Godfrey Radmore to give her such a present as a hat! Yet another thing puzzled her. She had understood that the three of them were going off some way into Sussex to look at a house, but they had evidently been up to London. Motor bonnets don't grow on country hedges.

"Where's the cat?" she asked, looking round.

"Godfrey has taken her up to the nursery," said Betty, "partly to show her to Nanna, and partly because we thought it would be better for her to be quiet up there than down here."

"Oh, Mum — do say that she can stay up there," cried Timmy pleadingly. "I hate the thought of her being in that dark old stable!"

"Very well; put her in the night nursery."

Even as she spoke, Janet was still gazing at her eldest step-daughter. Betty certainly looked extraordinarily charming this afternoon. It showed that the child required more change than she had had for many a long day. They had got too much, all of them, into thinking of her as a stand-by. After all she was only eight and twenty! Janet, with a sigh, looked back to the days when she had been eight and twenty, a very happy, independent young lady indeed, not long before she had met and married her quiet, wool-gathering John, so losing her independence forever.

"I suppose you haven't heard the great news," she exclaimed, forgetting that Timmy was there.

"What news?" asked Betty.

She glanced at her step-mother. Surely Janet hadn't been crying? Janet never cried. She had not cried since that terrible day when the news had come of George's death.

"What news?" she asked again.

"Mr. Barton — I really can't call him Lionel yet — came over this afternoon and — and —"

Timmy rushed forward in front of his mother, his little face all aglow: "Oh, Mum! You don't mean to say that he's popped?" he cried.

"Timmy, don't be vulgar!" exclaimed Janet severely.

Betty began to laugh a little wildly. "How very, very strange that it should have happened today —"

"I don't think it's strange at all," said Janet quietly. "The strange thing is that it hasn't happened before! But there it is — they're engaged now. He seems to have told her that he thought it wrong to make his offer until he had saved £100. She has gone over to Oakford, and they are busy making an inventory of the things they will have to buy."

"Has he actually saved £100?" asked Betty.

"No, he never could have done that. He's had a legacy left him, and he seems to think that £100 will start them most splendidly and comfortably on their married life. He *is* a fool!"

The door which gave on to the stairs which led from the scullery to the upper floor opened, and Godfrey Radmore stepped down. "Am I the fool?" he asked pleasantly.

Janet answered, smiling: "No, no; you're anything but that. I was only telling Betty that Dolly and Mr. Barton are engaged at last." She turned to Betty. "Of course, he's coming to supper tonight. I've been wondering what we can do in the way of something extra to celebrate the occasion. We *were* going to have cold mutton."

"At any rate I'll go and see what the village pub. can produce in the way of champagne," exclaimed Godfrey. He turned to his godson. "Timmy? Run up and look at Josephine and her kittens. I've put them in the old night nursery for a bit."

And then, when the boy had gone, he went up to Janet and, to her surprise, put his arm through hers: "I'm glad about Dolly," he said heartily.

"It proves how very little one really knows of human nature." She sighed, but it was a happy sigh. "I was beginning to believe that he would never what Timmy calls 'pop,' and yet the poor fellow was only waiting to be a little forward in the world. Someone's left him £100, so he felt he could embark on the great adventure. Your father and I have already talked it over a little" — she turned to Betty — "and we think we could squeeze out £100 a year somehow."

"I think we could," said Betty, hesitatingly. "After all, £1 is now only what 8/- was before the War."

"But not to us," cried Janet; "not to us!"

And then, to the utter discomfiture of both her companions, she began to laugh and cry together.

Godfrey rushed over to the sink. He took up a cup, filled it with water, rushed back to where Janet was standing, shaking, trembling all over, making heroic efforts to suppress her mingled tears and laughter, and dashed the water into her face.

"Thank you," she gasped; "thank you, Godfrey! I'm all right now. I may as well tell you both the truth. There's been a row — an awful row — between Jack and Timmy, and it thoroughly upset me. It was only over the cat — over Josephine — but of course it proved that what Betty and I were talking about this morning is true. Jack's madly in love with Mrs. Crofton — and — and — it's all so pitiful and absurd —"

"I doubt if you're quite fair to Mrs. Crofton, Janet," said Godfrey, in a singular tone. "I fancy she really does care for Jack. Of course it seems odd to all of us, but still, after all, odder things have been known! If you ask me whether they will marry in the end — that's quite another matter. If you ask me whether they're engaged, well, yes, I'm inclined to think they are!"

Even Betty felt violently disturbed and astonished.

"Oh, Godfrey!" she exclaimed. "D'you really think that?"

"I can't tell you what makes me think so, or rather I'd rather not tell you. But I don't think you need worry, if you'll only take a long view. They can't marry yet, and long before they could marry, she'll have got tired of him, and fond of someone else."

Betty gave him a quick look. Was he really unconscious of the reason why Mrs. Crofton had come to Beechfield?

Through her mind in a flash there crowded the many small, almost imperceptible, impressions made on her mind by the new tenant of The Trellis House. Enid Crofton in love with Jack? Betty shook her head. The idea was absurd. And yet Godfrey had spoken very decidedly just now. But men, even very shrewd, intelligent men, are at a hopeless disadvantage when dealing with the type of woman to which Enid Crofton belonged.

As for Janet she exclaimed, with sudden passion, "I would give anything in this world to see Mrs. Crofton leave Beechfield forever —" She stopped abruptly, for at that moment the staircase door to her right burst open, and Timmy stepped down into the scullery.

Chapter XXVI

*S*ince she had had the horrid accident which had laid her up, Timmy had not gone to see his old Nanna nearly as often as he ought to have done. Nanna herself, however, with the natural cunning of those who love, had made certain rules which ensured her a regular, daily glimpse of the strange little being she had had under her charge, as she would have expressed it, "from the month." Nanna did not desire his attendance before breakfast for she would not have considered herself fit to be seen by him till she herself was neat and tidy. Like all the women of her class and generation, the Tosswills' old family nurse was full of self-respect, and also imbued with a stern sense of duty. Timmy stood far more in awe of her than he did of his mother.

One of the stated times for Timmy's visits to the old night nursery was just before he had to start for church each Sunday, and on this particular Sunday, the day after that on which had occurred Dolly's engagement, and Mrs. Crofton's return from London, he came in a few moments before he was expected, and began wandering about the room, doing nothing in particular. At once Nanna divined that he had something on his mind about which he was longing, yet half afraid, to speak to her. She said nothing, however, and at last it came out.

"I want you to lend me your Bible," he said, wriggling himself about. "I want to take it to church with me."

This was the last thing Nanna had expected the boy to ask, for, of course, Timmy had a Bible of his own, a beautiful thin-paper Bible, which she herself had given him on his seventh birthday, having first asked his mother's leave if she might do so. The Bible was in perfect condition. It stood on a little mat on his chest of drawers, and not long before her accident Nanna had gone into his bedroom, opened the sacred Book, and gazed with pleasure on the inscription, written in her own large, unformed handwriting, on the first page:

Timothy Godfrey Radmore Tosswill on his seventh birthday from his loving nurse,

EMILY PEW

All this being so, his mother, or even his sister, Betty, would at once have enquired, "Why don't you take your own Bible to church?" But somehow Nanna thought it best not to put this question, for a lie, shocking on any day, is more shocking than usual, or so she thought, if uttered on a Sunday. So, after a moment's hesitation, she replied: "Certainly, Master Timmy, if such is your wish. But I trust you will be very careful with it, my dear."

"I will be very, very careful!" he exclaimed. "And I will bring it straight back to you up here after church."

He threw her a grateful look. He did more, and Nanna felt amply rewarded as he climbed up on her bed and, putting his arms round her neck, kissed her on each cheek.

"I hope," she said impressively, "that you are going to be a good boy in church — a boy that Nurse can be proud of."

Nanna never called herself "Nanna" to the children.

"I am always very good in church," cried Timmy, offended. "I don't see why you should go and spoil everything by saying that!" With these cryptic words he slid off the bed, taking with him the large old-fashioned Bible which always lay by Nanna's bedside.

Dolly, and Rosamund, who was Dolly's stable-companion, were attending the service held by Dolly's fiancé, Lionel Barton, in the next parish. As for Betty, her heart was very full, and as she did her morning's work and while she dressed herself for church, she still felt as if she was living through a wonderful dream.

Jack, who did not always go to church, had elected to go today; so had Tom and Godfrey; and thus, in spite of the absence of the two younger girls, quite a considerable party filed into the Tosswill pew.

All the people belonging to Old Place were far too much absorbed in their own thoughts on this rather strange Sunday morning to give any thought to Timmy. So it was that he managed, after a moment's thought, to place himself between his father and his godfather. He judged, rightly, that neither of them would be likely to pay much attention to him or to his doings.

When the rather nervous young rector had got well away with his sermon, and had begun to attract the serious attention of Mr. Tosswill and of Godfrey Radmore, Timmy very quietly drew out of his little, worn tweed coat a long sharp pin. Wedging the Bible, as he hoped reverently, but undoubtedly very securely between his knees, he thrust the pin firmly in the middle of the faded, gilt-edged leaves of Nanna's Bible, where there were already many curious little brown dots caused by similar punctures, the work of Nanna herself.

Having done this, Timmy carefully lifted the Bible from between his knees and let it fall open at the page the pin had found. The text where the point rested ran as follows:

Deliver my soul from the sword; my darling from the power of the dog.

His father's eyes flickered for a moment and fixed themselves on Timmy with a worried, disturbed expression. As a child he himself would have been sternly reproved for reading, even the Bible, during a sermon, but he supposed that Janet knew better than his own mother had done. Timmy certainly loved Janet far, far more than he, John Tosswill, had loved his own good mother. So he averted his eyes from his little son, and tried to forget all about him.

But John Tosswill did not know his Janet. Though three off from Timmy, she had become aware that her son was bending over a very big, shabby-looking book, instead of sitting upright, listening sedately. She gave him one glance, and Timmy, with a rather confused and guilty look, hurriedly shut Nanna's Bible, and turned his mind to the sermon. He had seen what he wanted to see; and further, he had made a mental note of the page and place.

At last the service was over, and the congregation streamed out of church. Timmy hung back a little, behind his mother. He did not wish her to see that he had Nanna's Bible instead of his own, but she was far too full of her own exciting and anxious thoughts to give any attention to her little boy. Rather to her surprise, she found her mind dwelling persistently on Enid Crofton. It was at once a relief and a disappointment not to see the young widow's graceful figure, and her heart ached when she saw the cloud come down over Jack's face.

All at once she felt a detaining gesture on her arm, and turning, she found Miss Pendarth at her elbow. They generally had a little talk after church, for it was often the only time in the week when these two, both in their several ways busy women, felt that they had a few minutes to spare for gossip.

"I wonder if you could come in to Rose Cottage for a minute? I want to show you something which I think will interest you as much as it has me."

Neither of them noticed that Timmy had crept up quite close and was listening eagerly. In a village community the gossip holds a place apart, and Olivia Pendarth, though by no means popular with the young people of Old Place, nevertheless had her value as the source of many thrilling tales.

Janet Tosswill hesitated. "I wish I could come back with you," she said at last, regretfully. "But I promised to go straight home this morning."

She debated within herself whether she should say anything here and now about Dolly's engagement; then she made up her mind not to do so yet.

Miss Pendarth, slightly lowering her voice, went on: "Perhaps I might come in this afternoon, and bring what I want to show you with me? It's a full report of the inquest held on Colonel Crofton."

Janet looked up quickly. "I confess I should very much like to read that," she exclaimed, and then she added, "but I shan't be in this afternoon. I've promised to go over to Oakford."

That much information she would vouchsafe her old friend.

A slightly satirical look came over Miss Pendarth's face. She told herself how foolish it was of Janet to suppose for a single moment that that good-looking young clergyman was ever likely to make an offer to tiresome, stupid, untidy Dolly Tosswill!

"I wonder if you would lend me the paper?" Janet suggested hesitatingly. "Timmy could go for it now, and I would send it you back the moment I had read it."

"Very well," said the other, not very graciously. "I suppose Timmy can be trusted to be careful of it? I went to great trouble to get a copy, and I don't think I should be able to get another." She added slowly: "I got it at the request of Colonel Crofton's sister, but I have not yet sent it to her because I thought it would distress her too much."

A few minutes later Timmy was gazing round the hall of Rose Cottage with eager, inquisitive eyes. Miss Pendarth did not care for children, and though Timmy frequently came to her door with a note, he was very seldom invited inside the house.

Even now his hostess said rather sharply: "Run out into the garden, Timmy, while I go upstairs and find an envelope big enough in which to put the paper for your mother. I daresay I shall be away five minutes, for I want you to take her a note with it."

The boy went through the glass door into the garden. He walked briskly up the path, kicking a pebble as he went, and then he sat down on the bench where, not so very long ago, Olivia Pendarth and Godfrey Radmore had sat discussing the curious and tragic occurrence which still filled Miss Pendarth's mind.

Timmy asked himself what exactly was the meaning of the word inquest? Why had a paper printed what Miss Pendarth called a full account of the inquest on Colonel Crofton's death? Was it "inquest" or "henquest?" His agile mind swung back to the mysterious words he had heard Mrs. Crofton's ex-man-servant utter in the stable-yard of The Trellis House.

At last Miss Pendarth opened the door giving into the garden, and Timmy, jumping up, hurried down the path toward the house. He then saw that she held a neat-looking brown paper roll in her hand, and over the roll was slipped an India-rubber band.

"I thought it a pity to waste a big envelope," she observed, "so I have done up the newspaper and my note to your mother into a roll. Will you please ask your mother to put it back exactly as it is now — with the rubber-rubber band round it? These bands have become so very expensive. She need not send it back. I will call for it tomorrow morning about twelve. Mind you give it to her at once, Timmy. I don't want to have a thing like that left lying about."

Timmy slipped into Old Place by a back way often used by the young people, for it was opposite a garden door set in the high brick wall which gave on to one of the byways of the village.

But instead of seeking out his mother, as he ought at once to have done, he went upstairs and so into what had been the day nursery. There he locked the door, and having first put Nanna's Bible on the big, round table, at which as a baby boy he had always sat in his high chair, he went over to the corner where Josephine was peacefully reposing with her kittens, and sat down on the floor by the cat's basket.

Very carefully he then slipped the rubber-rubber band off the roll of brown paper which had been confided to him by Miss Pendarth. He spread out the sheet of newspaper, putting aside the brown paper in which it had been rolled, as also Miss Pendarth's open letter to his mother. And then, with one hand resting on his cat's soft, furry neck, he read through the long account of the inquest held on Colonel Crofton's death. As he worked laboriously down the long columns,

Timmy's freckled forehead became wrinkled, for, try as he might, he could not make out what it was all about. The only part he thoroughly understood was the description of Colonel Crofton's last hours; the agony the dying man had endured, the efforts made by the doctor, not only to save his life, but to force him to say how the virulent poison had got into his system — all became vividly present to the boy.

Timmy felt vexed when he realized, as he could not help doing, that Mrs. Crofton had looked very pretty when she was giving evidence at the inquest; in fact, the descriptive reporter had called her "the dead man's beautiful young widow."

And then, all at once, he bethought himself of Miss Pendarth's letter to his mother.

Now Timmy was well aware that it is not an honorable thing to read other people's letters; on the other hand, his mother always left Miss Pendarth's notes lying about on her writing table, and more than once she had exclaimed: "Betty? Do read that note, and tell me what's in it!"

And so, after a short conflict between principle and curiosity, in which curiosity won, he began to read the letter. As he did so, he realized that it formed a key to the newspaper report he had just read, for Miss Pendarth's letter ran:

My dear Janet,

I am longing to talk over the enclosed with you. I was lately in Essex, and when we meet I will tell you all that was said and suspected there at the time of Colonel Crofton's death.

Someone we wot of got off very lightly. You will realize from even this rather confused report that *someone* must have put the bottle of strychnine into the unhappy man's bedroom — also that he absolutely denied having touched it. No one connected with the household, save of course Mrs. Crofton, had ever seen the bottle until after his death.

It is a strange and sinister story, but I remember my father used to say that Dr. Pomfrett (who for fifty years was the great medical man of *our* part of the world) had told him that not one murder in ten committed by people of the educated class was ever discovered.

I think you know that Mrs. C. has had a very handsome offer for The Trellis House from that foolish Mrs. Wallis, but I believe that up to yesterday she had not vouchsafed any answer.

Your affectionate,
OLIVIA PENDARTH

P.S. — Please burn this note as soon as read. I don't want to be had up for libel.

Timmy read the letter twice through. Then he very carefully folded up the newspaper in its original creases, put Miss Pendarth's letter inside, and made as tidy a roll as he could with the help of the brown paper. Finally he slipped on the rubber-rubber band, and scrambling up from the floor, unlocked the door. Taking Nanna's Bible off the round table, he went into his own bedroom and there laboriously copied out, with the help of a very blunt pencil, the text where the pin had rested in church. Then he took the Bible into Nanna's room.

"What's that you're holding?" she asked suspiciously.

"It's something I have to give to Mum."

Somehow the sight of Nanna, sitting up there in her big armchair, made him feel extremely guilty, and he was relieved when she said mildly: "You run along and give it to her, then."

He found his mother in his father's study, and they both stopped abruptly when he came in. Timmy supposed, rightly, that they had been speaking of Dolly and her engagement.

Janet took the roll of paper from her boy and slipped off the band absently: "What's this?" she exclaimed. And then, "How stupid of me! I remember now." She turned to her husband. "It's an account of the inquest held on Colonel Crofton. What a tremendous long thing! I shall have to put it aside till after lunch."

She did, however, read through Miss Pendarth's letter.

"Oh! John," she said, smiling, "this letter is *too* funny! Olivia Pendarth may be a good friend, but she's certainly a good hater. She simply loathes Mrs. Crofton." Then, deliberately, she went over to the fireplace and, lighting a match, set fire to the letter.

Timmy watched the big sheet of paper curling up in the flame. He was glad indeed that he had read the letter before it was burned, but he made up his mind that when he was a grown-up man, he also would burn any letter that he thought the writer would prefer destroyed. In a way Janet was her son's great exemplar, but he was apt to postpone following the example he admired.

Chapter XXVII

*I*t was after seven, on the evening of that same Sunday, that Enid Crofton, after having spent the whole day in her bedroom, came down to her pretty, cheerful, little sitting room.

She had returned from London in an anxious, nervous, strung-up frame of mind. For the first time in her life she did not know what it was she really wanted, or rather she was uncertain as to what it would be best for her to do.

The thought of seeing Jack Tosswill, of having to fence and flirt with him in her present disturbed state of mind, had been intolerable. That was the real reason why she had stayed upstairs all today. He had called three times, and the third time he had brought with him a letter even more passionately loving, while also even more angry and hurt in tone, than the one which she had received from him the day before.

As she read this second epistle she had told herself, with something like rage, that it was not her fault that what she had intended should be a harmless flirtation had caused such havoc. Still, deep in her heart she was well aware that but for the havoc she had caused, she could never have confided to him her urgent need of the five hundred pounds which he had procured with such surprising ease.

Jack had been quite honest with the woman he loved. He had told her of his talk with Radmore, of Radmore's immediate, generous response, and the check he had given which he, Jack, handed to her as a free gift.

She had gone up to London fully intending to see the Pipers after she had cashed the check. But when it came to the point she had shirked the second half of her program, telling herself, with perhaps a certain amount of truth, that by waiting till the last day of grace allowed her by that terrible old-clothes woman she would get better terms. Perhaps then they would be satisfied with three hundred pounds, or even less, and acting on that hope, she had expended a portion of the money in purchasing a few of the pretty dress etceteras which are so costly nowadays.

Apart from the time occupied by those pleasant purchases, she had spent every waking minute of the day with Harold Tremaine, lunching and dining at the big smart restaurants which both her soul and her body loved, going to the play, and listening in between to the most delightful love-making. . . .

Small wonder that during that long, dull Sunday, spent perforce in her bedroom, Enid Crofton's mind often took refuge in the thought of the only man now in her life with whom all her memories and all her relations had been, and were, absolutely satisfactory. Captain Tremaine was a simple, happy, cheerful soul. Though he was always what he called "dashed short," when with a woman he flung about his money right royally. Also he was an expert, not a teasing, lover. He knew, so Enid reminded herself gratefully, when to stop, as well as when to begin, making love. How unlike inexpert, tiresome Jack Tosswill! And yet he also was in dead earnest. He knew exactly what he wanted, and more than once, in a chaffing, yet serious, fashion, he had assured her that she had best submit at once, as he always "got there in the end." What he wanted was that they should be married, by special license, within a week from now, so that they might go back to India, a happy, honey-mooning couple, in a fortnight! And while he was with her, describing in eloquent, eager language what their life would be like and what a delightful, jolly time they would have, Enid had been sorely, sorely tempted to say "yes."

And yet? Though Tremaine was Enid Crofton's ideal of what a lover, even a husband, should be, and she had never liked any man as well, she knew with a painful, practical knowledge the meaning of the words "genteel poverty." Tremaine's regiment would not remain forever in India, and then would begin the enforced economies, the weary struggle with an inadequate income she had known with Colonel Crofton. No, no — it wasn't good enough! — or at any rate not good enough as long as there was a hope of anything better. Even so, it was comfortable to know that Harold Tremaine would still be there, a second string to her bow, in six months' or a year's time.

It was of all this that she thought, a little despondently, as she settled herself down in the easy chair close to the little wood fire. In a few moments her supper would be brought in by her pleasant-faced, rosy-cheeked parlor maid. Enid Crofton was dainty and particular as to her food. The bad cooking she had had to endure during those miserable months she had spent in Essex, after her husband had been demobilized, had proved a very real addition to her other troubles.

She had brought a nice sweetbread with her from London yesterday, and she was now looking forward to having it for her supper.

All at once there came a ring at the front door, and a feeling of keen, angry annoyance shot through her. Of course it was Jack — Jack again! He would ask tiresome, inconvenient questions about the mythical woman friend, the almost sister, for whom she had required the money, and she would have to make up tiresome, inconvenient lies. Also he would want to kiss her, and she did so want her dinner!

She stood up — and then the door opened and, instead of Jack, Timmy Tosswill came through it. For the first time in their acquaintance she was glad to see the boy, though she told herself that of course he had brought her a letter — another of those odious, reproachful letters from Jack.

"Good evening, Timmy," she spoke, as she always did speak, pleasantly. "Have you brought me a message from Rosamund? I hope she hasn't thrown me over? I'm expecting her to lunch tomorrow, you know."

"I didn't know," he said gravely, "and I've not brought a message from anyone, Mrs. Crofton. My coming is a secret."

"A secret?" Again she spoke easily, jokingly; but there came over her a strange, involuntary feeling of repulsion for the odd-looking child.

He came up close to her, and, putting his hands behind his back, began to stare fixedly beyond her, at the empty space between her chair and the white wall.

There crept over Enid Crofton a sensation of acute discomfort. She stepped back, and sat down in her low, easy chair. What was Timmy looking at with that curious, fixed stare?

It was in vain that she reminded herself that no sensible person now believes in ghosts, and that she had but to press the bell on the other side of the fireplace to ensure the attendance of her cheerful servant. These comforting reflections availed her nothing, and a wave of fear advanced and threatened to engulf her.

After what seemed to her an interminable pause, but which was really less than a minute, Timmy's eyes met hers, and he said abruptly, "Is it true that someone has asked you to go to India? Rosamund says it is."

She gave a little gasp of relief. On her way home from the station in the Old Place pony-cart, she had told her companion that while in London she had met a man who had fallen in love with her in Egypt, during the War. Further, that this handsome, brilliant, rich young soldier had urged her to marry him and go off to India with him at once. She was surprised as well as dismayed by this quick betrayal of her confidence. What a goose Rosamund was!

"Yes, Timmy," she bent forward and smiled a little, "it is quite true that I have been asked to go to India, but that doesn't mean that I'm going."

"I would, if I were you," said the child gravely.

"Would you?" Again she smiled. "But I've only just come to Beechfield. I hope you're not in a hurry to get rid of me?"

"No," he said, "I'm not in a hurry, exactly. It's you who ought to be in a hurry, Mrs. Crofton." He waited a moment and then added: "India is a very nice place."

"Yes, indeed. Full of tigers and leopards!" she said playfully.

"I should go as soon as you can if I were you."

She looked at him distrustfully. What exactly did he mean?

"Someone we wot of got off very lightly at the inquest."

His voice sank almost to a whisper, but Enid Crofton felt as if the terrible sentence was being shouted for all the world to hear.

Timmy's eyes were now fixed on the gay-looking blue rug spread out before the fender to his right. He was remembering something he had done of which he was ashamed.

Then he lifted his head and began again staring at the space between Mrs. Crofton's chair and the wall.

Enid Crofton opened her mouth and then she shut it again. What did the boy know? What had he seen? What had he been told? She remembered that Mr. Tosswill was a magistrate. Had the Pipers been down to see him?

"There were some people," went on the boy, and again he spoke in that queer, muffled whisper, almost as if the words were being dragged out of him against his will, "who thought" — he stopped — "who thought," he repeated, "that Colonel Crofton did not take that poison knowingly."

She told herself desperately that she must say something — something ordinary, something of no account, before a power outside herself forced her to utter words which would lead to horror incalculable.

Speaking in such a loud discordant voice that Timmy quickly moved back a step or two, she exclaimed: "I was not going to tell anybody yet — but as you seem so anxious to know my plans, I will tell you a secret, Timmy. I *am* going to India after all! A splendid strong man, an officer and a gentleman who would have won the V.C. ten times over in any other war, and who would *kill* anyone who ever said a word against me, has asked me to be his wife, and to go out to India very, very soon."

"And have you said you will?" he asked.

"Of course I have."

"And will you be married soon?" went on her inquisitor.

"Yes, very soon," she cried hysterically. "As soon as possible!"

"Then you will have to leave Beechfield."

She told herself with a kind of passionate rage that the child had no right to ask her such a silly, obvious question, and yet she answered at once: "Of course I shall leave Beechfield."

"And you will never come back?"

"I shall never, *never* come back." And then she added, almost as if in spite of herself, and with a kind of strange, bitter truthfulness very foreign to her: "I don't like Beechfield — I don't agree that it's a pretty place — I think it's a hideous little village."

There was a pause. She was seeking for a phrase in which to say "Good-bye," not so much to Timmy as to all the others.

"Will you go away tomorrow?" he asked, this time boldly. And she answered, "Yes, tomorrow."

"Perhaps I'd better not tell any of them at Old Place?" It was as if he was speaking to himself.

She clutched at the words.

"I would far rather you did not tell them — I will write to them from London. Can I trust you not to tell them, Timmy?"

He looked at her oddly. "Jack and Rosamund will be sorry," he said slowly. And then he jerked his head — his usual way of signifying "Good-bye" when he did not care to shake hands.

Turning round he walked out of the room, and she heard the front door bang after him, as also, after a moment or two, the outside door set in the garden wall.

Enid Crofton got up. Though she was shaking — shaking all over — she walked swiftly across her little hall into the dining room. There she sat down at the writing-table, and took up the telephone receiver. "9846 Regent."

It was the number of Harold Tremaine's club. She thought he would almost certainly be there just now.

She then hung up the receiver again, and, going to the door which led into the kitchen, she opened it: "Don't bring in my supper yet. I'll ring, when I'm ready for it." She then went back to the little writing-table and waited impatiently.

At last the bell rang.

"I want to speak to Captain Tremaine. Is he in the Club? Can you find him?"

She felt an intense thrill of almost superstitious relief when the answer came: "Yes, ma'am. He's in the Club. I'll go and fetch him."

She remembered with relief that Tremaine had told her that no one could overhear, at any rate at his end, what was being said or answered through the telephone — but she also remembered that it was not the same here, in The Trellis House.

Judging others by herself, as most of us do in this strange world, she felt sure that her two young servants were listening behind the door. Still, in a sense there was nothing Enid Crofton liked better than pitting her wits against other wits. So when she heard the question, "Who is it?" she simply answered, "Darling! Can't you guess?"

In answer to his rapturous assent, she said quietly, "I've made up my mind to do what you wish."

And then she drank in with intense delight the flood of eager, exultant words, uttered with such a rush of joy, and in so triumphant a tone, that for a moment she thought that they must be heard, if not here, then there, if not there, then here. But, after all, what did it matter? She would have left this hateful place forever tomorrow!

And then came a rather difficult moment. She did not wish to tell her servants tonight that she was leaving The Trellis House tomorrow, and yet somehow she must convey that fact to Tremaine.

As if he could see into her mind, there came the eager question, "Can you come up tomorrow, darling? The sooner, the better, you know —"

She answered, "I will if you like — at the usual time."

He said eagerly, "You mean that train arriving at 12.30 — the one I met you by the other day?"

And again she said, "Yes."

He asked a little anxiously, "How about money, my precious pet? Are you all right about money?"

For once her hard, selfish heart was touched and she answered truly: "You need not bother about that."

And then there came a whispered, "Call me darling again, darling."

And she just breathed the word "Darling" into the receiver, making a vague resolution as she did so that she would be, as far as would be possible to her, a good wife to this simple-hearted, big baby of a man who loved her so dearly.

Chapter XXVIII

*T*immy went straight home. He entered the house by one of the back ways and crept upstairs. Late that afternoon he had gratified Nanna by sharing her high tea, and so he was not expected in the dining room.

He felt intensely excited — what perhaps an older person would have called uplifted. He wandered about the corridors of the roomy old house, his hands clasped behind his back, thinking over and exulting in his great achievement. He felt just a little bit uneasy as to the contents of the letter Mrs. Crofton had said she would write explaining her departure. As to certain things, Timmy Tosswill was still very much of a child. He wondered why their enemy, for so he regarded her, should think it necessary to write to anyone, except perhaps to Rosamund, who, after all, had been her "pal." He was disagreeably aware that his mother would not have approved of the method he had used to carry out what he knew to be her ardent wish, and he wondered uncomfortably if Mrs. Crofton would "give him away."

At last he opened the door of what was now his godfather's bedroom, and walked across to the wide-open window. All at once there came over him a feeling of wondering joy. He seemed to see, as in a glass darkly, three figures pacing slowly along the path which bounded the wide lawn below. They were Godfrey Radmore, Betty, and with them another whom he knew was his dear brother, George. George, whom Timmy had never seen since the day, which to the child now seemed so very long ago, when, rather to his surprise, his eldest brother had lifted him up in his arms to kiss him before going out to France at the end of his last leave. And as he gazed down, tears began to run down his queer little face.

At last he turned away from the window, and as he went towards the door he saw the outline of a paper pad on the writing table which in old days George and Godfrey had shared between them.

Blinking away his tears, he took up the pad, and carried it down the lighted passage to his own room. There he sat down, and with a pencil stump extracted from his waistcoat pocket, he wrote:

Dear Mum,
This is from Timmy. I hope you don't still feel the pierce.
Your affectionate son,
TIMOTHY GODFREY RADMORE TOSSWILL

He put the bit of paper into a grubby envelope in which he had for some time kept some used French stamps; then, licking down the flap, he left his room and went into his mother's, where he propped up the envelope on the fat pincushion lying on her dressing-table, remembering the while that so had been propped an anonymous letter written many years before by a vengeful nursery maid, who had been dismissed at Nanna's wish.

Monday morning opened badly for more than one inmate of Old Place. Dolly and her lover had discovered with extreme surprise that one hundred pounds would only achieve about a fifth of that which they considered must be done before his vicarage would be fit for even the most reasonable of brides. With Dolly this had produced an extremely disagreeable fit of bad temper — of temper indeed so bad that it had been noticed by Godfrey Radmore, who had followed Janet into the drawing room after breakfast to ask what was the matter.

Jack Tosswill had gone off as early as he felt he decently could go, to The Trellis House, only to find its mistress gone — and gone, which naturally much increased his disappointment and anger, only ten minutes before his arrival! He had interviewed both servants, they only too willing, for his infatuation was by now known to the whole village. But what they had to say gave him no comfort — indeed, it was almost exactly what the house-parlor maid had said last week, when Enid had gone off to town, leaving no address behind her. This time, however, she had said she would telephone from town.

As he was turning away, feeling sick at heart, the cook suddenly vouchsafed the information that her mistress had left a letter for Mrs. Tosswill, and that The Trellis House odd man, on his way back from the station, where he had gone with Mrs. Crofton, for she had taken two large trunks this time, would deliver it at Old Place.

But when he reached home the letter had not yet been delivered, and Jack, half consciously desiring to visit his misery on someone else, hunted up Timmy in order to demand why Josephine and her kittens had not been sent back to Epsom ere now. There had followed a lively scrap, leaving them both in a bad mood; but at last it was arranged that Godfrey, Betty and Timmy should motor to Epsom with the cat and her kittens after luncheon.

The morning wore itself slowly away. Only two of the younger people were entirely happy — Betty, doing her usual work, and Godfrey Radmore. Even he was more restless than usual, and kept wandering in and out of the kitchen in a way which Rosamund, who was helping Betty, thought very tiresome. As for Timmy, his mother could not make him out. He seemed uncomfortable, and, to her practiced eye, appeared to have something on his conscience.

Three times in one hour Jack came into the drawing room and asked his step-mother whether she had not yet had a letter from The Trellis House. Now Jack Tosswill had always been reserved, absurdly sensitive to any kind of ridicule. Yet now he scarcely made an effort to conceal his unease and suspense. Indeed, the third time he had actually exclaimed, "Janet! Are you concealing anything from me?" And she had answered, honestly surprised, "I don't know what you mean, Jack. I've had no communication from Mrs. Crofton of any kind. Are you sure she wrote me a letter?" And he had answered in a wretched tone: "Quite sure."

And then, about five minutes before luncheon, and luncheon had to be a very punctual meal at Old Place, for it was the one thing about which its master was particular, Timmy came in with a letter in his hand, and sidling up to his mother, observed with rather elaborate unconcern: "A letter for you, Mum."

She looked at him quite straight. "Has this letter only just been left, my dear?"

He answered rather hurriedly: "It came a little while ago, but I put it in my pocket and forgot it."

Janet broke the seal, for the letter was sealed, and then she called out to her son, who was making for the door: "Don't go away, Timmy. Betty will ring the lunch bell in a moment."

Unwillingly he turned round and stood watching her while she read the four pages of closely written handwriting. But, rather to his relief, she made no remark, and the bell rang just as she put the letter back in its envelope. Then she slipped it in her pocket, for Janet Tosswill was one of the very few women in England who still had a pocket in her dress.

Giving him what he felt to be a condemnatory look, but in that he was wrong, for she was too surprised, relieved, and, yes, disturbed, to think of him at all, she motioned the boy to go before her into the dining room.

As the Sunday joint was always served cold on Monday, they were all there, even Betty, but owing, as at any rate most of them believed, to the unfortunate discovery made by Dolly that the pre-war pound was now only worth about seven and six, it was rather a mournful meal.

At last Rosamund went out to get the coffee, and then Janet addressed her son: "Timmy," she observed, "I have something I wish to say to the others, so will you please go and have your orange with Nanna?"

Timmy obeyed his mother without a word, and then, after the coffee had come in and been poured out, Janet said slowly:

"I've had a letter from Mrs. Crofton, and as she asks me to tell you all what is in it, I think it will be simpler if I read it out now."

She waited a moment, gathering up her courage, wondering the while whether she was doing the best thing by Jack. On the whole she thought *yes.* There are blows which are far better borne among one's fellows than in solitude.

She wished to make her reading as colorless as possible, but she could not keep a certain touch of sarcasm out of her voice as she read aloud the first two sentences:

"Dearest Mrs. Tosswill,

"You have always been so kind to me that I feel I must write and tell you why I am leaving the dear Trellis House and delightful Beechfield."

She looked up, but no one spoke; Jack was staring straight before him, and she went on:

"To my *utter* surprise a very old friend of my late husband's and mine has asked me to be his wife. He is going back to India in a fortnight, and so, much as I shrink from the thought of all the bustle and hurry it will involve, I feel that as it must be now or never, it must be *now,* and the fact that I have a good offer for The Trellis House seemed to me a kind of sign-post.

"Though perhaps I ought not to say so, he is a splendid soldier and did extremely well in the war. He won a bar to his M.C., which my husband once told me would have won him a V.C. in any other war.

"He is anxious that I should not come down to Beechfield again. The time is so short, and there is so much to be done, that I fear I shall not see any of you before I leave for India. I would have liked Rosamund to come to my wedding, but we shall be married very quietly, and the day and hour will probably be fixed at the last minute.

"I am purposely not telling you where I am staying as I do not want to give you the bother of answering this rather unconventional letter. As for presents I have always hated them.

"All the business about The Trellis House is being done by a kind solicitor I know, who arranged about the lease for me.

"Might I ask you to remember me very kindly to everybody, and to give my special love to Rosamund and to sweet Miss Betty? I wish I had known her better.

"Again thanking you for your kindness, and assuring you I shall always look back to the happy days I spent at Beechfield,

"Believe me to remain,

"Yours very sincerely,

"ENID CROFTON"

There was a long pause. Jack was now crumbling up his bread and then smoothing out the crumbs with a kind of mechanical, steam-roller movement of his right-hand forefinger.

Rosamund was the first to speak. "Why, she hasn't even told us his name!" she exclaimed. "How very funny of her!"

And then Godfrey Radmore spoke, just a thought more sharply than usual: "I'm not at all surprised at that. She wants to start quite clear again."

Betty said quietly: "That's natural enough, isn't it?" But her heart was full of aching sympathy for her brother. She felt, rather than saw, his rigid, masklike face.

They all got up, and slowly began to disperse. After all, there was only one among them to whom this news was of any real moment.

Janet, feeling curiously tired, went into the drawing room. The moment she had finished Enid Crofton's letter she had begun to torment herself as to whether she had done right or wrong after all?

To her relief Godfrey Radmore came into the drawing room. "I want to put those two unfortunate people out of their misery, Janet. Shall I tell Dolly, or will you tell her, that I want to give her a thousand pounds as a wedding present?"

Janet had very strong ideas of what was right and wrong, or perhaps it would be better to say of what was meet and proper.

"I don't think they could take a present of that sort from you," she said very decidedly. "These are hard times, Godfrey, even for rich people. But you always talk as if you were made of money!"

"Do I?"

He looked taken aback, and even hurt.

"No, no," she said, "I don't mean that, but I'm upset today. What with one thing and another, I hardly know what I'm saying." She caught herself up. "I'll tell you what I think would be reasonable. As you are so kind, give Dolly a hundred pounds. It will make a real difference."

"No," he said, "it's going to be a thousand."

"I'm quite sure that John would not allow Dolly to accept it."

Radmore knew that when Janet invoked John, it meant that she had made up her mind as to what must be.

He went to the door, opened it, and called out in what seemed to Janet a very imperious tone: "Betty?" And yet no glimmer of the truth came into Janet's mind.

"It's no good sending for Betty," she said sharply. "There are things that can be done, and things that can't be done."

As she uttered that very obvious remark, Betty appeared.

"Yes," she said a little breathlessly. "Yes, Godfrey, what is it? We have just started washing up —"

He took her hand and led her in front of Janet. "We have got to tell her *now*," he said. "We must do it for Dolly's sake; I never saw anyone looking so woebegone as she has looked all the morning."

And then, at last, Janet began to understand.

"I don't think Mr. Tosswill will be able to object to Dolly's *brother* giving her a thousand pounds," he said, and then, very much to Janet's surprise, he suddenly threw his arms round her, and gave her a great hug.